BOOK CLUBBED

BOOK CLUBBED

Lorna Barrett

BERKLEY PRIME CRIME, NEW YORK

THE BERKLEY PUBLISHING GROUP
Published by the Penguin Group
Penguin Group (USA) LLC
375 Hudson Street, New York, New York 10014

USA • Canada • UK • Ireland • Australia • New Zealand • India • South Africa • China

penguin.com

A Penguin Random House Company

This book is an original publication of The Berkley Publishing Group.

Berkley Prime Crime Books are published by The Berkley Publishing Group.
BERKLEY® PRIME CRIME and the PRIME CRIME logo are trademarks of
Penguin Group (USA) LLC.

Library of Congress Cataloging-in-Publication Data

Barrett, Lorna.
Book clubbed : a Booktown mystery / by Lorna Barrett. — First edition.
pages cm
ISBN 978-0-425-25257-4
1. Miles, Tricia (Fictitious character)—Fiction.   2. Women booksellers—Fiction.
3. Receptionists—Crimes against—Fiction.   4. New Hampshire—Fiction.   I. Title.
PS3602.A83955B65 2014
813'.6—dc23
2014005611

FIRST EDITION: July 2014

PRINTED IN THE UNITED STATES OF AMERICA

10   9   8   7   6   5   4   3   2   1

Cover illustration by Teresa Fasolino.
Cover design by Diana Kolsky.
Interior text design by Laura K. Corless.

For Patricia Ryan,
thank you for your enduring friendship

ACKNOWLEDGMENTS

I had so much fun writing *Book Clubbed* and I hope you will enjoy reading it just as much. Part of the fun was comparing notes with friends and keeping track of our daily word counts. My thanks to J. B. Stanley and Leann Sweeney, for keeping me on track. My pal Dru Ann Love not only solves all my Word and Excel problems, she's also been helpful with research. I couldn't do this without all you guys.

Of course writers find support in group situations, too. I'm so lucky to be a member of the Cozy Chicks blog. We are: Ellery Adams, Kate Collins, Mary Kennedy, Mary Jane Maffini, Hannah Reed, Maggie Sefton, and Leann Sweeney. Check us out at cozychicksblog.com.

As always, I'm grateful to have a wonderful editor in Tom Colgan, and my agent, Jessica Faust, is always there with help on the business side of things.

Did you know I have an author page on Facebook? You can find me there, as well as on Goodreads and Twitter. Don't forget to sign up for my periodic e-mail newsletter on the contact page of my website: lornabarrett.com.

Happy reading!

Book Clubbed

ONE

For once the winter weather seemed to be co-operating, meaning that unless any unforeseen complications arose, Tricia Miles, owner of the mystery bookstore Haven't Got a Clue, would get a lot accomplished on that particular Saturday in February. No ice, no snow, and though the sun had not yet made an appearance in Booktown, otherwise known as Stoneham, New Hampshire, the skies were due to clear before lunchtime—hopefully bringing plenty of book-buying customers with it.

Meanwhile, Tricia and her sister, Angelica, who owned not only the Cookery bookstore, but a charming retro café, Booked for Lunch, and had a half share in a local bed-and-breakfast called the Sheer Comfort Inn, had a date to look over a private book collection. These kinds of sales were few and far between, and their window to make a bid on the collection was narrow—between ten and eleven o'clock.

Tricia glanced at her watch. It was 9:55 and Angelica wasn't yet ready to leave.

"Ange, will you hurry," she called, but Angelica was deep in conversation with her new receptionist. In actuality, Betsy Dittmeyer *wasn't* Angelica's personal secretary, but she was employed by the local Chamber of Commerce. Angelica had won the election for the presidency back in November and had officially taken office some five weeks before. Things hadn't gone so well during that time. The former Chamber president, and Angelica's former lover, had made the transition as difficult as possible. So had the Chamber's receptionist.

"I don't know how much longer I can tolerate this impossible situation," Betsy cried, and sighed dramatically.

"I'm sorry," Angelica apologized as she struggled into the sleeves of her leather jacket, "but you, more than anyone else, should understand the Chamber's predicament. When Bob Kelly terminated our lease on the former Chamber building, we had to scramble. I'm giving up a large portion of my storeroom until other arrangements can be made."

"It's embarrassing and inconvenient to have to share restroom facilities with the general public," Betsy huffed, setting her wastebasket filled with candy and other junk-food wrappers, as well as a load of dirty tissues, on the floor, and her key ring on the counter. She must have been on her way to tote the trash out back when she stopped to berate Angelica. Prim and proper, Betsy lived her life by Robert's Rules of Order. At fifty-something, she was barrel shaped with brown hair streaked with gray. She took no guff from anyone, and she didn't encourage frivolity of any sort. Tricia doubted the woman had ever smiled, let alone laughed. She watched as, with exaggerated care, Betsy yanked the sleeves of her maroon sweater over her wrists, then pulled it down over her rather large derriere.

Tricia glanced at her watch once more. Thanks to Betsy, they'd hardly have time to look at the books before they would have to make a decision on whether or not to buy them. Betsy had a penchant for being annoying. And according to Angelica, the woman spent an inordinate amount of time tying up the Cookery's facilities, usually timing her bathroom breaks for when the store was full of paying customers in need of a restroom visit.

"I've got feelers out on several properties that might be available for rent, but Mr. Kelly hasn't been helpful about setting up the appointments," Angelica explained. And it was irritating that the property owners insisted that Angelica go through Bob. How long could they afford *not* to rent to the Chamber, and was Bob subsidizing them in the interim out of spite? He couldn't do it forever, but meanwhile Angelica's patience was near the snapping point, which was evident by the tightness in her voice.

And it wasn't surprising that Angelica had a hard time holding on to her temper. Betsy constantly complained, despite the fact they'd been over the same ground at least a hundred times since Angelica had won the election, beating Bob by a handful of votes to become Chamber president on the first of the year. Meanwhile, the Chamber's former digs up the street had remained empty and unrented. Spoilsport Bob had declined to even contemplate negotiating a new lease.

Luckily the door opened, interrupting what was sure to be another tense conversation. Unfortunately it was Frannie Mae Armstrong who entered the Cookery. Frannie had been the Chamber's previous receptionist. Bob had fired her, but not only had Angelica hired her to manage the Cookery, she'd given her a fat raise and health-care benefits, too. Betsy resented that fact and made no bones about it.

"Good morning, all," Frannie called cheerfully. "Isn't it a lovely day?"

It was not. The sky was steel gray, but she knew the sound of her Texas twang set Betsy's teeth on edge. She zeroed in on the Chamber's only employee. "And how are you today, Betsy, dear?"

"Just fine," Betsy grated. "I have work to do. I'd best get to it," she said, pivoted, and flounced toward the back of the store to empty her wastebasket.

Angelica waited until Betsy was out of earshot before she spoke. "Really, Frannie, must you tease her so?"

Frannie feigned innocence as she shrugged out of her leather bomber jacket and set it on the sales counter. "Why I'm always as sweet to her as my mama's homemade peach pie. I can't help it if Betsy is such a disagreeable person."

Angelica frowned. "No, I suppose you can't."

The door opened again and two women dressed for the arctic entered the store. Customers were so rare these days that both Angelica and Frannie practically leapt to attention. "Welcome to the Cookery," Angelica said rather enthusiastically.

"Please don't hesitate to ask if you need assistance," Frannie called out.

The women nodded and stepped farther into the store to browse.

Angelica picked up the conversation where she'd left off. "I've got a hard decision in front of me. The Chamber can have a full-time receptionist who does little else but take potty breaks and complains, or we can have a part-time employee and rent office space. At this moment I'm leaning heavily toward that second alternative. All we need is a tiny storefront and there isn't one available right now."

"What about renting a bungalow at the Brookview Inn?" Tricia suggested.

Angelica shook her head. "The cost would be prohibitive."

The bell over the door jingled again and Tricia looked up to see Charlie, the sixty-something mailman, come through the door. He was bundled in his regulation coat and hat, with a big leather pouch slung over his shoulder. "Mail call!" he said cheerfully. He handed the bills and junk mail to Angelica.

"Thanks." She set them on the counter and turned her attention back to Tricia and Frannie.

"If Bob is keeping you from his clients, maybe you should just forget about him. Why not place an ad in the *Stoneham Weekly News?*"

Angelica sighed. "Yes, I suppose I could. I'll call Russ today. Better yet, maybe I should just go over there."

They heard a bang from the floor above and instinctively looked up. Had Betsy just slammed a file drawer shut?

Tricia looked at Frannie—the eyes and ears of Stoneham. "I'm surprised you don't know of any places to rent in the area."

Frannie crossed her arms over her bright green aloha shirt decorated with parrots, and frowned. "Believe me, I'd like to get rid of Betsy just as much as anyone else around here, but most of the available rentals I know about are in Milford— and I know you want the Chamber to stay here in the village," she said, focusing on Angelica. "It's just too bad Bob Kelly owns just about all the rental property in town."

They heard another bang and instinctively looked up at the painted tin ceiling. Betsy really was riled.

"That has got to change," Angelica said, ignoring the sounds above and frowning. "I wonder if I should go to the town hall and look up all the property in town—see who owns it, and ask if I can rent something, even just a room for a few months, until we can figure out where the Chamber's new home will be."

They heard a tremendous crash that seemed to shake the whole building.

"What on earth is Betsy up to?" Tricia asked. "Dumping bookshelves?"

Angelica sighed and shook her head just as the door opened, allowing four or five people to crowd into the store, which suddenly made it feel that much smaller. Where had they come from? And more important, were they going to visit Haven't Got a Clue before they left the village?

"I should go hang up my coat," Frannie said, excused herself, and threaded her way through the customers.

"Ange, we really need to leave. We're already late to look at that book collection," Tricia said.

"I'm sorry. With everything that's going on around here, I almost forgot." She pulled on her gloves and grabbed her purse from the sales counter.

Tricia shivered and crossed her arms over her coat. "Did you forget to turn the heat up this morning?"

"It's on an automatic timer. It comes on half an hour before the store opens."

Frannie approached. "That darn Betsy. She left the back door wide open when she took out the trash."

"That's not the first time she's done that," Angelica groused. "Looks like I'm going to have to have another little talk with her."

"It's okay. I shut and locked it, and reset the alarm," Frannie said, taking her accustomed station behind the cash desk.

They heard more banging, but it didn't seem to be directly overhead.

Angelica looked up at the ceiling. "What in the world is going on up there?"

"I don't think it's coming from the storeroom," Tricia said.

"You don't think Betsy was angry enough to go up and trash my apartment, do you?" Angelica asked.

"From what you've said, anything is possible when it comes to Betsy."

"I'd better go up and see," Angelica said, already heading for the back of the store and the door marked PRIVATE.

"Ange, we're already late," Tricia called.

"It'll only take a minute," Angelica called over her shoulder.

Tricia knew if she wasn't around to speed things along that Angelica might get distracted once again, and hurried to follow.

The two of them rushed up the stairs. It had suddenly gotten very quiet. Was Betsy over her snit and goofing off with her feet up on the desk and a romance novel open on her lap? Betsy was the only person Tricia had ever met who could look industrious while doing absolutely nothing.

"Something's not right," Angelica said as they rounded the landing and saw that the door to the storeroom was ajar. From the floor above, they heard muffled barking from Angelica's bichon frise, Sarge. Tricia felt Angelica's index finger poke her shoulder. "Go on in," she urged.

Tricia's stomach knotted, but despite her misgivings she also knew if she wanted to assess those books for sale she'd have to move things along. She charged ahead and entered the storeroom-turned-office and cringed at the sight of the mess. How on earth had Betsy created so much chaos in so little time? Chairs were overturned, files were dumped on the floor, the computer tower had been knocked over, and the monitor screen had been smashed, with cracks radiating in a kind of starburst pattern. In the back of the storeroom was an overturned bookcase that had been filled with Angelica's excess stock of vintage cookbooks.

And underneath it lay Betsy Dittmeyer . . . squashed flat.

TWO

Without conscious thought, Tricia whipped out her cell phone and punched in an all-too-familiar number—911—to report the accident.

When she ended the call, she looked straight at her sister. "You stay here, and I'll go down and wait for the police."

"Me?" Angelica practically squealed. "I don't want to stay with her—she's . . . she's dead. And dead people creep me out. *You* stay here. You're used to finding and dealing with dead people."

"I am not," Tricia protested, but by the time the words had left her mouth, Angelica had hightailed it out of the storeroom and down the stairs to her shop.

Tricia glanced back down at Betsy. She hadn't been attractive in life, and death hadn't made any improvements.

Her eyes bulged, and her mouth was open, her chin bloodied, exactly what Tricia would have expected from someone who'd been crushed. It seemed incredible that Tricia had spoken to the woman only minutes before and now she was so thoroughly dead. She looked away, taking in the storeroom. How on God's earth did Betsy make all that mess before she toppled the bookcase on herself?

The sound of a siren broke the quiet. Tricia turned away and took several deep breaths to quell her queasy stomach. Soon the sound of footsteps on the stairs caused her to look up, and her ex-lover, Chief Grant Baker of the Stoneham Police Department, appeared before her with Angelica right behind him. "The ambulance is on its way," he said, nearly breathless.

"You can cancel it. Betsy's dead," Tricia said.

"How do you know?" he asked, hustling past her to get to the body.

"Dead people cease to bleed."

The chief looked down at Betsy's lifeless form, then up, his gaze darting around the room. "What happened here?"

"Betsy and I had a tiny tiff before she came up here to work," Angelica sheepishly admitted. "We heard a lot of noise and figured she was throwing a tantrum up here. Then there was a terrible crash, and it got really quiet. Tricia and I ran up the stairs and . . . this is how we found her."

Baker nodded grimly, and then began to pick his way through the room, presumably looking for clues.

Tricia shivered in a draft. "It sure is nippy up here. Is the heat up here on a timer, too?"

"It was toasty warm the last time I was in here—which was last night," Angelica said.

"This doesn't feel normal," Tricia said, frowning, while Baker continued his circuit around the storeroom.

Angelica darted into the open stairwell and looked up. "Good grief! My apartment door is wide open. I never leave it unlocked. Oh, my! Sarge!" she cried, and bolted up the flight of stairs.

"Wait! Grant!" Tricia hollered, but instead of waiting for him, she ran up the stairs after Angelica.

Bursting through the doorway to the back of the apartment, Tricia saw no trace of Angelica and pounded down the hall toward the kitchen, where she found her sister cradling her tiny bichon frise.

"Mommy's little boy," Angelica crooned as she kissed the top of the fluffy dog's head while he furiously tried to lick her in return.

"I take it he's okay," Tricia said with relief. Sarge had once been kicked like a football, causing internal injuries. She didn't wait for an answer. "Why is it so cold in here?" She looked around the kitchen. None of the windows were open. She wandered from the kitchen to the living room and into the bedroom. Sure enough, the window that overlooked the alley was wide open. She went to shut it and saw that the fire escape ladder had been extended. If she touched the window, she might obliterate fingerprint evidence.

Chief Baker barreled into the room. "Don't touch that!"

Tricia whirled. "I wasn't going to."

Baker practically knocked her over as he shoved her aside. He stuck his head out of the window, looking from right to left. "Damn. No one in sight. But there may be footprint evidence in the snow. I'd better call in the sheriff's tactical squad to check things out."

"A lot of people walk their dogs along the alley," Tricia said, knowing Angelica was among them.

"Will you please close that window!" Angelica said sharply. "I'm not heating the great outdoors, you know."

"This window will stay open until the lab team dusts it for fingerprints," Baker ordered.

"That will make my bedroom uninhabitable. I've seen the way you guys throw that stuff around and it's damn hard to clean up—and goodness knows none of your men ever clean up the messes they leave."

"This apartment, and especially this bedroom, is off-limits, so why don't you ladies go back downstairs."

"And do what? Twiddle my thumbs while you and your men keep customers out of my store?" Angelica demanded.

"May I remind you that your secretary was just found dead on your premises—"

"She was the Chamber's receptionist—not secretary," Angelica interrupted.

"—and possibly due to foul play?" Baker continued. "You don't seem very concerned."

"Of course I'm concerned—and very upset. Whoever did that to Betsy also kicked in my apartment door, invaded my home, and could have hurt or killed my dog. And now your men are going to blitz my bedroom and keep me out of my own home for goodness knows how long."

"It'll only be for a few hours. Now, go over to Tricia's store. I'll be over there as soon as I can, and you'll be back in your store and apartment by tonight," Baker said with more consideration.

"Very well," Angelica agreed, but not at all graciously. "Tricia!" she called.

"Go on ahead. I want to talk to the chief."

Angelica frowned, pivoted, and left the room. Tricia turned back to Baker.

"What did you want to tell me?" he asked.

"Don't even bother to consider me, Angelica, or even Frannie as suspects in what now looks like a possible murder."

"Are you saying you all had motives to kill Mrs. Dittmeyer?" he asked wryly.

"Of course not. We were all in the Cookery when all the noise broke out. And there were customers there who can corroborate that, too."

"Did you get their names? Because when I got here Frannie was the only one in the store. And as far as I'm concerned, *everyone* is a suspect until I can rule them out."

"Thank you once again for your unwavering belief in me," Tricia said with heavy sarcasm. "May I go?"

"No. I didn't see the back entrance open."

"Betsy had just emptied her wastebasket and left the back door open. Frannie shut and locked it."

"Then you don't know for sure that Frannie was telling the truth."

"We could feel a draft, and I don't doubt Frannie *was* telling the truth."

"Did you see the open door?"

"No, I was standing at the front of the store with Angelica."

"Did you see anyone else you recognized in the store at the time of the . . . upset?"

Tricia shook her head.

"That means Mrs. Dittmeyer could have let her killer into the shop."

"I guess. As I said, there were a bunch of customers in the store at the time, and Charlie the mailman was there a few minutes before we heard the ruckus."

"Did you see him leave?"

Tricia thought about it. "No. But that doesn't mean any-thing. Angelica and Frannie and I were talking. We weren't paying attention to anything else that was going on—until all the noise started upstairs."

"And you thought the victim was making it?"

Tricia nodded. "As Angelica said, she and Betsy had been discussing the limitations of using the storeroom as the Chamber headquarters. Betsy made it plain she was not happy with the situation, and we figured she was throwing a tantrum."

"Did she regularly do such things?" Baker demanded.

Tricia shrugged and heard others tromping around the apartment. "I don't know. I didn't hang out with the woman."

"And why was that?" Baker asked.

"Because she wasn't very nice. Or at least not very warm and welcoming."

"What about the mailman?"

"Charlie? He's a sweetheart. I suppose you can find him at the post office—after he's finished his route, that is."

"Chief?" Officer Henderson called.

Baker held up a hand to stall him. "We'll talk later," he told Tricia in dismissal.

She nodded, turned, and waited for the officer to move away from the doorway so she could escape. So much for getting anything accomplished during the rest of the morning—and there was no way she'd be able to visit the estate sale to look at the books on offer.

Tricia found the Cookery crowded with the entire Stone-ham police force, who demanded she stay until Chief Baker verified that she was allowed to leave, which took another ten minutes—minutes in which she was not allowed to speak with Frannie, Angelica, or anyone else. When she was finally allowed to return to her store, Tricia pondered the fact that Stoneham seemed to have become the death capital of southern New Hampshire. And why, oh, why, did she always seem to be the one to keep stumbling over the newly deceased?

While she loathed being called the village jinx, Tricia was beginning to think the title might just be apropos.

THREE

With all the chaos going on at the Cookery, Tricia was happy to return to her own store and its relative peace. Relative because her assistant, Pixie Poe, was singing. As she studied the order forms before her, Tricia desperately tried to ignore her employee's slightly off-key rendition of "Yankee Doodle Dandy." As it was, Tricia had been afraid Angelica might wait out the police presence at her own store by hanging out at Haven't Got a Clue, but instead she'd chosen to go across the street to Booked for Lunch, the tiny retro café she owned and operated.

Pixie dressed exclusively in vintage togs, so one never knew what era she was likely to represent on any given day. Today she seemed to be channeling the Andrews Sisters, looking like a rather long-in-the-tooth Patty, with shoulder-length blonde hair, pancake makeup, and ruby-colored lips and nails. The customers loved her, and sales had skyrocketed since she'd come to work at Haven't Got a Clue. Tricia had rewarded her with several raises and was thinking of giving her another.

While Tricia's other employee, Mr. Everett, dusted the back shelves, Pixie once again wandered over to the big display window to look outside, checking out what she could see of the mix of official cars and people, and the investigation into Betsy Dittmeyer's death.

"They haven't taken the body out yet," she said with what sounded like disappointment.

"And when they do, there'll be nothing to see," Tricia chided her.

"I know. It's just . . . well, with the screws blocking the sidewalk, we aren't going to have any customers, so I've gotta do something to keep from getting bored."

"Why don't you go read a book," Tricia encouraged.

"Really?" Pixie asked with delight. "Great. I'm working my way through Dashiell Hammett once again. Love that *Maltese Falcon*." Tricia watched her go over to one of the shelves, pluck out a book, and then flop down into the readers' nook.

Tricia sighed and went back to her paperwork. Pixie might not be working, but neither was she singing.

The little bell over the door rang cheerfully, causing both Tricia and Pixie to look up, but instead of a customer it was Ginny Wilson-Barbero who entered Haven't Got a Clue. Unfortunately, her demeanor was anything but cheerful. Tricia didn't bother with the usual pleasantries. "Is something wrong?"

"Not at all," Ginny said, her voice high and squeaky.

"Hi, Ginny!" Pixie called without looking up from her book.

"Hi, Pixie. How are you?"

"Just Yankee Doodle dandy!" she said and, unfortunately, began to hum as she read. From the back of the store, Mr. Everett waved his lamb's-wool duster in greeting and went back to work.

Ginny inched closer to the sales desk. "I saw the police cars. Well, who could miss them? Rumor has it that Betsy Dittmeyer was killed this morning over at the Cookery."

"I'm afraid it's true."

"By a bookcase?" Ginny asked.

Tricia nodded grimly. "Fully loaded."

"Messy," Ginny said and winced.

"Yes," Tricia agreed. She noted that Ginny's eyes were bloodshot and her nose was red, although she didn't sound like she had a cold. "Are you sure there's nothing wrong?"

Ginny's eyes filled with tears. "Have you got a couple of minutes to talk?"

Tricia looked over at Pixie, who had turned to look their way. "Sure, Mr. E and I can hold down the fort," Pixie said. As usual, she'd been eavesdropping.

"Come on," Tricia said and came out from behind the cash desk and wrapped an arm around Ginny's shoulder. "We'll go upstairs and have a nice cup of cocoa."

Ginny sniffed and allowed herself to be guided through the shop. Miss Marple joined them, scampering up the stairs, while Tricia and Ginny followed until they reached the third floor and Tricia's loft apartment. Tricia unlocked the door and let them in. "Let me take your coat."

Ginny shrugged out of the sleeves of her coat, handing it to Tricia, who hung it on the coat tree by the door. She hurried over to the kitchen counter and filled the electric kettle with water, then got out mugs and packets of cocoa mix. "I hope you don't mind instant. Of course, Angelica would make it from whole milk, and the finest Swiss ground chocolate."

"She does tend to go overboard," Ginny admitted, then dug for a tissue in the pocket of her skirt and blew her nose.

"I'm afraid I don't have much to serve a guest. I don't really keep cookies or desserts up here. But we've got some thumb-print cookies down in the store. I could dash down and—"

Ginny shook her head. "No, thanks. The last thing I need right now are more calories."

"What's wrong?" Tricia asked. "Have you and Antonio had a fight?"

"Oh, no. He's the sweetest, nicest man in the world—well, apart from Mr. Everett. I love him to death. I've never had an unhappy minute with him."

"But you don't look very happy right now. Is it the job?" Tricia prompted, since Ginny didn't seem to be in a hurry to explain.

Again Ginny shook her head. Her gaze fell and her lower lip trembled, and then she nodded. "I guess it is my job I'm worried about." She nodded once more. "Yes, that's exactly it. I'm afraid I'm going to lose the Happy Domestic."

"Why? I thought it was doing well. That you were in the black and your boss, Nigela Ricita, was very happy with your work."

"She is. Or so Antonio tells me."

"Then what's the problem?"

The kettle chose that moment to come to a boil, and Tricia turned her attention to the cocoa at hand, pouring the water into the cups and mixing the contents with spoons. She grabbed a couple of paper napkins from the holder, set them on the kitchen island, and placed the mugs on them.

Tricia waited, but Ginny didn't seem able to meet her gaze. "Ginny, please, tell me what's wrong."

Ginny looked up, her eyes filling with tears, her face screwing into an expression of total misery. "I'm . . . I'm pregnant."

"Pregnant?" Tricia cried and leapt forward to embrace her friend. "That's wonderful. Oh, I'm so happy for both of you."

But Ginny didn't move. She stood rock still.

Tricia pulled back, studying Ginny's face. "This is wonderful news. Why aren't you happy?"

"Part of me is happy," she cried, "but most of me didn't plan for this to happen for another couple of years."

"What does Antonio think about it?"

Ginny looked away. "I haven't told him."

"Oh, Ginny."

Ginny waved her hands in the air as though to stop an oncoming scolding. "I can't tell him. Not when I feel this way."

"Okay, so the timing isn't what you'd originally planned, but you'll make the best mama in all of Stoneham."

"But what about the Happy Domestic?" she cried.

"What about it?"

"As far as I'm concerned, it belongs to me. Maybe not on paper, but I've put my heart and soul into that store."

"And you've done a wonderful job—"

"But what if they take it away from me?"

"Who?"

"Antonio and Nigela Ricita."

"Why would they take it away from you?"

"Because," she said and sat down at the island, placing her hands around the steaming mug, "I just have this feeling . . . maybe it's the name of the store . . . the Happy Domestic. I don't want them to force me to be just a housewife."

"What makes you think they'd do that?"

"Let's face it; the former owner didn't have a happy domestic life. She and her husband fought about the business after their son arrived. And then a plane dropped out of the sky and killed her. What if the place is cursed?"

"Hey, I'm supposed to be the village jinx, not you," Tricia reminded Ginny.

"Deborah Black wasn't good at juggling her business and her home life. What if I can't do it, either?"

Tricia sighed, exasperated. "I have faith in you. And if you'll let them, I'm sure Antonio and Nigela Ricita will, too."

Ginny picked up her cup, blew on the hot liquid, and took a tiny sip. "This wasn't supposed to happen. Not now. The timing just isn't right."

"You weren't thinking of . . ." Tricia found she couldn't even say the words.

Ginny raised her gaze just a trifle, looking guilty. "I did . . . for about a second and a half. This is something I want. But not right now."

"Why did you tell me first?" Tricia asked. "Are you looking for advice?"

"Not exactly," Ginny admitted, taking another sip. "I know what you're going to say: 'Talk to Antonio.'"

"He is your husband," Tricia reminded her.

"Like I could forget that," Ginny said with a shadow of her old laugh.

"Talk to him. I'm sure your fears are all blown out of proportion. It's probably the hormones."

Ginny shrugged, and drank more of her cocoa. "I feel so selfish."

"Motherhood is a big responsibility," Tricia said. "It will change your life, but not for the worse."

"You think?"

"I'm sure of it."

Ginny nodded wearily and tipped her head to take in the last of her cocoa. "I really need to get back to my store."

"Me, too."

The women set their dirty mugs in the sink and Ginny retrieved her coat before they headed to the stairs that took them back to Haven't Got a Clue. Still seated in a chair in the nook, Pixie looked up over the top of her book. "Is everything okay?"

"It will be," Tricia said and forced a smile. Before she and Ginny made it halfway to the exit, the door burst open and Nikki Brimfield-Smith entered.

"I've got the most wonderful news!" she cried, zeroing in on Tricia and rushing forward. "Russ and I are having a baby!"

Stunned, Tricia stood rock still with her mouth agape. Ginny, the poor soul, burst into tears.

Nikki appeared unsure of herself. "Isn't anyone going to say anything?"

"Congratulations," Tricia managed, but Ginny made a break for the door Nikki had just entered. She and Tricia watched as Ginny slammed the door behind her.

Nikki frowned. "She could have at least pretended to be happy for us."

"I'm sure she is," Tricia said, "but Ginny is pretty upset this morning. If you'd told her the moon was made of green cheese she probably would have had the same reaction."

Nikki stared at the closed door, miffed, then turned back to Tricia. "And what do *you* think about my news?"

Tricia forced a smile. "I think it's terrific. How far along are you?"

"Two months."

"Have you picked out any names?" she asked, trying to sound thrilled.

"We won't even consider names until after we find out the baby's gender."

Tricia nodded. She wasn't sure what to say next.

"Since I found out earlier this morning, all I can think about is selling the Patisserie and becoming a stay-at-home mom."

"Oh," was all Tricia could think of to say.

"You don't think I should?" Nikki challenged, not sounding at all sure herself.

"You should do whatever makes you happy. But are you sure you want to do that? You trained so hard to become a pastry chef. You worked so hard to take possession of the bakery."

"Nothing is more important to us than giving our child the most nurturing environment. And that means devoting my entire life to him or her."

The door opened and an older man entered, his cheeks chapped from the wind. He paused, pulled off a pair of brown leather gloves, and retrieved a slip of paper from his coat pocket. "Can someone help me find these books?"

Pixie was about to get up from her chair, but Tricia shook her head and she sat back down. Likewise, Mr. Everett, who'd been about to bound forward, did an abrupt about-face.

"I'd be glad to." Tricia turned back to Nikki. "I'm sorry, but I've got a customer—and as I'm sure you already know, they seem to be a rarity these days. Congratulations to both you and Russ. You'll make fine parents."

Nikki frowned and turned for the door without another word. She'd obviously expected a more enthusiastic reception to her announcement. Shoulders slumped, she left the shop without another word and quietly closed the door behind her.

Tricia sighed. Two women, two announcements—two very different reactions. And Tricia found she didn't envy either Ginny or Nikki.

The morning's only customer turned out to be a good one. After browsing for just under an hour, he'd purchased nearly three hundred dollars' worth of books. Since it was nearly their lunchtime anyway, Mr. Everett and Pixie helped carry the books to the customer's car before they headed off for the Bookshelf Diner to eat.

Tricia settled behind the cash desk, determined to battle the pile of paperwork before her when the shop door opened once again. This time, it was not a customer but Christopher Benson, Tricia's ex-husband, who'd taken up residence across the street in the apartment over the Nigela Ricita Associates office where he worked.

"What brings you to Haven't Got a Clue?" Tricia asked, looking straight into Christopher's mesmerizing green eyes. She always thought they were his best physical trait. Dressed in jeans, a bulky sweater, and a ski jacket, he looked like he might be about to pose for a spread in an L.L. Bean catalog.

"I happened to be looking out my office window when I saw Pixie and Mr. Everett go out for lunch. I thought you might want some company."

Tricia looked over her shoulder at Miss Marple, who was asleep on her perch behind the cash desk. "I'm never lonely when I'm with my cat. You see, she stuck with me through thick and thin. Like when my husband left me," Tricia said, keeping her tone light and even.

"Touché," Christopher reluctantly agreed.

"Now, why did you *really* come here today?"

"I've seen the police and rescue vehicles come and go, and I've heard all the gossip. And I know how wrapped up you get whenever there's a crime in Stoneham."

"What's that supposed to mean?"

"Everybody knows you like to think of yourself as a much younger and prettier Agatha Christie."

"I do not." She frowned. "Well, I will accept the 'prettier' part."

"From what I hear, you've helped the cops solve several crimes in the past couple of years."

"I was just being a good citizen."

"I hoped that when your employees return from their lunch that we could go somewhere to eat and maybe talk about Betsy Dittmeyer."

"And what did you know about Betsy?"

"I am the only financial advisor in town. You'd be surprised how many clients I've accumulated in such a short period." He'd moved to town only two months before.

"I thought you worked for Nigela Ricita Associates."

"Not exclusively. I'm on a retainer, but I still have several hours free every day."

"What about client confidentiality? Aren't you afraid that if you talk to me about a client's financial situation that your other clients might find out and take their business away from you?"

"I happen to trust you. I know you wouldn't go blab whatever I tell you to anyone—except maybe Angelica, and she can keep a secret, too."

"How would you know that?"

He shrugged. "We've talked."

"Has Angelica hired you to give her financial advice?" Tricia asked, surprised.

"Yes."

"Okay, so what is Angelica's financial status?"

Christopher shook his head. "I can't tell you that."

"Why, because she's still alive?"

He nodded. "Pretty much."

"Have you spoken to Chief Baker about Betsy?"

He nodded. "I thought it might be pertinent."

"And was it?"

"He seemed to think so. And so will you."

"Okay, I'm game."

"Great, then you'll go out to lunch with me?"

"I didn't say that."

"You do need to eat," he said reasonably.

"Why can't you just tell me now?"

"I don't mind being seen with you. Do you mind being seen with me?"

Tricia sighed. She was getting tired of the runaround. "Level with me. Please?"

"Okay." Christopher shoved his hands into his jacket pockets. "But only because I feel I owe you. I realize now it was downright cruel of me to leave you the way I did."

"Yes, you hurt me, but I'm over it now. I like my life the way it is. Believe it or not, I'm not pining for you. You don't have to buy me expensive jewelry or do anything else to make up for it. It's behind us now. I've moved on. It's time you did, too."

"You're absolutely right. But is it wrong for me to still enjoy your company? We have a history. If nothing else, I'd like us to be friends."

"We are friends. Just not close friends."

Christopher frowned. "I suppose you're right."

"And does this mean you aren't going to tell me about Betsy's finances?"

He sighed. "I guess I could, at least until a customer comes in." He straightened. "You might not believe it, but Betsy Dittmeyer was a multimillionaire."

Dumpy, unattractive, Betsy? The one who was afraid the Chamber of Commerce might reduce her from a full-time to a part-time employee? "You've got to be kidding," Tricia said, flabbergasted.

Christopher shook his head. "It seems she'd had several large judgments from civil suits. Not only that, but not long ago she'd changed the beneficiary for nearly all of her accounts."

"And who was the unlucky person to lose Betsy's favor?"

"Her sister."

"Joelle Morrison?" Tricia asked.

"Do you know her?"

"We've spoken on a number of occasions," Tricia admitted, neglecting to add that she'd led the wedding planner to believe she and Christopher might be on the verge of reconciliation— all in the name of gathering information on a previous murder investigation. "Do you know if Betsy told Joelle she'd been cut out of the will?"

Again, Christopher shook his head.

"Do you think the loss of such a large inheritance could be the reason Betsy was murdered?" Tricia blurted.

"Not necessarily. Betsy assured me her sister had no idea of her personal worth, but Chief Baker was sure interested. Apparently he thinks it makes a good motive for murder."

It certainly did. "Who was the lucky new benefactor? Anyone we know?"

"The Stoneham Food Shelf, several charities involved in cancer research, and a living trust."

"Wait a minute. Betsy always acted like she was broke. She certainly didn't dress the part of a millionaire—or flaunt the fact she had the kind of money you're suggesting. So unless she was just spiteful, Joelle had no real reason to kill her sister."

"Perhaps Betsy taunted her about the disinheritance. If she did, I have no knowledge of it—and maybe no one else did, either. They may never have spoken about it. Do you talk money with Angelica?"

Angelica had once told Tricia that she'd written a will leaving all her worldly goods to Tricia—and vice versa, but they hadn't spoken of it since. "No. And she rarely mentions it to me, either."

"There you go."

"So does this make Joelle a truly viable suspect, or would you rule her out?" Tricia asked.

"That's not up to either of us to decide. But I'm sure your boyfriend, Chief Baker, will."

Tricia felt her insides tighten. "I wish you wouldn't refer to him that way. We are no longer an item . . . not that we ever really were."

"Too bad for him. You're a remarkable woman, Tricia. The kindest I've ever come across."

She certainly didn't feel that way today. Not after her encounter with Nikki . . . and now with Christopher. Still, she replied, "Flattery will get you nowhere."

"No, I really mean it."

But before he could elaborate, the shop door opened and an elderly female customer entered.

Tricia made eye contact with the woman and managed a smile. "Good afternoon. Welcome to Haven't Got a Clue. I'm Tricia. Please let me know if you need any help."

"Thank you," the old lady said and moseyed over to one of the bookshelves.

"I guess that's the end of our conversation," Christopher said with yet another shrug.

"I guess," Tricia agreed, and for some unfathomable reason she actually felt a pang of regret.

"That lunch invitation is still good. I mean, you do need sustenance to stay alive. If none of the local restaurants appeal to you, I make a mean risotto."

There was no way Tricia would allow herself to visit her ex-husband's apartment. She worried that, plied with enough wine, she might finish the evening in his bed—and she really didn't want that to happen. "Thank you, but no thank you."

"No matter how much you deny it, it's not over between us, Tricia. One day we will get back together."

Tricia said nothing. She didn't want to encourage him. And she didn't want to admit that somewhere in her heart of hearts she still cared more for him than she wanted or would ever admit. She didn't want to give him that much power over her ever again.

Christopher cast a glance toward the back of the shop where Tricia's lone customer still browsed. "Well, I guess I'd better go. If you won't eat with me, can I at least bring you a sandwich or something?"

"I usually have lunch with Angelica at Booked for Lunch after it closes."

"I know. I often see you cross the street around two o'clock."

"Have you been spying on me?" Tricia asked, although she wouldn't be at all surprised if he had. He certainly lived close enough to observe her comings and goings.

"Not spying. I just happen to look out my window when I'm not busy. If you're there—I see you. If you're not, I don't."

"And do you find yourself without something to do on a

regular basis?" she asked and found herself smiling. Good grief, was she actually flirting with her ex-husband?

Christopher's smile was wistful. "Sometimes."

The door opened and another customer entered the store. Tricia gave her usual canned line about giving assistance before turning back to Christopher.

"Are you sure I can't get you something? A cappuccino? Espresso? A big greasy burger and a slice of cheesecake?"

"No, nothing, thank you."

Christopher's smile morphed into something a little more sly. "I guess I'll be seeing you around, then."

"I guess so," Tricia said.

"I'm going now," he said, backing toward the door.

"I see that you are."

"Honest, I'm almost out of here."

"Have a nice lunch."

With nowhere left to go, Christopher opened the door, gave her a cheerful wave and a smile, and then he was gone.

Tricia sighed. After all the unhappiness he'd caused her, why did she still love that man so much?

FOUR

Tricia watched as the clock's minute hand inched closer to the hour. Already the east side of Main Street was bathed in shadows. Every day the sun stayed above the horizon for just a minute or so longer, promising that spring was only another five weeks away. Still it gave her hope, however dumb that sounded.

Main Street seemed strangely quiet after the unnatural bustle during the morning and most of the afternoon caused by Betsy Dittmeyer's death. After the medical examiner had finally removed her body, and all the other official vehicles had departed, the village seemed deserted and forlorn.

"Another eventful day in Stoneham," Pixie declared and sighed as she placed yet another removable price sticker on a paperback. She'd been working on a box of books Tricia had bought from an online auction.

From her position on the other side of the cash desk, Tricia looked over the top of her reading glasses. "After this morning, I think I could do without any more eventful days, thank you very much."

Pixie shrugged and slapped a sticker on a Tami Hoag novel. "My parole officer thinks I have a vivid imagination. He doesn't believe a word I tell him about what goes on here in Stoneham."

"Maybe you shouldn't tell him those tales. He might decide the village is a bad influence on you and force you to quit your job and leave us. Then what would Miss Marple, Mr. Everett, and I do?"

"Gee, I hadn't thought of that. I'll keep my mouth shut from now on," she promised.

Tricia gave Pixie what she hoped was a warm smile. She'd actually become quite fond of the ex-prostitute who happened to have an encyclopedic memory when it came to vintage mysteries. Besides her habit of eavesdropping, there was only one other thing about Pixie that Tricia couldn't abide: her affection for the large, ugly, vinyl baby doll she'd given to Tricia as a gift several months before, and had adopted as the store mascot. Pixie had named her Sarah Jane and liked to dress the doll for holidays and special occasions. Since Valentine's Day was only a week away, the doll now sported a frilly red dress decorated with pink hearts and black piping. Pixie had recently bought the thing a vintage pram—an item she'd won on an eBay auction. Sarah Jane often held a book in her little plastic hands, but they didn't stay there for long. For some reason, whatever Sarah Jane recommended was quickly snapped up by Tricia's customers.

Oddly enough, the customers weren't freaked out by the doll like Tricia was.

"What have you got on tap tonight, Pixie?" Tricia asked, knowing she had no plans of her own.

"I'm taking up the hem on a new dress." *New* was a relative term when it came to Pixie's clothes. "It's red with a taffeta slip—just gorgeous. Now if I just had a gentleman friend to dress for," she said wistfully.

"I hear you," Tricia agreed.

"Oh, come on, you've got two guys dogging your tracks. Odds are you'll have both of them badgering you for a date for the most romantic night of the year."

Tricia didn't comment. The fact that one of the guys was her ex-husband who had dumped her to find himself, and the other was a cop who couldn't make a commitment, had a lot to do with her lack of enthusiasm. Valentine's Day was less than a week away and, though she'd spoken to both men that day, neither had mentioned it.

Mr. Everett wandered up to the cash desk. "Is there anything you'd like me to do before the end of the day, Ms. Miles?"

"Would you please empty the wastebaskets?"

"I'd be glad to," he said and she handed him the one that resided behind the cash desk.

The door to Haven't Got a Clue opened, letting in a blast of cold air, and Betsy Dittmeyer's sister, a haggard-looking Joelle Morrison, her knee-length coat unbuttoned, wearing no hat or gloves despite the frigid weather, staggered in. "Betsy's dead," she cried. "She's dead!"

Tricia took off her reading glasses, scooted around the counter, and hurried to Joelle's side, giving her a gentle hug. Joelle stood there, sobbing hysterically. Tricia's cheeks warmed in embarrassment as Pixie watched her gently pat Joelle's heaving back. "I'm so sorry," she crooned over and over again, wondering if it was her day to console weepy women.

The last time Tricia had seen Joelle, she'd been at least fifty pounds heavier, but the weight loss had made her face look gaunt—or did it just seem that way because of her emotional state? She was about the same age as Tricia, but the years hadn't been so kind. A wedding planner by trade, Joelle had been hired by Antonio Barbero's stepmother, Nigela Ricita, to help Ginny plan her wedding the previous fall. Joelle had also been a suspect in Stan Berry's murder. He'd liked his women on the heavier side, and when Joelle would no longer eat the sumptuous chocolates and cupcakes he liked to stuff her with, they'd had a parting of the ways.

Eventually Joelle's sobs began to subside and Tricia pulled back. "Come sit down," she encouraged, and led Joelle to the comfortable upholstered chairs in the store's readers' nook. "Pixie, would you please get Joelle a cup of coffee?"

"Sure thing," Pixie said and hurried over to the beverage station.

"Black with two sugars," Joelle said as if by rote. She sat down and pulled a used tissue from her coat pocket and blew her nose several times, sounding remarkably like a honking goose.

"I wanted to see the spot where dear Betsy died, but the Cookery is closed," Joelle declared.

Tricia took the adjacent seat. "How did you find out about . . . what happened?"

"Well, it sure wasn't the Stoneham police who called me. It was Frannie Armstrong," Joelle said, wiping at her eyes.

"I didn't know the two of you were friends."

"We're not. But it was very kind of her to call. Otherwise

I might have found out by watching the six o'clock news, and that would have killed me."

That seemed unlikely. The thing was, Tricia hadn't seen a TV news truck roll past her big display window at all that day. Poor Betsy's death hadn't been at all newsworthy . . . at least to the nearby TV stations.

"Frannie said Betsy was squashed like a bug by a heavy bookcase," Joelle went on with a catch in her voice.

"Oh, dear. I hope she didn't use those words," Tricia said, appalled.

"Well, no, she didn't. She said she'd been crushed to death, and that it wasn't an accident."

"I'm afraid that might be true," Tricia admitted.

"But who could have wanted dear Betsy dead?" Joelle cried.

At one time or another, probably every member of the Chamber of Commerce. The woman was not well loved, and Tricia doubted anyone here in Stoneham would miss her, either. "Did Betsy have any enemies?" she asked.

Joelle sniffed. "Well, her ex-husband, Jerry, wasn't very fond of her. It was a bitter divorce. They fought over everything. In the end, they had to sell a lot of their assets just to pay their attorney fees."

That certainly wouldn't have endeared Betsy to her ex. "Anyone else?" Tricia asked.

Joelle wiped away another stray tear that had leaked from her left eye. "Well, there was that nasty incident with her former neighbors."

"Oh?" Tricia prompted, her interest piqued.

"They put up a fence without having their property surveyed. Betsy couldn't abide such carelessness and had her own yard surveyed. She found the fence was three inches over the property line. Naturally she had a hissy fit and reported them to the town. They made the neighbors pull down the fence. It cost them thousands. They never forgave Betsy. She could never prove it, but someone would egg her windows on a regular basis and Betsy was sure it was them."

"Oh, my," Tricia said. Somehow she felt more sympathetic toward the neighbors than Betsy.

"And then there was the guy who hit her car at a stop sign while texting. She sued him and got all kinds of damages. She was lucky that way." So Christopher had mentioned. Yet to Tricia it sounded more like Betsy was just spiteful.

"Did Betsy and her husband ever have children?"

Joelle nodded but looked away, her expression dour. "A daughter. Poor little Amy was born with an extra chromosome." She looked thoughtful. "Or maybe she was born with a missing chromosome. I never could get that straight." She shook her head. "That little angel was only eight years old when she died."

"Oh, my. Poor Betsy," Tricia said, genuinely saddened. Maybe the loss accounted for her sour disposition.

"Betsy was always a little bit loony after she lost Amy. She kept her baby's room just the way she'd left it. I thought it was kind of creepy, but I guess it wasn't that unusual." Joelle sighed. "Betsy was my only living relative. Now I'm all alone in the world."

From her tone, Tricia surmised that Joelle hadn't yet heard she'd been cut out of Betsy's will. "I'm so sorry," she said sincerely. From the corner of her eye, she noticed Pixie was hovering. Though she'd tried, Tricia hadn't been able to break her newest employee of the habit. "It's getting late, Pixie. Could you please finish pricing the rest of those paperbacks?"

"Sure thing," Pixie said affably, and went back to the cash desk.

Tricia turned back to Joelle. "Is there anything I can do to help you?"

Joelle sniffed once again. "No, I guess I just needed to talk to someone. I suppose I need to think about the arrangements. I'm not sure what Betsy would have wanted. We never spoke of it."

"I'm sure you'll make the right decisions," Tricia said kindly.

Joelle nodded. She sighed, and then sat up straighter in her chair. "Have you and Mr. Benson set a date yet?"

Oh, dear. Joelle certainly hadn't forgotten the fantasy Tricia had spun for her the previous fall that she and Christopher might reconcile. But Joelle had a memory like a steel trap and she reminded Tricia of her promise every time they met. She also mailed Tricia promotional material on a monthly basis.

"Sadly, Mr. Benson and I are still at an impasse when it comes to a reconciliation," Tricia said; a blatant lie, since not only hadn't they discussed the topic, but, except for earlier that day when they'd spoken for the first time in several weeks, Tricia had only seen Christopher to wave to—not plan a renewal of vows—and that suited her just fine.

"You *will* keep me in mind when the time comes," Joelle insisted.

"Yes, of course."

Joelle heaved a loud sigh. "I suppose I'd best be on my way. I'm on my way to the gym. Maybe if I work out hard enough, I'll be able to sleep tonight. Goodness knows I'll be alone—just like every other night."

Though she felt like a heel, Tricia did not invite Joelle to join her for dinner. She had no clue about how she'd feed herself, let alone a guest. She stood, hoping the gesture wouldn't be taken as rudeness. "It's just about time to close the shop for the day."

Joelle also rose to her feet. "I'm sorry. I hadn't noticed how late it is. Thanks for listening to me whine, Tricia. When I get home, I'm going to drown my sorrows in a bottle of pink Catawba."

Tricia had to restrain herself from shuddering at the thought of drinking such a cheap wine. She walked Joelle to the door. "Get some rest. These next few days are sure to be stressful for you."

"I will, thank you." Joelle gave a wave before she pulled the door closed behind her.

Tricia let out a weary breath, feeling ready to collapse.

"That poor woman," Pixie said from her seat in the readers' nook.

"Who? Joelle or Betsy?"

"Both. That Betsy sounded like a class A bitch, but I guess having a sick kid die on her coulda been a contributing factor. She was lucky to have a sister who loved her so much. Well, there's no accounting for taste," she added under her breath. Then she looked thoughtful. "I feel like I know the sister from somewhere. Do you think she ever did time?"

"I don't think so," Tricia said.

Pixie shrugged.

Mr. Everett, who'd made himself scarce since Joelle's arrival—emotional scenes complete with tears made him extremely uncomfortable—reappeared, returning the empty wastebaskets to their rightful places.

Pixie glanced at the clock then down at the pile of paperbacks in front of her. "These are done. Do you want me to stay and shelve them in alphabetical order?"

"No, we can do that in the morning."

"Okay." Pixie headed for the back of the shop and returned with her own and Mr. Everett's coats. She handed his off, then donned her own, taking a moment to put on her black wooly hat before ducking behind the sales counter to claim her purse. She and Mr. Everett headed for the door. "See you tomorrow," Pixie called.

"Good night, Ms. Miles," Mr. Everett said.

"Good night," Tricia said and closed and locked the door behind them. She stood for a long moment soaking up the silence.

"*Yow!*" Miss Marple said loudly. Her kitty stomach could tell time, too.

"Yes, it is time for your dinner."

The cat jumped down from her perch behind the register and watched as Tricia turned the OPEN sign to CLOSED and drew the blinds. But before she could take more than a couple of steps away from the sales counter, the phone rang. She turned and answered it. "Angelica?"

"How did you know?"

"I just had a feeling. Is everything back to normal at the Cookery?"

"Well, as normal as it can get after someone is murdered on your premises; something you well know."

Yes, Tricia did.

"The police are all gone. Come over and keep me company for a few hours, will you? I'm only making omelets for supper, but I'm making some nibbly bits as a test for my next cookbook. Are you game?"

That was certainly better than scrounging the cupboards as Tricia had been planning to do. More likely Angelica just didn't want to be alone, and Tricia couldn't blame her. "Of course. Let me feed Miss Marple and I'll be right over."

"See you in a few," Angelica said and hung up.

Tricia and Miss Marple headed up the stairs to Tricia's loft apartment. As she opened a fresh can of cat food and changed the water, Tricia thought back on her visit with Joelle. Something about it didn't sit right with her. Perhaps it was because in her moment of terrible grief Joelle had pitched her wedding planning services. But then who could blame the woman for her chaotic thinking. She'd just lost her only living relative. If Tricia lost Angelica she was sure she'd suffer an emotional collapse. She'd do it quietly, and alone, but the thought was too painful to contemplate. If it had happened four years before she would have been sad but soldiered on.

Stop it! she told herself. Those types of thoughts were morbid.

She petted Miss Marple, locked her apartment, and went back down to her store.

Unless Angelica really irritated her, she would enjoy her company and try not to think about the terrible expression on Betsy Dittmeyer's face, or ponder just who wanted the woman dead.

FIVE

Tricia unlocked the door to the Cookery and let herself in. She walked a little slower as she headed up the steps and passed the second-floor landing, pausing a moment to look at the locked door that led to Angelica's storeroom, where Betsy had drawn her last breath, and then hurried up the rest of the stairs, eager to leave the place of death.

The door to Angelica's apartment was unlocked and Sarge met her, barking happily and jumping up to try to lick her face. She'd come prepared with an Angelica-approved doggy treat, and he raced back to the kitchen while she hung up her coat. She frowned as the sound of slightly off-key singing wafted through the loft apartment. *Shades of Pixie,* she thought.

As she entered the kitchen, Tricia found Angelica all dolled up—in a pretty, ruffled pink cocktail dress, makeup, with her hair curled, looking like she'd spent half the afternoon primping.

"Did you get dressed up just for me?" Tricia asked.

Angelica immediately stopped singing "That's Amore," but continued to smile, her eyes sparkling with merriment. "I always feel better when I look my best."

"You do remember that someone died in your building today," Tricia said.

Angelica's smile faded. "Don't you dare go throwing a bucket of cold water on my carefully engineered good mood. Of course I feel terrible about Betsy's death. Don't forget, whoever killed her kicked in *my* door and raced through my home. I have been violated!"

Tricia hadn't even noticed that the door had been fixed. "I'm sorry. That was really thoughtless of me."

Angelica pouted. "I forgive you. But please, could we talk about anything *but* Betsy this evening? Just for a few hours, I'd like to pretend that it never happened."

Tricia nodded. She could share what she'd learned about Betsy from Christopher and Joelle another time. "Sure."

Angelica managed a ghost of her former smile. "Thank you."

"Can I ask what put you in such a happy mood?" Tricia said.

Angelica turned to face the oven, opened the door a crack, and peeked at its contents. Whatever it was smelled heavenly. "I take it you haven't heard the wonderful news!"

"What news?" Tricia asked, noting two martini glasses on the counter, along with an ice bucket, a bottle of Bombay Sapphire gin, vermouth, and olives skewered by frilly toothpicks, the kind Tommy at Booked for Lunch used to skewer club sandwiches.

"There's a new real estate office opening in Stoneham. Finally someone will give Bob Kelly a run for his money. And you'll never guess who's behind it."

"Not Nigela Ricita Associates," Tricia said with a groan. That particular development company not only owned a share of the Brookview Inn and another in the Sheer Comfort Inn, but had bought out the local roach coach, and now owned the resident watering hole, the Dog-Eared Page, *and* the Happy Domestic.

"Yes."

"Then why are you happy? You hate them."

"What a terrible thing for you to say. I do not hate them," she said, picked up the tongs, and placed some ice in the chrome cocktail shaker. "I'm in partnership with them at the Sheer Comfort Inn. And I think it's brilliant that they're opening a real estate office. I intend to be their first customer, or at least I intend for the Stoneham Chamber of Commerce to be their first customer."

"Who told you about it?"

"I do get cc'd on some of their e-mails, you know. As soon as I got that one late this afternoon, I made an appointment to see their new sales manager." She measured the gin and added it to the shaker. "Her name is Karen Johnson and we're going to meet for tea tomorrow afternoon. I've already got my menu planned. I'll have Tommy help me pull it together tomorrow morning before we open the café."

"That's nice," Tricia said and leaned against the kitchen island, watching the drink-making operation. "When did all this come about?"

"I called Antonio and he admitted that it's been in the works for some time."

"Will they have any clients? I thought Bob had all the sale and rental properties in the area locked in."

"Yes, but most of those contracts are usually only for three months. And let's face it, those clients can't be happy that Bob has deliberately avoided showing their properties to prospective clients—like me. I'll bet quite a few of them will be ready to jump ship when their contracts run out."

"And who's going to tell them?"

"Oh, I don't know. Maybe a little bird," she said and giggled.

"A five-foot-six-inch bird with blonde hair who sings a trifle off-key?" Tricia suggested.

"Could be," Angelica said, added the vermouth, covered the shaker, and shook it vigorously. She poured equal amounts into the two martini glasses, added the olives, and then handed one to Tricia, taking the other. "To Betsy. And to the NRA real estate office. May they find the Chamber a home in record time."

The sisters clinked glasses. "Amen." They both took a sip, Angelica with relish, and Tricia with a bit of a wince. Perhaps if she drank enough of them, she'd actually come to enjoy a classic martini.

"Have you heard the latest about Nikki and Russ?" Angelica said excitedly, grabbed a pot holder, and turned for the oven door. She withdrew a baking sheet filled with little triangles—spanakopita, one of Tricia's favorite appetizers.

"Oh, I heard it all right. Nikki came straight to my store to announce her happy news."

"Mine, too." Angelica retrieved a couple of plates from the cupboard and transferred several of the appetizers to them while Tricia grabbed some napkins from the holder on the shelf, taking them and her drink to the kitchen island. Meanwhile, Angelica turned for the refrigerator, withdrew a mini muffin tin, and placed it straight into the oven, closing the door once again.

"It's just as well we're drinking martinis," Tricia said when Angelica joined her. "I've got a piece of good news to share, too, but you have to promise me you won't say a word to anyone," Tricia said.

"Do you think I'm some kind of a blabbermouth?" Angelica asked, wounded, and set her glass down on the island.

"Of course not, but . . . this was told to me in confidence—"

"Most secrets are," Angelica muttered.

"—and, though I'm sure it'll be making its way around the village any day now, I think the happy couple ought to be the ones making that announcement to the world in general."

"Someone's getting married?" Angelica guessed, delighted.

Tricia took another sip of her martini. "Not married, but the next best thing."

"Another baby?" Angelica asked.

Tricia nodded and picked up one of the triangles, taking a bite. Terrific!

"But the only ones we know who are young enough to . . . Oh, my God! Ginny and Antonio are pregnant?" Angelica squealed with delight.

Sarge, who'd retreated to his bed, looked up, startled by her outburst.

"Shhh! Don't say it so loud. But, yes, they are."

"This is wonderful! We must start making the plans for Ginny's baby shower. What's she having? A boy or a girl?"

"She doesn't even know yet. And knowing her, she won't

want to know before the birth. And you can't give a baby shower when the baby isn't even due for at least another six months."

"We have to wait that long?" Angelica asked, disappointed.

"I'm sure that's just what Ginny will be saying a few months from now."

Angelica looked positively delighted and Tricia could almost hear her sister's thoughts buzzing with plans for a baby shower. If there was one thing Angelica did exceptionally well, it was throw a party—any kind of party.

"That's not all the news I have to share," Tricia said.

"Twins!" Angelica guessed.

"No! Will you calm down?"

"I can't help myself. Our Ginny having a baby."

"*Our* Ginny? You didn't even like her until last year."

"Well, I like her lots now. What's behind us is behind us. And anyway, if you hadn't used her as a living shield from my phone calls to you, I would have liked her a whole lot better right from the start."

"Let's not bring up the past," Tricia implored.

"You started it," Angelica muttered crossly, taking another sip of her drink.

"Let's just be happy for her, because she's not exactly thrilled with the news."

"Why not?"

"Because. She's afraid Antonio and Nigela Ricita will force her to stop working."

"Why would they do that?"

"I don't know. Maybe out of some outdated sense of morality, or family values, or something."

"I hardly think so. I mean, Ms. Ricita is a businesswoman, and a shrewd one at that. I can't imagine anyone with her experience and foresight would force a new mother out of a job. Not in this day and age."

"I don't think so, either, but Ginny is terrified someone else will be hired to take over the Happy Domestic."

"We've got to talk to Antonio," Angelica said firmly.

"No, we don't. This has nothing to do with us. It's a family matter."

"*We're* family. Maybe not by blood, but with her mom and dad living down south, we're all she's got here in New Hampshire."

"It's a nice thought," Tricia conceded. "Ginny shared her concerns, and now she's got me wondering if she'll make the same mistakes Deborah did when she owned the Happy Domestic."

"Oh, don't be silly. Deborah didn't know when she had a good thing."

"I'm not so sure the thing she had was any good at all," Tricia said, taking another bite of her appetizer.

"Whatever," Angelica said dismissively. "The circumstances are totally different. As soon as she lays eyes on it, Ginny will love her baby like a mama bear loves her cub. All women feel that way."

"Not our mother."

Angelica sighed. "You're not going to start that again, are you?"

"Start? It'll never end, not until she tells me what it was that I've done wrong. What I am that never suited her."

"Please, Trish, you've got to stop torturing yourself about Mother. She is who she is."

Tricia glanced at the clock. "What's the time in Rio? I've a mind to just pick up the phone and ask her right now."

"Please don't," Angelica said.

Tricia looked at her sister with suspicion. "Why not? Because it would upset her? What about me? I've been upset my entire life by our relationship—or lack thereof."

Angelica sighed and looked away. "I just have a bad feeling."

"About what? That she might actually tell me why she treats me the way she does? That she might hurt my feelings if she did? She once told me that she never thought they'd have a second child, but that can't be it. Couples do get over that. And whatever it is she'd have to say couldn't hurt much more than years of her indifference."

"That's what you say now," Angelica said quietly, and picked up another appetizer.

"Then you *do* know what's at the heart of all this," Tricia accused.

Angelica sighed. "I suppose you won't be happy until I've told you everything—and broken Mother's heart once again."

"How can telling *me* break *her* heart?"

"Because you're going to want to talk to her about it, and I'm telling you right now—she will not talk to you about it. If you call her and bring it up, she will hang up on you. If you flew down there and asked her in person, she would just run away."

"Good grief. What on earth could be so terrible she can't even speak about it? Please, Ange, just tell me."

Angelica sighed and picked up her drink, taking a hearty sip. She set the glass down. "What you don't know is that after you were born, Mother had what was then called a nervous breakdown."

"Don't you mean postpartum depression?"

Angelica shook her head. "No, it wasn't brought on by a birth; it was brought on by a death."

"Who died?" Tricia asked. She certainly hadn't heard this story before.

Angelica sighed. "For years I've wrestled with my conscience about telling you the whole sordid tale. No good can come of your knowing, and talking about it to our parents would only reopen old wounds."

Tricia's stomach did an immediate flip-flop. "Are you saying Daddy isn't my biological father? That Mother—?"

"Oh, don't be ridiculous," Angelica chided. "Of course Daddy is your biological father. We've both got the Miles nose, after all. And anyway, if that were true, it would've been Daddy who'd taken a tailspin, not Mother."

"Then what in God's name are you talking about?"

"Our brother!"

Tricia glared at her sister. "We never had a brother."

"Yes, we did."

"I'm certain I would have remembered him if we had."

"Not unless your memory spans back to your time in the womb or shortly after birth."

"Are you saying . . . ?"

"You were a twin. Fraternal, but you had a twin brother."

"I did? And he died at birth?" Tricia asked, aghast.

"No, about two months later. Little Patrick was a SIDS baby."

Tricia had heard all about perfectly healthy babies suddenly dying with no apparent cause. The number of SIDS deaths had plunged once parents were encouraged to never let their babies sleep on their tummies, but when Tricia and everyone else in her generation was born, all babies slept that way.

"Patrick," she murmured, trying the name on for size.

"Patrick and Patty. That's what we called the two of you."

Patty. Tricia grimaced. That was what their mother had

called her when she was most exasperated. "*Oh, Patty*," she'd lament, which had always set Tricia's teeth on edge.

"So why did Mother treat me so shabbily after Patrick's death? I would have thought as the surviving twin she'd have felt I was precious."

Angelica seemed to squirm. "Patrick was her favorite. I mean, it was obvious even to me, and I was only five. That little prince certainly knocked me off the princess throne."

As far back as Tricia could remember, their mother had doted on Angelica, while she'd always felt like an unwanted member of the family—that is, except for by her grandmother Miles, who had loved her unconditionally.

"You see," Angelica continued, "Mother had longed for a son. When she found out she was pregnant with twins, she hoped they'd be identical boys. She bought all kinds of matching outfits. Of course, they didn't do ultrasounds in those days, so when you were born, she was a bit disappointed."

"What would my name have been if I'd been born a boy?" Tricia asked.

"Paul."

Paul Miles. Rather a boring moniker, Tricia decided. "I suppose Mother blamed me for Patrick's death."

Angelica nodded sadly. "You were both sleeping in the same crib."

"Why?"

"I don't know. Remember, I was only five years old at the time."

"Did she think a two-month-old baby would deliberately smother her sibling?" Tricia asked.

Angelica shrugged and reached for her drink once again.

"But Mother once told me that I was a mistake—that she hadn't wanted a second child," she reiterated.

"She wanted Patrick," Angelica whispered.

"And not me," Tricia finished for her, bitterness gnawing at her soul.

"I'm so sorry, Tricia," Angelica said with tears in her eyes. "And I feel so ashamed."

"Why should you feel that way?"

"Because I let Mother's resentment color the way I felt about you for far too many years. You're my sister and I love you—no matter what."

"And our mother doesn't." It wasn't a question.

"I'm sorry. Nothing can make up for what she's done or how she feels."

Tricia sighed. This was all too much information to take in all at once, and yet it seemed to echo what she'd learned not an hour before from Joelle. Betsy Dittmeyer had changed—soured—after the death of her child. Was it so surprising that Tricia's mother had had the very same experience? But oddly enough Tricia didn't feel angry toward her mother. Instead, she felt sorry for her. And more, she felt a strong sense of relief. Nothing she had done in the past or could do in the future would ever make a difference to her mother. If she still loved her dead child . . . well, who could blame her?

"Are you okay, Trish?" Angelica asked, sounding worried.

"Yes. I am. And thank you for finally telling me."

"You have to promise me that you won't tell Mother I told you."

"I promise."

"And that you'll never bring it up."

Tricia wasn't sure about that one. "I don't know."

"Please," Angelica pleaded.

"I don't know!" Tricia repeated. "I'm going to have to

think about this long and hard. And I do mean long. Days. Weeks. Maybe even months."

Angelica lifted her glass and drained it, her expression distraught. "I knew I should never have told you."

"How could you keep such a terrible secret to yourself for so long?" Tricia asked.

"You'd be surprised how good we are at keeping secrets in this family," Angelica said tartly.

"Does that mean there are more?" Tricia demanded.

Angelica pursed her lips, not taking the bait.

"Did Mother make you swear not to tell me?"

"No, she didn't."

If that was true, had their mother been waiting for decades for it to come out? What if she had? What if she'd wanted Angelica to tell the truth so she wouldn't have to? And why had their father never said a word?

"What are you thinking?" Angelica asked.

"That our family might have healed from that terrible loss if only someone had spoken the truth a long, long time ago."

"I don't disagree with you. But it wasn't my secret to tell; it was Mother and Daddy's."

Tricia turned away, taking another sip of her drink. Did the news of her infant brother's death really change things between her and her parents? Their father had always been pleasant but distant. Why hadn't he insisted her mother get counseling? But then her mother was not known for taking suggestions from anyone.

Tricia heard Angelica open the oven door, felt the rush of heat on her back, and inhaled the aroma of something wonderful. She took another sip of her drink. It was all too much to take in in one evening. She needed to think it all through, but now wasn't the time.

Tricia turned back to the kitchen and found Angelica standing with a silver tray in hand, a dainty white paper doily offsetting the golden popovers she'd taken from the oven. She looked like she was about to cry.

"I'm sorry, Tricia. Mother was wrong not to tell you. But I may have been wrong *to* tell you. Please don't do anything rash."

Tricia sighed. "I will not mention any of this to Mother. At least not tonight. And not tomorrow, either. With everything that's already happened today, it's all just too much to contemplate."

"Here, have a blue cheese popover. It'll make *me* feel better."

Tricia reached out and took one of the still-steaming appetizers. She blew on it, and then nibbled. As with almost everything Angelica cooked, it was delicious, and she said so.

Angelica blew out a harsh breath. "I think I could use another martini. How about you?"

Tricia shook her head. "I'm still working on mine."

Angelica nodded and turned back to the counter, picking up the gin bottle.

Tricia stared into her glass, admiring the golden frill on the toothpick that pierced the olives. It looked so festive . . . the way Angelica had felt before Tricia had come over and ruined her mood, and probably her evening. Feeling the need to lighten the mood, she started to hum.

As Angelica shook the cocktail shaker she absently joined in . . . and Tricia was sure if she looked outside, the moon might just look like a big pizza pie.

SIX

 Despite hearing the distressing news about a deceased baby brother the night before, Tricia slept heavily and ended up waking later than she'd anticipated. She tried to put those thoughts out of her mind as she went through her usual morning routine and concentrated on the tasks that needed to be accomplished during the day. One of them was to stock up on coffee for her customers, and to purchase some kind of tasty treat to go along with it. Mr. Everett was particularly fond of the Patisserie's thumbprint cookies, but Pixie had grumbled the last few times Tricia had put them out for her staff and customers. It was time to find something that Pixie would enjoy as well.

Tricia donned her knit hat and wrapped a heavy scarf around her neck before she braved the fierce wind and trudged down the sidewalk toward the Patisserie. She glanced across the street and saw the lights were already on at the Happy Domestic and decided she'd visit Ginny to see how she was doing before she returned to Haven't Got a Clue to open for the day.

She paused to look through the heavy glass door before entering. The bakery was empty, save for Nikki, who sat on a stool behind the big glass display case filled with all sorts of wonderful baked goodies. The day before she'd been ecstatic when spreading her happy news. Now she looked anything but happy.

Tricia wrestled with the door before she could wrench it open, and had to jump inside before the door slammed on her hand. Startled, Nikki looked up. "Good morning, Tricia." The words were cheerful, but the delivery was not. It looked like she'd been crying. Her eyes were bloodshot and puffy and Tricia wasn't sure she should mention it.

"Hi, Nikki. Boy, that's some wind. I hope it doesn't keep potential customers from visiting us today."

"Same here. I've been open for more than an hour and you're only my second customer."

"Things will pick up soon," Tricia said optimistically. In reality, she knew sales wouldn't get better until April—a full two months away—but there was no sense dwelling on what couldn't be changed.

"What can I get you this morning?" Nikki asked.

Tricia looked over the offerings. There were gaps in the big glass refrigerated case that also served as Nikki's sales counter. Instead of several dozen cupcakes, only twelve were displayed, and they were plain—with no beautifully piped decorative flowers in pastel shades. Several loaves of bread were stacked on the shelf behind the counter, but nowhere near the usual amount or variety. What was going on? Worst of all—there were absolutely no thumbprint cookies! Mr. Everett would be so disappointed, but that so much was absent meant something was definitely up.

"I'll take a couple of bran muffins and how about a dozen of those almond cookies."

"Coming right up," Nikki said, her voice cracking.

Tricia could no longer ignore Nikki's beleaguered state. "Is everything okay?"

Nikki shook her head. "I thought I'd be beyond morning sickness by now. But I've felt queasy all morning." Was that all?

"When's your due date?"

"September eighth," Nikki said as she plucked two muffins from the rack behind her. "It seems so far away right now, but we have a lot of decisions to make before the baby comes."

"What kind of decisions?"

"Mostly financial." Nikki sniffed several times as she loaded the cookies into a separate white bakery bag. As she handed Tricia the sacks, she burst into tears.

Tricia moved closer to the case, wishing she could get around it and give the poor distraught woman a hug. "Is there anything I can do to help?"

Nikki looked up and shook her head. "Not unless you've got the name of a good marriage counselor."

Tricia clamped her teeth shut and tried not to wince. Nikki and Russ Smith had been married just over three months and already they were in trouble? Tricia didn't want to get in the middle of their marital problems, but if she didn't say anything—would that make her seem cold and indifferent to the poor woman's suffering?

"Things can't be that bad," she said.

"But they are. Russ says I have to keep working after the baby arrives. That we can't afford to live on only one income.

I think he's wrong, but he's adamant. I want to be with our baby every moment of the day. I don't want to miss that first step or first word. I'm going to breast-feed and later make my own baby food. Nothing will be too good for my child."

Did she intend to be a helicopter mom—constantly hovering over the poor kid? Oh, well, it wasn't Tricia's place to judge. "I'm sure the two of you will work everything out—and soon."

Nikki shrugged, looking unconvinced, and sniffed again.

Tricia paid for her purchases and started for the door. She needed to give Nikki a shot of hope—or at least the promise of another sale. "I'll see you tomorrow. I hope you'll be feeling better by then."

"I'd sure appreciate the business," Nikki said as she commandeered the stool once again.

The door closed with another bang and Tricia hung on to her bakery bags for dear life as she battled the wind and crossed the street, heading for the Coffee Bean, where she bought a cup of French roast for herself and a decaf for Ginny. She had to work up her courage to leave the shop and slog through the gale to the Happy Domestic. She rang the bell and quickly turned her back to the wind. Seconds later, Ginny came out from the store's back room, crossed the shop, and unlocked the door.

"I thought it might be you," she said in greeting. "Come in out of that wicked cold before you shatter."

Tricia welcomed the warmth that enveloped her, not completely sure if it was the temperature or the pretty merchandise that was for sale all around her. "I bring you a decaf coffee and a bran muffin. No more cupcakes for you—you've got to eat healthy for the next few months."

"How did you know I skipped breakfast this morning?" Ginny asked.

Tricia smiled. "Just a hunch."

Ginny took the coffee tray from her. "Come on back to the office where we can sit."

The Happy Domestic's combination storeroom and office was tidy, with a place for everything. The folding metal seats weren't exactly comfortable, but they'd do. Ginny doled out the coffee while Tricia took off her coat, tossed it onto a stack of cartons, and sat down. She opened the bag and removed the muffins, handing one of them to Ginny.

"Thanks. I think I've got some napkins," she said, scrounged through her desk, and came up with a couple stamped with the Coffee Bean's logo.

"How's business?" Tricia asked.

"Slow."

"Same here. Same everywhere in Stoneham. Nikki said I was only her second customer of the day."

Ginny nodded. She and Nikki hadn't talked much since Ginny had scored the Brookview Inn for her wedding reception, the same day as Nikki's. Nikki had had to settle for the party room at the American Legion hall, which wasn't anywhere near as swank. "How's Angelica holding up after yesterday?"

"She's fine. You know what a trouper she is."

"That she is. If it were me who'd had to deal with an employee being killed on the premises, I think I'd be ready for a padded room."

"Angelica is made of tough stuff. Her biggest problem now is keeping things together for the Chamber until she can hire someone to do Betsy's job."

"What about Frannie?"

Tricia shrugged. "She has her duties at the Cookery."

Ginny nodded and sighed. She broke off the top of her muffin but instead of eating it, just stared at it. "I'm so embarrassed about the fuss I caused at your store yesterday. But when Nikki came busting in with her happy news, it just made me feel like such a heel."

"You are not a heel. And Nikki isn't as happy as you might think."

"What do you mean? When I saw her she was absolutely ecstatic."

"Apparently Russ didn't share her joy. It seems they're having financial difficulties. Unless things change, Nikki probably won't be able to stay home with the baby as she'd like." Tricia didn't care to say more.

Ginny frowned. "Here she wants to stay home with her baby and can't, and I can afford to, but don't want to. What a pair we make."

Tricia took a sip of her coffee. "Have you told Antonio yet?"

Ginny shook her head and looked guilty. "But I'm going to have to soon. I know he'll be happy about it, but I can't tell him until *I* feel happy about it."

"Give yourself a few more days. Once the shock wears off, you'll be fine." Tricia broke off a piece of her muffin and nibbled on it.

"Since I haven't been able to work up the courage to say something about the baby, I'm actually glad Antonio has been working late almost every night lately. Something very hush-hush"—she rolled her eyes at the words—"is going on at NRA and there's going to be an announcement at any time now."

"He hasn't let you in on the big secret?" Tricia asked, surprised.

Ginny shook her head. "The big boss—Nigela Ricita—says it's on a need-to-know basis, and I don't need to know."

Oh, dear. How was it Angelica knew about the NRA real estate agency and not Ginny? Perhaps they weren't copied on the same e-mails.

Ginny took another bite of her muffin and swallowed. "I suppose it's too soon to hear if Chief Baker has any good leads on Betsy Dittmeyer's murder."

"He hasn't shared any news with me," Tricia admitted.

"I've tried to remember when I last spoke with her. I guess it was at the January Chamber breakfast. She chided me for not finishing my third cup of coffee. She told me in future I should finish everything I took from the buffet table or not take seconds at all."

"That sounds like Betsy all right," Tricia agreed.

"But what's funny is, after the meeting was over, I hung back to talk to Antonio and saw Betsy pilfering paper napkins. She must have stuffed about a hundred of them into her purse."

"That *is* rather rude," Tricia said, especially for someone who she'd been told had millions squirreled away.

"I mentioned it to Antonio, but he said to forget it. That she always took something after every Chamber breakfast. Once, she swiped a linen tablecloth. He said paper napkins were cheaper and easier to replace."

They both polished off the last of their muffins and Ginny glanced up at the clock, stood, and sighed. "I hate to be a killjoy, but we both need to get to work."

Tricia rose, too. Good old Ginny, always the pragmatist. Tricia disposed of her coffee cup, buttoned her coat, and headed for the door, with Ginny right behind her. "We'll talk again soon," Tricia promised, gave her former employee a quick wave, and headed out the door.

The sky was overcast with the threat of snow when Tricia arrived back at Haven't Got a Clue. No sooner had she hung up her coat when the shop door opened, the little bell over it tinkling cheerfully. "Good morning," Chief Baker called as Tricia approached from the back of the store.

"What brings you out bright and early this not-so-fine morning?" Tricia asked.

"Not much. I just thought I'd pay you a visit. We *are* friends. And besides, you seem to know everything that goes on around the village."

"I hope you don't think of me as the resident gossip."

"Not at all. We all know Frannie Armstrong has that title cinched. But you do seem to get around, and people are far more willing to talk to you than they are to me."

"And you want me to share what I've heard?" she asked.

"If you think it might help my investigation, yes. Have you heard anything of interest?"

"I'm not sure I know anything you don't already know. Are you willing to compare notes? Have you got any suspects?" she asked.

"I've spoken to your friend Charlie, the mailman."

"Charlie? How can you even suspect him? He's a sweet old man."

"You, Angelica, and Frannie all said he was in the Cookery before Mrs. Dittmeyer's death. But no one can corroborate where he was at the time she was actually killed."

"What do you mean? He delivers to all the stores. He walks into *every* store and hands the shop owner his or her mail. Somebody has to have seen him Saturday morning."

"The shopkeepers know they got their mail that day, but none of them can seem to remember the exact time he delivered it."

"What possible motive does he have for murdering Betsy?"

"We don't know. We're still investigating."

Tricia couldn't imagine Charlie hurting a fly—let alone

dumping a heavy bookcase on anyone. And running up the stairs to Angelica's apartment, kicking in the door, and then fleeing down the fire escape to escape? The rather chubby, older gent wasn't any kind of an athlete.

"Do you have any other suspects?" Tricia asked.

"We're continuing to investigate," Baker reiterated, which meant he wasn't going to share whatever else he knew—despite his hint just minutes before. "There is another reason I stopped by. I wanted to let you know that I've heard from the state crime lab with their analysis of the fingerprint evidence from the break-in at Stan Berry's home last fall."

Tricia had to think about what he'd said before she remembered the incident. Three months before, Stan Berry had been murdered at the Brookview Inn. Days later, his home had been broken into and ransacked in what appeared to be an attempt to eradicate evidence.

"And?" Tricia asked.

"Well, you didn't hear it from me, but the fingerprints match a set already on file with the state: Bob Kelly."

"Bob?" Tricia repeated, aghast.

Baker nodded.

"Are you going to arrest him?"

"If I can track him down—yes. If you see him, would you please call me?"

Tricia scrutinized Baker's face. "Why are you telling me this? Shouldn't this be confidential until after the deed is done?"

"I felt I owed it to you. You were involved in the case, and you helped bring Berry's killer to justice."

And he wanted very desperately to get back in her good graces.

"What else?" she asked, knowing there had to be more to it.

"The man seems to have gone to ground. I went to his

office on Thursday. He saw me coming and slipped out the back, as though he knew why I had come to see him. Since then, neither I nor my officers have been able to pin him down. Not at his house or his place of business. His business, home, and cell phone numbers all go to voice mail."

Tricia digested all that he'd said. "It won't work, you know."

"What won't work?" Baker asked, sounding puzzled.

"Telling me about Bob. And all the other silly excuses you make to see me. Grant, we're not getting back together again."

"I know that. But I consider us friends. Can't a man talk to his friend? Can't he elicit her help to track down a criminal? Can't he invite her to lunch once in a while just to talk? And maybe to dinner, too?"

Tricia frowned; it sounded like he and Christopher were quoting the same script. "As long as that's all there is to it."

"Are you free for dinner tonight?" he asked hopefully.

"As a matter of fact, no."

"Is it true, or are you just saying that to blow me off?"

"I'm telling you I am *not* free for dinner tonight. I've made other plans."

"Will you be free tomorrow?"

"I don't know."

"Would you be free if Christopher asked you?" he asked, sounding like a willful child.

"We're not talking about Christopher."

"Have *you* been talking to him?"

"This is beginning to sound an awful lot like an interrogation," Tricia said unhappily.

"I'd just like some company when I eat. Is there anything wrong with that?"

"Have you considered adopting a pet?"

It was Baker's turn to frown. "Very funny."

"I'm not trying to be."

"I'm sorry I brought up the whole subject," Baker said diffidently.

Tricia sighed. "Grant, have you noticed that every time we talk lately it ends up feeling like an argument?"

"I don't mean for that to happen," he said, defending himself.

"And neither do I. I just wish . . ." She let the sentence hang for a long moment. "I just wish things had turned out differently. It seems like we connected at the wrong times in our lives."

"You mean we never quite connected," he said.

"Exactly."

"Are you absolutely sure there can *never* be a future for us?"

Tricia felt a smile creep onto her lips. "I never say never."

"But?" Baker asked.

"Your job doesn't make it easy."

"Nor does your propensity to find trouble. Trouble in the form of murder."

"My life revolves around solving puzzles—be it in a mystery book or in life." She shrugged. "And I'm beginning to think I really was born under an unlucky star."

"Is that why they call you the village jinx?"

Tricia sighed once more. "I guess so."

"If it's any consolation, I don't believe it. Not for a minute."

"Thank you."

The shop door opened once again, this time admitting Pixie. "Good morning!" she called, sounding insanely cheerful.

"Hi," Tricia called back.

Baker pursed his lips. "I'd best get back to work. I'm sure we'll speak again in the coming days."

"No doubt," Tricia said.

Baker touched the brim of his hat in good-bye and left the store.

Pixie returned from hanging up her coat. "What did he want? To take you out to dinner—again?"

"Yes."

"And you said no."

"Yes."

Pixie shook her head. "It's been so long since either one of us has been with a man, I'll bet we've both forgotten how to do it."

"Do what?" Tricia said, knowing full well what Pixie was getting at.

"The deed. Getting our bones jumped. Having red-hot, sweaty, wonderful sex."

Tricia sighed. She wasn't about to talk about her sex life with someone who had performed the act for a living. "Why don't you shelve those bargain books you priced last night?" Tricia suggested.

Pixie's smile was wide. "I don't know why you don't want to talk about sex. I mean, it's as natural as . . . well, getting laid."

"Pixie, conversations such as that are not conducive to maintaining a good employer-employee relationship."

Pixie frowned. "Gee, I thought we'd gone beyond all that. I thought by now we might actually be friends."

Again Tricia sighed. "We are, but—"

Pixie held up a hand to stave off the explanation, but Tricia could tell by her expression that Pixie's feelings had definitely been hurt. "Never mind." She turned, picked up an armful of books, turning her back on Tricia, and headed for the bargain shelf, leaving Tricia to feel like some kind of repressed prude.

Three of the four conversations she'd had that morning had ended on rather unhappy notes, and Tricia wondered if that was an omen of things to come.

SEVEN

Mr. Everett arrived for work at precisely two o'clock, just as Tricia grabbed her coat and headed across the street for Booked for Lunch. The place was deserted, and Bev, the waitress, had already gone home. That left just Angelica and her short-order cook to clean up the café and make it ready for the next day's customers.

"Bev left early?" Tricia asked, taking off her coat and setting it on one of the booth seats.

Angelica nodded. "She wasn't feeling well. If she has the beginnings of the flu, I don't want her spreading it to me or Tommy—and especially not to my customers." She picked up a couple of mustard-stained plates and a glass. "Don't mind me. I'll take these dishes in to Tommy and be right with you." And with that, Angelica backed through the swinging door into the kitchen.

Tricia hung up her coat and moved behind the counter, crouching before the small fridge. But when she opened the door, the tuna plate that was usually waiting for her was nowhere to be seen. She stood.

Angelica reappeared. "What a rotten day. It was dead slow, and then we had a bit of a rush at the end, but not enough to make a difference for this month's bottom line." She poured herself a cup of coffee and one for Tricia, too. "So, what's the latest gossip around town?"

"Um, Ange, there's no tuna plate for me."

"Of course not. We're having tea with Karen Johnson in less than an hour over at Haven't Got a Clue."

"At my store? Why?" she asked, irritated.

"Business has been at a standstill, and you've got that lovely readers' nook just sitting there doing nothing."

"What if I have customers?"

"I'm sure Pixie or Mr. Everett can wait on them while we talk to Karen."

Tricia's stomach grumbled in annoyance. "If this shindig is less than an hour away, shouldn't you be getting ready for it?"

"I need to sit down for five minutes and rest," Angelica said and slid onto one of the counter stools.

"Why can't you meet with your Realtor here?"

"Much as I love this place, it isn't the ambience I want to project when I speak to Karen."

"Then why don't you entertain her in your apartment?"

"This is a *business* meeting. And besides, my place is a mess. There was so much of that messy fingerprint powder all over my bedroom that I ended up sleeping in the living room. That stuff got everywhere. My dry cleaning bill is going to be three or four pages long. Thank goodness Antonio asked one of the ladies on his housekeeping staff if she'd like to earn a few extra bucks. It should be clean before the Cookery closes today."

It was no good arguing with Angelica. She usually got her way no matter what. Tricia decided not to press it.

"So, have you heard anything new about Betsy's murder?"

"You didn't want to talk about it last night, but I had news yesterday. Did you know Christopher was Betsy Dittmeyer's financial advisor?"

"No, but I'm not surprised. He's the only one in town," Angelica said and slipped off one of her three-inch heels, rubbing her foot.

"Yes, but he works for Nigela Ricita Associates."

"So?"

"So, wouldn't that be a conflict of interest to take on other clients?"

"I don't see how," Angelica said reasonably.

Tricia shrugged and her stomach growled. She wondered if there were any stray potato chips or dill slices hanging around the place, but everything looked tidy. And as usual, Angelica was probably right about her ex. "Christopher told me Betsy was a multimillionaire."

"Honestly?" Angelica asked, wide-eyed.

Tricia nodded.

"I'm sure he shouldn't have mentioned that."

"That's what I thought. But like Grant Baker, he's trying to get back in my good graces."

"I imagine it would take a lot more than that, although I suppose it's a good start," Angelica said.

"He said he thought I could keep a secret."

"Then I guess you just proved him wrong," Angelica said and sipped her coffee.

"He knew I'd only tell you, and that you wouldn't tell anyone else."

"I certainly won't. But how is this news relevant?"

"Betsy recently changed her beneficiary from her sister to a bunch of charities."

"So, you think Joelle's a suspect?"

"Maybe. But she's not a very big person—at least not since she lost all that weight. Could she have pushed that book-shelf over? And if Betsy had let her in the back door, wouldn't we have seen her in the shop just before the murder occurred?"

"We were a bit distracted," Angelica reminded her.

Tricia frowned once again, wondering if she should mention to Angelica that she'd found herself flirting with Christopher. No, she decided, that would only encourage Angelica to try to get them back together and, despite her conflicted feelings toward the man, Tricia didn't want that. Perhaps she'd flirted just to see if she still appealed to him. It wasn't something she wanted to think about, so she changed the subject.

"Did you know Betsy had a daughter with some kind of congenital health problem, and that she'd died at a young age?"

"No, I didn't. She wasn't one to blab about herself. Perhaps I would have had a bit more patience with her if I'd known."

Tricia wondered if she should bring up the sore subject of her relationship with their mother, but feared Angelica might have to admit divided loyalties and she didn't want to argue about it. She'd have to find some way to come to peace with the situation without Angelica's input.

"Have you called an employment agency to find a replacement for Betsy?" Tricia asked at last.

Angelica eased her foot back into her shoe. "It's Sunday,"

she reminded Tricia. "Besides, out of respect for Betsy, I decided to wait until after the funeral."

"When is that?"

"I have no idea. I'd better give Baker Funeral Home a call."

"Betsy's sister, Joelle, came to visit me yesterday."

"What for?"

"She wanted to see where Betsy had died, but you'd already closed the Cookery."

Angelica frowned. "I am not holding tours for people to see the death site—and especially not for Betsy's relatives."

"She told me she needed to make funeral arrangements. She doesn't live in Stoneham, so maybe she'll move the burial to Milford or Nashua."

"Either way, I suppose I'd have to go—at least to the funeral parlor," Angelica said without enthusiasm. "I mean, she *did* work for the Chamber and I *am* its president."

"I keep thinking about Betsy having deep pockets. Why do you think she continued to work after coming into all that money?"

"Maybe she didn't have anything else to do with her time. I never heard her talk about having any hobbies. She never brought a book to read during her lunch break. And she did not want the Chamber receptionist job to be reduced to a part-time position."

"Maybe working was the only time she had contact with people," Tricia suggested, and picked up her cup.

"Betsy never mentioned having any friends. I don't think she had a pet, either."

"What a terribly lonely life," Tricia said.

"You know, I'm very sorry the woman is dead, but it gives me a chance to start fresh with the Chamber. I never did feel that Betsy had any loyalty to me. And I'd better spend some serious time trying to figure out what needs to be done to keep the Chamber going for the next week or so until I can hire someone else."

"At least you have Frannie as a sounding board. She had the job for over a decade."

"I hate to do that, but I don't know where the Chamber stands on something as simple as the reservations for the next breakfast meeting. And there's the monthly newsletter. Betsy took care of that, too. If nothing else, she was extremely efficient."

"What an epitaph. Surely she had more going for herself than that."

"If she did, she kept it to herself," Angelica admitted.

Tricia pushed her cup away. She didn't want any more coffee and she didn't want to talk about Betsy's death anymore, either. "Did Patty come in for lunch today?"

"Patty?" Angelica asked. "Patty who?"

"You know, Patty Perkins—from Russ Smith's office."

"Oh, that Patty. Yes."

"So what does Russ think about being a daddy?" Tricia asked, eager to know the answer.

"Apparently it was quite a shock. Patty said he's been walking around like a zombie. Before the wedding, he and Nikki never talked about starting a family. He told Patty he thought they were both past it. Now he's worried about money. If Nikki sells the Patisserie, she won't make much on the deal. She owes too much and has almost nothing in equity. And ad revenue is down at the *Stoneham Weekly News,* too."

"Oh, dear," Tricia said. "It seems like the two of them never get a break."

"I wonder if I should talk to Nikki," Angelica mused.

"And say what? That you think she should keep her business?"

"She doesn't have to be on the premises twelve hours a day to keep it and make a profit. My success with the Cookery is proof of that."

"She wants to be a stay-at-home mom."

"Right *now* she does, but how will she feel when the little tyke is ready for school?" Angelica asked.

"Maybe she'll have a couple more kids by then," Tricia said.

"Or maybe in the future Russ will take a more active role with birth control."

"Now that's a subject I don't want to get into," Tricia said, remembering her earlier conversation with Pixie. She looked at her watch. "I'd better get back to my store. Do you want me to take anything over to Haven't Got a Clue for your afternoon tea?" she asked as she got up from her seat at the counter, shrugged into her jacket, and donned her hat.

"Thanks, but Tommy and I can handle it," Angelica said and rose from her seat. "I'm going to change and I'll be at your place in about half an hour."

Tricia nodded, waved, and exited the café. She had to wait for a lone car to pass, and then crossed the street. Before she opened the door to Haven't Got a Clue, she felt the hairs on the back of her neck bristle and turned to look up at Christopher's third-floor office window. Sure enough, he stood there, as if waiting for her. He waved and, although disconcerted, she found herself waving back before she hurried into her store. She didn't like living in a fishbowl.

Angelica was as good as her word. Within half an hour, she and her short-order cook had assembled several plastic-wrapped trays on the beverage counter at Haven't Got a Clue. "Want me to help set things up?" Tommy asked.

"Yes, please," Angelica said and then dispatched Tricia to make a pot of tea. By the time Tricia arrived back at the shop, the readers' nook had undergone a complete transformation. The dog-eared issues of *Mystery Scene* magazine had disappeared, and the big square table sported a linen tablecloth with three settings of a beautiful pink rose-patterned china upon it and a matching three-tiered plate filled with delectable goodies: finger sandwiches, scones, and what looked like handmade dainty chocolate cups filled with mousse and crowned with fresh raspberries—at this time of year?

Tricia set the teapot down on the table and looked at her watch. "If your Realtor doesn't arrive soon, the tea will be stewed."

As if on cue, the shop door opened, the little bell above it tinkling merrily, and all eyes turned to see who'd entered. The tall, handsome black woman with a blue wool coat and matching fur-trimmed hat spoke. "Ms. Miles?"

Tricia and Angelica both piped up, "Yes?"

Angelica turned her head to glare at Tricia, and then back to the visitor. "I'm Angelica Miles. You must be Karen Johnson. Please come in."

Pixie and Mr. Everett, who'd been hanging around and watching the food setup with hungry eyes, turned away, heading in different directions, trying to look busy.

"May I take your coat?" Tricia asked.

"Thank you," Karen said and began to unbutton it. Under it she wore a pink wool suit and black knee-high leather boots. She took off her hat, revealing close-cropped natural hair, and handed it, too, to Tricia.

"Won't you sit down?" Angelica asked, offering Karen the

seat of her choice. She took the one that faced west, overlooking Main Street.

Tricia headed for the back of the store to hang up the coat, noting the hat's fur trim was real—mink, by the feel of it. By the time she returned, Angelica was also seated, and pouring the tea. "Karen, this is my sister, Tricia. She owns Haven't Got a Clue."

"It's a charming store," Karen said with admiration. "I love what you've done with its restoration."

Tricia felt a blush warm her cheeks. She never tired of hearing praise for her store. "Thank you."

"I must admit, the first time I set eyes on Stoneham, several years ago, I wasn't the least bit impressed, but it sure has changed—and for the better," Karen continued.

"Thank you," Angelica said, accepting the credit and causing Tricia to frown. "In summer, there are pots of flowers in front of all the stores. It's really very lovely. Last year we were a runner-up as one of the prettiest villages in New Hampshire."

"I've seen the pictures on the village website," Karen said, picking up the sugar tongs and adding two cubes to her cup. Angelica (or had it been Tommy?) had piped dainty pastel flowers on each of them. Karen picked up her spoon and gently stirred the tea. "Everything looks lovely. You really shouldn't have gone to all this trouble."

"It was no trouble at all," Angelica said. "I'm so pleased to welcome NRA Realty to the Stoneham Chamber of Commerce. Have you decided where to set up your offices?"

"For the moment, I'll be operating out of one of the bungalows at the Brookview Inn, but I hope it's only temporary. Ideally, Ms. Ricita would like the business to own its own building, but that's problematical at this point."

"Bob Kelly doesn't want to rent space to the Chamber. I'm almost positive he won't want to rent to his direct competition," Angelica said.

"I've called and left messages, but it's been difficult pinning the man down," Karen admitted.

"What are your plans for the agency?" Tricia asked.

Karen turned her attention to Tricia. "My team and I will visit everyone in the village who has a Kelly Realty sign on their lawn or window and ask them if their business needs are being met."

"You have a team?" Tricia asked.

"Right now, just a receptionist. But Ms. Ricita intends to branch out into neighboring towns. She feels there's a real need in the area that isn't being properly addressed."

"I've been saying that for years," Angelica piped up, and passed the plate of finger sandwiches to Karen, who took one of the salmon sandwiches. Angelica selected an egg salad sandwich, a scone, and one of the chocolate goodies. When the plate made its way to Tricia she selected tuna, happy to finally get her lunch.

Angelica picked up her cup and took a sip. "I want the Chamber of Commerce to sign on as your very first client. We've had a devil of a time finding office space."

Karen sobered. "Yes, I heard what happened yesterday. Very unsettling."

"It happens all the time around here," Pixie said from her post at the cash desk.

As one, Tricia and Angelica turned to glare at her. Pixie found somewhere else to look. Tricia turned back to Karen. "That's my assistant, Pixie Poe."

"Oh? Related to the mystery master Edgar Allan Poe?"

"So she says," Angelica said sweetly, and promptly changed

the subject. "How long do you think it will take for you to wrestle up some clients willing to sell or lease?"

Karen looked thoughtful. "That depends on how long they've signed with Kelly Realty and if they're happy. Although from the grumblings I've already heard around the village, people aren't at all happy with Mr. Kelly—especially his tenants here on Main Street."

"You've already spoken with them?" Tricia asked and selected a raisin scone. Angelica had thoughtfully provided sweet butter, clotted cream, and raspberry jam to go with them.

Karen smiled. "Last evening I visited that cute little tavern across the street. The manager treated me to a drink on the house and we had a very nice chat. Some of her customers eavesdropped and offered their own opinions."

Tricia chewed a bit of her scone and looked up, noticing Pixie still had one ear cocked in their direction. She swallowed, and picked up her teacup. "It seems to be a village habit."

"All good-natured," Karen assured her.

"Try one of these chocolate mousse treats. I made them myself," Angelica said, offering the plate back to Karen.

She selected one and took a small bite, savored it for a moment, and swallowed. "Mmm. Delicious."

"Have you officially put out your realty shingle?" Tricia asked.

"Yes." Karen reached down for the purse at her feet, opened it, and withdrew several business cards. She handed one each to Tricia and Angelica.

"If you'd like to officially sign up for Chamber membership, I have the paperwork right here," Angelica said, reaching for her own briefcase.

"I would, thank you."

Angelica handed her a clipboard with the registration forms, as well as a ballpoint pen. She smiled. "It's so nice to see a new business opening here in Stoneham. And nice that someone is giving Bob Kelly some real competition."

"We wouldn't be opening the agency if we didn't feel there was a need in the community," Karen said with conviction.

Angelica's smile broadened. Tricia knew that smile—and didn't for a minute trust it. Was it possible Angelica had suggested to Antonio—or even Nigela Ricita herself—that the development company should invest more of its time and assets in Stoneham . . . just to bug Bob?

Knowing Angelica, anything was possible.

EIGHT

Angelica was just as efficient at collecting her tea party paraphernalia as she'd been at disseminating it across Haven't Got a Clue. Tricia and Pixie helped her take the boxes back to the Cookery, where she assured them that, thanks to her dumbwaiter, she could handle things from there on her own. She'd left all the leftovers for Pixie and Mr. Everett, who spent a pleasant half hour sharing their hopes that Angelica might stage more tea parties in the shop and on a regular basis. Tricia's fridge was full with the rest of the leftovers that her employees planned to take home, as well.

The clouds seemed to press down harder on Stoneham as the day wound down. Tricia stood behind the cash desk, reading Ngaio Marsh's *Death in a White Tie,* while Mr. Everett dozed in the readers' nook and Pixie fussed with Sarah

Jane in her carriage, strategically placing yet another Nancy Drew mystery in her tiny plastic hands.

All was peaceful. So when the phone rang, shattering the silence, all three of them started. Tricia grabbed the phone before it would shriek again. "Haven't Got a Clue. This is Tricia. How may I help you?"

"By not mentioning me by name," said Grace Harris-Everett, Mr. Everett's bride of two years. "I don't want William to know I'm calling."

"Very well. What can I do for you?" Tricia said, playing along.

"Did you know that William has never had a birthday party?" Grace said, sounding appalled.

"No, I didn't."

"His birthday is on Valentine's Day and I would dearly love to give him one, but I need help."

"I'd be glad to offer my assistance," Tricia said, hoping her words made it sound like this was an actual business call.

"Oh, good. Could you come over to my office to talk about it?"

Tricia turned her back on her employees and lowered her voice. "Do you think that's a good idea? I mean, he might see me enter your building."

"Oh, dear. I hadn't thought about that."

"Perhaps we could meet on neutral ground," Tricia suggested. "How about at the pub?"

"Oh, that sounds positively decadent. Yes, let's meet there. How about in five minutes? Would that be convenient?"

"Yes, certainly."

"I'd best get there first, in case William looks out the window and sees me. Can you keep him occupied for the next few minutes?"

"Of course."

"Good. I'll see you there. Good-bye."

"Thank you for calling," Tricia said and hung up the phone as Pixie wandered up to the sales counter.

"What was that all about?" she asked.

Tricia decided not to admonish her for eavesdropping—not this time, at least. "Nothing much."

Pixie gave her a suspicious look. Since Mr. Everett had his back turned to them, Tricia held a finger to her lips to indicate Pixie shouldn't speak. Then she grabbed a pen and a scrap of paper and wrote: *Don't let on. Working on a surprise for Mr. Everett. Will tell you all about it later.*

Pixie nodded and twisted an imaginary key to lock her lips.

Tricia smiled and nodded. "I need to run an errand. Do you think you can hold down the fort while I'm gone?"

"Sure thing," Pixie said. "I mean, it's not like we've been inundated with customers all day."

Tricia looked out the window and saw Grace exit the building that not only housed the offices of the Everett Foundation, which Grace had established to distribute the money Mr. Everett had won from a Powerball lottery drawing, but was also where Angelica's café, Booked for Lunch, resided.

"I'll just get my coat and be on my way," Tricia said.

"How long will you be gone?" Pixie asked.

"Not long. I'll be back before we close for the day."

"Okay."

As Tricia left the store, she paused at the edge of the sidewalk and looked up. Sure enough, once again Christopher was standing in front of his office window. He waved, but this time Tricia didn't wave back. He *was* spying on her.

She looked both ways before crossing the empty street. The wind was bitter cold, blowing tiny icy snowflakes into

Tricia's eyes. She squinted as she made her way to the Dog-Eared Page. When she opened its door, she was instantly enveloped in its cozy atmosphere. She hung up her coat and rubbed some warmth into her hands as she searched for Grace, who sat at a booth in the back.

Happy hour wasn't set to begin for at least another hour, but already there were four people sitting at the old oak bar conversing with the pub's manager, Michele Fowler. Michele waved a quick hello before she turned her attention back to her patrons.

Tricia hurried down the length of the pub and sidled into the booth, across from Grace.

"I'm so glad you could come," she said. "I took the liberty of ordering cream sherry for the both of us. I hope you don't mind."

"Not at all. But I was surprised to see you're working on a Sunday."

"Just catching up on paperwork while William is at work for you."

Tricia nodded. "Now tell me, what are you planning for Mr. Everett's party?"

"That's just it—I haven't had a chance to do anything as of yet. I only found out this morning that William has never had a birthday party, and that's a crime for anyone nearing his seventy-eighth year on this earth."

"How have you celebrated in the past?"

"For the past two years we've gone out for a quiet dinner. Ideally, I'd love to throw him the biggest, most lavish party Stoneham has ever seen, but I know he'd be embarrassed by the fuss and attention."

"Last year Ginny bought cupcakes and we sang 'Happy Birthday' during a lag in business, which isn't hard to do at this time of the year," Tricia said, picked up her drink, and took a sip. The sherry was sweet and its warmth seemed to immediately spread through her. "How about dinner at the Brookview with just a few close friends?"

"That's what I thought, too. Who do you think I should invite?"

"Ginny and Antonio, Pixie and me. It's not a lot of people, but we're all his friends. It would be a low-key celebration, but nice."

"That's an excellent idea. I wish my secretary hadn't had her appendix out yesterday, otherwise she could have helped with the arrangements."

"Poor Linda. I hadn't heard."

"She'll be off work for a week. I have a temp coming in tomorrow, but it'll be all she can do just to keep us from going under."

"I'd be glad to help any way I can. What would you like me to do?"

"William sticks to me like glue when we aren't both working. If I order a special cake from the Patisserie, perhaps you could pick it up and deliver it to the restaurant on Friday."

"Of course. Is there anything Pixie and I can give Mr. Everett as a gift?"

"No gifts," Grace insisted. "We're at the point in our lives when we're shedding material things, not acquiring new ones. A birthday card and a warm hug should suffice." Grace took another sip of sherry and sobered. "I hate to bring up an unpleasant subject, but is there any news about Betsy Dittmeyer's death?"

"Not that I heard."

"I can't say I'll miss her. She was quite abrupt with me the last few times we spoke."

"When did you last talk to her?"

"A few days ago. She contacted me, asking how she could go about setting up a charitable foundation."

"Oh?" Tricia prompted. She wasn't about to tell Grace about Betsy's financial situation, but this sounded interesting. "Did she explain why?"

Grace shook her head and took another sip of sherry. "I started to tell her how I'd gone about setting up the Everett Foundation, but she kept interrupting me with questions, and then she wouldn't let me answer them. She was really quite rude."

"Did she tell you what kind of charity she wanted to start?"

Again Grace shook her head. "We never got into the details. I got the feeling she might want to protect her assets, perhaps through a trust. I tried to explain the difference to her, but she cut me off, quickly said good-bye, and hung up."

"How odd." Tricia drained her glass.

"Would you care for another?" Grace offered.

Tricia shook her head. "Thank you, but I'd better get back to the store. We'll be closing soon."

"And I'd better suck on a breath mint. I wouldn't want William to think I've taken to drinking during the day, although I must admit I could get used to slipping in here every afternoon as a treat."

"Why don't the two of you try it now and then?"

"Oh, William never drinks and drives."

"They also serve soft drinks," Tricia reminded her.

"So they do," Grace said with a smile. "Thank you for the suggestion."

Tricia stood. "I'll talk to you soon and we'll firm up the arrangements."

"Thank you. Have a good evening."

"You, too."

Tricia retrieved her coat and hat from a peg by the front door and left the pub. Once she'd crossed the street, she turned to look up at Christopher's office window. No light illuminated the gloom, and there was no sign of him lurking about, either. *Good.*

Tricia had been stalked once before and wasn't keen on a repeat performance. What was it Christopher had said the day before? *"No matter how much you deny it, it's not over between us, Tricia. One day we will get back together."*

A shiver ran down Tricia's back and it had nothing to do with the temperature.

NINE

Only ten minutes had passed since Tricia had returned from her visit to the Dog-Eared Page and in that time the snow had changed from minuscule crystals to thick, heavy flakes. Pixie stood in front of the big display window at Haven't Got a Clue, eyeing the street with growing concern. "Ya know, I really oughta think about getting some new tires on that old buggy of mine."

Tricia looked at her watch. It was 4:55. "Why don't you leave now? Beat the traffic," she said, noting there weren't even any tire tracks on the street. Stoneham in February was so dead someone might as well toss an RIP wreath on the street.

"You can go, too, Mr. Everett."

Neither of her employees needed coaxing. They both hurried to get their coats, hats, and scarves from the pegs at the back of the store, while she retrieved the tea party leftovers from her refrigerator. "I'll walk you to your car," Mr. Everett told Pixie. "I wouldn't want you to slip on the sidewalk."

"Aw, you're a peach, Mr. E."

"Good night, Ms. Miles," Mr. Everett said.

"See ya tomorrow," Pixie called rather cheerfully, having either forgotten, or more likely chosen to forget, their conversation from earlier that day. Tricia turned the lock on the door behind them, turned the OPEN sign to CLOSED, and then pulled down the shades on the big display window, taking note that Christopher's office window was dark, and his apartment blinds had been drawn. *Good*.

It only took a few minutes to make sure the store was shipshape for the next day's opening. Tricia decided to wait until morning to vacuum, and called to her cat. "Let's make an early night of it, Miss Marple," she said, but before she could turn off the lights and head for the back of the store and the stairs leading to her loft apartment, the phone rang. Tricia picked up the receiver. "Ange, is that you?"

"It sure is. Don't you just hate this weather? Come on over. I'm making soup for dinner."

"How can you even think about food after that tea you put on this afternoon?"

"It won't be ready for at least an hour. I could use a little company, and figured you could, too."

"We saw each other only an hour or so ago."

"Yes, but we didn't actually get to talk."

No, they'd done that before their tea. But then, Tricia had nothing else penciled in on her social calendar.

"Soup is comfort food," Angelica continued. "And it's not all that filling."

"Knowing you, that's not all that'll be on your table," Tricia commented.

"Okay. I've got a baguette and a pound of butter. What else would anyone need?"

"A glass of wine?" Tricia suggested.

"Bring your own bottle."

Tricia smiled. "I'll be over in a few minutes."

Miss Marple followed Tricia up to the apartment, where she was promptly fed, watered, and petted. "Be good. I'll be home in a few hours."

Tricia grabbed a bottle of wine and headed back down the stairs. She put on her jacket, but didn't bother to button it, locked the door, and was surprised how much the snow had accumulated in only the few minutes since Pixie and Mr. Everett had left. There weren't even any signs of their footsteps on the sidewalk.

Tricia let herself into the Cookery and stamped the snow from her feet before crossing the store and heading up the stairs to Angelica's apartment. Once again she paused at the storeroom on the second floor. She tried the door handle, found it still locked, and felt better. Not that a wooden door was much of a barrier against a ghost, and not that she even believed in ghosts . . . still, she hurried up the rest of the steps and let herself into Angelica's apartment. Once again Sarge was waiting and was apoplectic with joy at her arrival. She made a fuss over him and he raced to the front of the apartment to announce her arrival.

"Yes, yes, I know she's here," Angelica said and laughed, while Sarge jumped up and down as though on an invisible mini trampoline.

Angelica looked up. "Honestly, wouldn't life be grand if everyone we knew was that excited to see us?"

"I have to admit, Miss Marple is a tad more aloof in her greetings, but she's just as nice to come home to."

"Unscrew the cap and pour the wine. It's been a long day," Angelica said and turned back to her stove. A pot simmered with tendrils of steam rising from it into the air.

Tricia took two glasses from the kitchen cabinet, cracked the seal, and poured the wine, handing Angelica a glass. "Don't we make a pair. We have dinner together more often now than when we were kids."

"It was all those after-school piano lessons, dance classes, and everything we were involved in that kept us from the dinner table."

"That and the fact that Daddy didn't get home until after eight most nights."

"When you own a business, you stay until the work is done."

"You didn't tonight."

"I did," Angelica insisted. "But since the Cookery hadn't had a customer in well over an hour, I let Frannie go early and came up here to cook. I always feel better with a wooden spoon in my hand," she said, and with said wooden spoon stirred the soup then took a tentative taste. "Needs more pepper." She grabbed the grinder from the top of the stove and gave it several good twists. "What did you think of Karen Johnson?"

"I like her. I have a feeling she's going to be good for Stoneham."

"Me, too," Angelica agreed. "And isn't it nice that so many women are stepping up to make this little village a destination point?"

"Stoneham, New Hampshire's home for entrepreneurial women," Tricia said.

Angelica tipped her glass in Tricia's direction. "I'll drink to that."

They did. But then Tricia stared mournfully at the condensation on the side of her wineglass. "I couldn't help but think about Betsy as I came up the stairs."

"She's been on my mind a lot today, too," Angelica said. "Her death has put all Chamber business on hold. It's very inconvenient. I suppose I'll have to process Karen's membership myself."

"It's not like Betsy asked to get killed," Tricia said.

"I don't know. She must have really pissed someone off—which apparently wasn't all that difficult," Angelica said, tested the soup again, and found it more to her liking.

"It's too bad Grant confiscated the Chamber's computer. It would have been nice to see if Betsy had anything to hide. I don't suppose she saved her work to an online storage site."

"We talked about procuring one, but I don't think Betsy took it upon herself to do anything without explicit instructions from either Bob or me. But it doesn't really matter."

"Why?"

"Because I have nearly the entire hard drive saved on flash drives—just in case."

Tricia's eyes widened with delight. "Are you kidding?"

"Why would I?"

"When did you last back up the files?"

"About a week ago, thank goodness. The police took the computer. Without those files, I wouldn't be able to run the Chamber."

"I don't suppose Grant would have taken it if he didn't think he might find something incriminating."

"I suppose," Angelica said and took a sip of wine.

"Aren't you curious to see if there's something there that could've gotten Betsy killed?"

"I guess," Angelica admitted.

"Then what are we waiting for? Boot up your computer and let's have a look."

Tricia's delight soon turned to irritation as she and Angelica slogged through the Chamber's computer files, taking only a few minutes' break to eat their soup before starting in on the task once again. Spreadsheets kept track of the Chamber's income and expenditures, including those members who paid their dues on time and those continually in arrears. Some spreadsheets had multiple worksheets, and they had to check them all, too, which made the task even more labor-intensive.

Angelica got up from her seat, taking their empty wineglasses with her, with Sarge trailing behind her. Tricia took the opportunity to slip into her seat, and scrolled through the flash drive's contents. Angelica returned a few minutes later with their refilled glasses and a plate piled high with buttered baguette slices.

Tricia grabbed one, nibbling on it while manipulating the mouse with her other hand, and tried not to look down at Sarge, whose eyes watched her every move, no doubt hoping she'd drop a piece of bread into his waiting mouth.

Angelica pointed to a list of names in the documents file. "Click on that one."

Tricia clicked on the document titled MEMBER RE-PORT. The first page contained a list of the Chamber members' names in alphabetical order. Each had been bookmarked so that clicking on a name caused the cursor to jump deeper into the document to a corresponding paragraph.

"Looks like it lists the entire Chamber membership. Click on the link for my name. Let's see what it says," Angelica said.

Tricia clicked on her sister's name and began to read.

"*Angelica Miles Samuels Collins Beck Prescott Miles*—whew! That's a mouthful. *Born*—"

"Skip that part," Angelica instructed.

"—*went to school at* . . . blah blah blah. *Graduated from Dartmouth.* Yada yada yada. *Joined the Chamber of Commerce over two years ago. Owns the Cookery, Booked for Lunch, and has a share in the Sheer Comfort Inn.*"

"So far no dirt," Angelica said with relief.

"Oh, yeah? Listen to this: *Ms. Miles is a selfish, opinionated bitch with an interfering nature. She's been known to break and enter*—Hey, this is the exact date we snuck into Grace Harris's house and found the evidence against that rotten no-good bastard who had her committed to a nursing home." Tricia looked over at her sister. "Did you ever tell Bob about it?"

"Well, of course."

"And he must have told Betsy—the date and all."

"That rat," Angelica practically growled. "Is there anything else in there?"

Tricia rolled the little wheel on the mouse, her gaze darting back and forth as she silently read the text. Angelica read along, too.

"Good lord—it even lists my panty size," Angelica cried, appalled.

"Whoa, that's a low blow," Tricia agreed. "Let's see what it says about me." Tricia scrolled down to reveal her own name.

Angelica began to read. "It says you're a—"

"*Goody Two-shoes!*" Tricia read.

"And a nosy one at that," Angelica said.

"*Nosy, bossy, condescending, smug.* Did Betsy consult the thesaurus to write this?" Tricia asked, taking a healthy and rather sloppy sip of wine.

"No panty size," Angelica commented dryly, pulling Tricia out of the chair and retaking command of the computer, "but it does say that you're the village jinx and lists—wow—twelve separate incidents to back it up."

"Let me see that," Tricia said, grabbing the mouse from Angelica's hand. Sure enough, the dates and details of every unfortunate incident had been recorded. What was Grant Baker going to think when he read it?

"Let's check out some other names," Angelica said, rescuing the mouse and scrolling back to the top of the list and clicking the mouse on Michele Fowler's name. *"Born and schooled in London, England. Her first marriage broke up when she found her husband in bed with her best friend. She took him to the cleaners and opened her first business, a tearoom in Brighton."*

"How did Betsy find out all this information?" Tricia asked.

"Michele is pretty much an open book. If she told anyone local that story, I'm sure it's been repeated a number of times."

"I never heard it."

"It's because you lead such a sheltered life," Angelica said, and not for the first time. She read on. *"Fowler lost that business to bankruptcy and married her second husband soon after. He owned a pub, which she helped run."*

"So that's why Nigela Ricita Associates hired her."

"We already knew she had restaurant experience. She told us she once managed Nemo's in Portsmouth."

"And ran an art gallery," Tricia put in and took another piece of baguette. "She's a woman of all trades."

Angelica turned her attention back to the computer screen and continued to read. *"Fowler is a woman of loose morals and most recently slept with David Black and Will Berry.* Good grief. Betsy even had dates!"

"That's rather catty of Betsy to name names," Tricia commented.

"She named your former lovers, too, and speculated you'd remarry Christopher."

"What? He's the last man on earth that I'd want to be with," she protested. "Where did Betsy get that idea?"

"Didn't you hint to her sister the wedding planner that you and Christopher were getting back together?"

"That was only so I could get some information out of her after Stan Berry's death. She must have blabbed it to Betsy. But it isn't true. Not in the least. I have no more feeling for Christopher than I'd have for a dead trout."

Angelica raised an eyebrow. "Methinks thou doth protest too much."

"Give it a rest," Tricia grated.

Angelica scrolled back up to the list of Chamber member names. "Do you see who's missing from the list?" She passed the mouse back to Tricia, who went through the list of names much more slowly.

"Bob Kelly."

"Which says to me that he asked Betsy to put this list together." Angelica reached for the last piece of baguette on the plate and polished it off. "I don't want to kick you out . . . but I have things to do and the night isn't getting any younger."

"I'm sorry. It must be a drag to have me over here nearly every night mooching dinner from you."

"On the contrary, it's almost always the highlight of my day."

Tricia stared down at the keyboard, embarrassed but pleased. "I'm not juggling two businesses and a writing career, so I've got more free time than you. Why don't you e-mail the files to me? I can study them and let you know if I come up with anything else."

"Great idea," Angelica said and rose from her seat. Sarge

stood, too, looking hopeful. "I've got to take Sarge out anyway, so I'll walk you back to your place."

The three of them bundled up (Sarge wore his jaunty tartan coat—all he needed was a deerstalker hat and a pipe to complete his Sherlock Holmes impersonation) and headed down the stairs for the Cookery. Once outside, they paused to look skyward. The clouds had disappeared, revealing the beautiful starry sky.

"Just lovely," Angelica said, "but cold. Let's move on; Sarge has a date with a fire hydrant."

"Go on ahead. I'll be fine," Tricia said.

"See you tomorrow," Angelica said, giving Tricia an air kiss, and she and Sarge headed down the sidewalk in the opposite direction. Tricia kicked at the snow on the sidewalk as she walked the ten or so feet to her storefront. Again she looked up to see if she was being watched. She wasn't. Taking out her keys, she let herself into her store, part of her wondering if Christopher was reading or watching TV . . . and the other part wondering why he hadn't been looking to catch a glimpse of her.

Miss Marple demanded to be made a fuss over, and Tricia gladly obliged. But soon the cat tired of basking in Tricia's unbridled affection and retreated to the couch for a much-needed nap. Tricia then booted up her laptop and clicked on her e-mail program. She hadn't accessed it in a couple of days and found her in-box was nearly full. Half an hour later, she'd deleted most of it (after all, she didn't need Viagra or a Russian bride, or expect to collect money from a distant relative in Nigeria), and finally opened Angelica's e-mail and downloaded the Chamber of Commerce files, opening the one called MEMBER REPORT.

She felt vaguely sick as she read through the slurs and despicable character assassinations. Was it possible Betsy had used the information she'd gathered for blackmail purposes? Was that how she'd padded her bank account? If so, that was certainly a motive for murder, although Tricia couldn't imagine any of her fellow Chamber members squashing Betsy. The memory of Betsy lying in Angelica's storeroom, her lips bloodied—terminally crushed—caused Tricia to shudder once again.

To distract herself from the unpleasant recollection, Tricia scrolled through and found what Betsy had written about Ginny. *A slut whose former lover was a murderer, and whose current love (UPDATE: now her husband) is an opportunist with a shady (unverifiable) background. (See Antonio Barbero.) Wilson and Barbero worked to rob Elizabeth Crane of the opportunity to purchase the Happy Domestic just days after the death of its owner, Crane's daughter, Deborah Black.*

Tricia closed the file. Ideally she would have liked to have deleted it but thought she might need it in the future—why, she wasn't quite sure. Instead, she opened a spreadsheet that chronicled the Chamber's income and expenditures. Tricia looked at the list of numbers and did a rough bit of math in her head. Something didn't quite add up. She clicked onto a cell and examined the formula. Tricia was no expert, but it seemed like Betsy's long and complicated formulas were faulty. She clicked on a free cell, typed in a simple formula to add cells two through sixty-five and pressed enter. Sure enough, the new total was much higher than the total from Betsy's formula. It didn't take much expertise to figure out that Betsy had been skimming the Chamber's accounts.

On impulse, Tricia picked up her cell phone and punched in the number of the only financial consultant in Stoneham.

"You have reached Christopher Benson Financials. I can't come to the phone right now, but if you leave your name and number, I'll get back to you as soon as I can."

Tricia decided to go for it. "Christopher, it's Tricia. I've been looking at the Chamber of Commerce's books and they look funny to me, except I'm not laughing. Would you have time to—" *Beep!*

Tricia set her phone aside. Oh, well. Perhaps what she should have done was call Angelica—not her ex-husband.

She picked up her cell phone once more, prepared to call her sister, when the ringtone sounded. She answered it. "Hello?"

"It's Christopher. You rang?"

"I'm surprised you didn't pounce on it when you heard or saw it was me calling."

"Better a minute late than never. What were you saying, that someone cooked the Chamber's books?"

"I'm no expert, but that's what it looks like to me. I don't suppose you have a few minutes to take a look in the next couple of days."

"Hey, I'm free right now. Are you in your apartment?"

"Yes, but I can run down the stairs to wait for you."

"Be over in a minute," he said and ended the call.

By the time Tricia trundled down the stairs and crossed the length of the store, Christopher stood huddled in his unzipped jacket, waiting for her to open the door. Had he risked life and limb and run across the slick street to get there so fast?

"Thank you for coming over," she said.

"I've been dying to see where you and Miss Marple live."

"I'm sure Miss Marple will be pleased to see you. Follow me."

Christopher seemed to clomp up the three flights of stairs, which Tricia thought might frighten her cat, but apparently Miss Marple could sense who had come to visit. As soon as Christopher entered the kitchen, she was purring like a motorboat and winding around his legs in adoration.

"Hey, Miss Marple, will you let me pick you up?" The cat practically leapt into Christopher's arms. She rubbed her face against his chin and her purring went into overdrive. "I can see I'm going to have to come and visit you more often."

Please, no! Tricia thought. "The computer is in the living room."

Christopher ruffled the cat's ears, set her back on the floor, and wriggled out of his jacket, setting it on one of the stools. "That cat always did have good taste in men."

Tricia ignored the comment and ushered Christopher to take her seat in front of the computer. He did, snatched up the mouse, and started clicking through the spreadsheet. Next he checked the other work pages in the document before he leaned back in the chair. "So, who do you think doctored the books? Betsy Dittmeyer?"

Tricia nodded. "Angelica would never stoop to petty theft, and I'm pretty sure Bob Kelly wouldn't, either."

"I wouldn't call this petty theft. It looks more like she'd been skimming the Chamber's income for a couple of years now. Did the former president ever have the Chamber's books audited? This kind of tampering would be evident to anyone with half a semester of Accounting 101."

"I don't think so. What do we do next?"

Christopher shrugged. "If you want the money back, there's only one thing to do: sue Mrs. Dittmeyer's estate."

"How long is that likely to take?"

"It could take years," he admitted. "But I also know that

the estate has enough to repay the embezzled funds. Hell, I helped her invest a large chunk of that money."

"But you said she'd left the bulk of her estate to charity."

"The Chamber will want to be at the top of the list of creditors who'll all want to be reimbursed."

"Could you take on the case for the Chamber?"

He shook his head. "It might be construed as a conflict of interest."

"Can you direct us to someone we can trust?"

"I've only been in the area for a few months, but the least I can do is find you someone with similar credentials."

"Thank you." *Okay, you can now leave,* Tricia thought, but Christopher didn't seem like he was in a hurry to go.

"Nice place you've got here, Trish." He let his gaze travel around the room until it came to rest on the open door to Tricia's bedroom.

"Can I offer you a cup of coffee or perhaps some cocoa to warm you up before you head for home?" she asked in hopes of distracting him.

He turned to face her. "Are you trying to get rid of me?"

"Not at all. I just figured we've both worked a long day and that you might want to turn in early." *And not with me!*

He mulled over the invitation. "I haven't had cocoa in ages. Do you have any marshmallows?" Tricia shook her head. "Whipped cream in a can?" Again she shook her head. "Plain is fine," he said with what sounded like defeat, and got up from the chair to follow Tricia and Miss Marple back to the kitchen.

Tricia put the kettle on, took out two mugs, two packets of cocoa mix, and two spoons, just as she'd done with Ginny the day before.

Miss Marple immediately jumped up on the stool where

Christopher had dropped his jacket, folded her legs under her, closed her eyes, and began to purr louder than ever.

Traitor! Tricia thought. She stepped away from the island and leaned against the counter, waiting for the water to heat. She couldn't think of anything to say to Christopher. They'd said it all several years before.

"Nice loft," Christopher said, taking in the exposed brick and the custom cabinetry.

"Thank you."

"It's nothing like what we had in the city."

"I made a conscious decision to avoid reminders of the past," Tricia said.

"So I see."

"How are you getting on in Stoneham?" she asked, more out of politeness than curiosity, or at least she wanted to believe it.

"Well. Very well, in fact. It's not too crowded. It's actually just what I've been looking for."

"In a couple of months the town will explode with tourists. They'll be pounding the streets from ten until seven. Maybe even longer now that the Dog-Eared Page is open. You might wish you'd never come back East."

"I don't think so. I was here at Christmas. How much more crowded can it get than that? And the soundproofing in the building is terrific. I never hear the music that's playing down below."

Tricia nodded and turned away, wishing she hadn't asked. Instead she concentrated on emptying the cocoa packets into the mugs.

Christopher cleared his throat before speaking again. "The word circulating around the village is that the girl who runs the Patisserie is pregnant."

"She's a woman in her thirties, not a girl," Tricia admonished.

"So she is," he said, nodding.

"And she's not the only one around here who's having a baby."

"Do I know the other girl—er, woman?"

"I've been asked not to talk about it until after she's had a chance to tell her family." That was mostly true.

Christopher smiled. "The fact that you even mentioned it means you must trust me implicitly."

"I wouldn't go that far." The kettle began to whistle, so Tricia unplugged it and poured hot water into the mugs and then stirred them.

"Do you ever wish we'd had a child?" Christopher asked.

Tricia sighed, resigned. This was not a conversation she wanted to have, but ignoring the question might just force him to ask again. And yet, she decided to keep her back to him when she answered. "It wasn't going to happen. Not the way we lived. I had my career and you had yours, although when I lost my job at the nonprofit I thought we might talk about it. But at nearly forty, the odds weren't in our favor, and then . . . well, you made the announcement that you were leaving me." She sighed yet again, but decided it was time to let him know just how much she'd suffered because of his selfishness. She faced him, looking him straight in the eye. "Rehashing what might have been isn't a productive use of time. And it's heartbreaking, too. I'm sorry, Christopher, but I've had more than enough heartache for one lifetime."

"No, Trish, I'm sorry. I was a fool. I—"

She laughed mirthlessly. "Don't flatter yourself. You broke my heart, but you weren't the only one, and even though I sometimes have to fight the urge to weaken, I will not allow it to happen again." At least she hoped that last part was true.

Christopher looked crestfallen. "Does that mean you've given up on love?"

She shook her head. "Not at all. But I refuse to rush into any relationship ever again. Angelica tells people that this is her time in life to do as she pleases. I've decided to adopt the same philosophy."

"And what will that entail?"

She shrugged. "I'm not sure. Yet." *But not you.* She felt a pang of something . . . regret? *Most likely.*

Tricia picked up one of the cocoa mugs and plopped it in front of Christopher. "Careful. It's very hot."

He lifted it and blew on it to cool it. "You know, we would have been great parents," he said at last.

Tricia didn't acknowledge the comment. Why did he want to talk about it now, when it was far too late? She picked up her own mug and took a tentative sip—and burned her tongue. It served her right for inviting him over in the first place. And now how was she going to get rid of him?

They drank their cocoa in silence, with Tricia avoiding his gaze. Christopher had the most beautiful, mesmerizing green eyes, and she knew if she looked at them she'd melt. He still had that much power over her.

Finally, Christopher drained his mug and stood. "I guess I'd better get going. It's really cold out there. The wind chill makes it feel like it's forty below."

She didn't doubt that.

"A man could suffer from hypothermia, and all for nothing, since the girl he loves—excuse me, woman—has a nice warm apartment and a queen-size bed, just the right size for sharing on such a bitter cold night."

"You only live across the street and I'll bet you have a perfectly fine bed."

"But it's lonely sleeping by yourself."

"From what I understand, you've been doing it for four years now. I would have thought you'd gotten used to it by now. I certainly have."

He frowned. "I don't remember you being so coldhearted."

"I'm a businesswoman. I've had to grow a thicker skin just to survive."

Christopher shrugged, stepped around the counter to remove a sleepy Miss Marple from his coat, and put it on. "You'd better walk me downstairs and lock up."

At last! Tricia held out a hand to usher him to the door. He complied and they went back down the stairs to the shop in silence.

At the door, Christopher turned. "Can I kiss you good night?"

"No."

"Please?"

Tricia stood her ground. "No. It seems you have a poor memory. We're divorced. You initiated the separation. Why on earth would I want to kiss you?"

Christopher stood that much taller. "Because you still love me."

Tricia was determined not to dignify that fantasy with a reply. "Thank you for looking at the Chamber's files. Feel free to bill them for your time. I'm sure Angelica will approve the expenditure, and if not—then I'll pay you."

"I came over to help a friend, but I guess we can't even claim that anymore, can we?"

"I consider you a friend, but not a close one."

"Then good night, acquaintance."

Tricia unlocked the door and held it open for him. He went through it and she shut and locked it before he could change his mind—or she could change hers.

TEN

As soon as Tricia saw that Christopher had returned to his own apartment, she stepped over to the cash desk and picked up the heavy receiver of the circa 1930s telephone that she kept in homage to the golden age of noir pulp mysteries. It seemed to take forever for the old rotary-dial phone to connect. "Hello?" said Angelica.

"Ange, I went through some of those Chamber files you sent to me."

"What did you find?" she asked, sounding distracted.

"It seems that Betsy had sticky fingers when it came to managing the Chamber's funds."

"Are you kidding me?" Angelica asked, sounding both astonished and angry.

"No. In fact, I asked Christopher to come over and have

a look. He suggests we sue her estate to try and get the money back."

"That cheating little bitch," Angelica muttered tersely.

"Don't go saying that to anyone else. It might just make them think you had a motive for killing her."

"I don't think so," Angelica declared. "For one thing, it wasn't my money. And for another, I have an ironclad alibi."

"Yeah, and it's the same as mine and Frannie's. And knowing Grant, he's likely to dismiss everything we've told him just so that no one can accuse him of being prejudiced."

"That man exasperates me," Angelica groused.

"He's exasperated me for over two years."

Angelica sighed. "How much money are we talking about?"

"At a bare minimum—ten grand."

"Oh, dear." Tricia had a feeling Angelica had had to bite her tongue to keep from saying what involved a multitude of swear words. "What do you want me to do?"

"Tomorrow you should call Christopher. He said it would be a conflict of interest for him to do the audit, since he was Betsy's financial advisor, but that he could help us find someone to go over the books."

"Thank goodness for that. By the way, did you know that they're supposed to announce the results of Betsy's autopsy tomorrow? Although it seems like a waste of time to me—she was crushed to death. But I suppose the police have to do things by the book."

"And Grant is a stickler for following the rules," Tricia agreed.

"Oh, I know what I forgot to ask you. What's this I heard about a surprise birthday party for Mr. Everett on Valentine's Day?" Angelica asked.

"It isn't much of a surprise if you know about it. Who told you?"

"A little bird." Tricia could imagine Angelica smirking.

"Since there are only four guests, it had to be one of them," Tricia said, and she had a good idea who: a certain Italian fellow that Angelica seemed to be consulting on a regular basis. Of course, that was to be expected as they both had ties to Nigela Ricita Associates.

"It was," Angelica said, "but I am sworn to secrecy—and I want to come, too."

"I'm not the one making up the guest list. But don't ask Grace for an invite; you'll only put her on the spot. I'll talk to her tomorrow and see what she says."

"Thank you. Goodness knows nobody else has invited me out on Valentine's Day," Angelica said with chagrin.

Me, either, Tricia thought. "Speaking of Bob," she said, though they hadn't, "have you seen him lately?"

Angelica shook her head. "After the mess he left for me with the Chamber of Commerce, I hope I never see that man again."

"Do you think he knew about Betsy's pilfering?"

"I can't imagine he did. He'd have fired her on the spot—and made sure she was prosecuted. Bob was always very careful where money was involved."

At least his own, Tricia thought. "Grant's been looking for him and hasn't been able to track him down, and Ginny mentioned she hasn't seen him walk past the Happy Domestic for a couple of days. Has he contacted you?"

"No, I haven't spoken to him for at least a month, and as I mentioned, I don't want to, either." Angelica sighed. "I don't know about you, but I'm tired. I must get some shut-eye. I'll talk to you in the morning."

"Sleep well," Tricia said. She hung up the phone and stared at it for long seconds, wondering if she should try to call Bob, even though Baker had had no luck in contacting him. Maybe she'd drop by Bob's real estate office in the morning. After all, if he wasn't at home, or showing the properties he handled, where else could he possibly be?

Mr. Everett was jovial when he reported for work the next morning, arriving with a song on his lips and a bag full of still-warm bagels from the Patisserie. Not a minute later, a cold blast of air preceded Pixie's arrival. "Good morning," she called, her smile wider than Stoneham Creek after a heavy rain. In her hand was a rumpled plastic shopping bag. "Look, I've bought another new outfit for Sarah Jane." Tricia refrained from rolling her eyes, and after coats were shucked and the coffee was poured, they all sat down in the readers' nook to have a pleasant breakfast and talk about plans for the day.

Tricia always enjoyed these conversations, which were longer and more gratifying when not interrupted by customers. Life in Stoneham was much slower during the winter months and in some ways Tricia preferred it. At least, she felt that way on cold blustery mornings such as this.

It was only five minutes to ten when the door rattled open and Tricia looked up to see Grant Baker enter Haven't Got a Clue. Mr. Everett and Pixie exchanged disappointed glances as they realized the morning coffee klatch was over. Tricia felt a trifle resentful, too, as she watched her employees pick up the discarded napkins, plastic knives, and the empty butter and cream cheese packets, and head for the back of the store to wash their cups.

"To what do I owe the pleasure?" Tricia asked, forcing a smile as she joined Baker at the front of the store.

He stepped farther into the shop and took off his hat, brushing off the light coat of snow on the brim. He must have walked from the station up the street. "I thought you might like to hear the results of Betsy Dittmeyer's autopsy."

"Death from being crushed," Tricia said dully.

"As a matter of fact, no. She died of strangulation."

Tricia stared blankly at her former lover. "I don't understand."

"Neither do I. She was dead—or nearly dead—when the bookshelf was pulled onto her. That's why there was so little blood at the scene."

So the noise she, Angelica, and Frannie had heard was Betsy thrashing around, trying to escape someone's crushing hands on her throat.

"She fought her attacker," Baker said. "Judging from what they found under her fingernails, she must have scratched him or her quite badly."

Tricia frowned. "Why are you telling me this?"

He gave no answer for a long moment. "Because I thought you'd want to know."

Was he trying to get back in her good graces? Did it really matter? "Thank you."

A long quiet moment followed.

"Angelica said you'd confiscated the Chamber's computer. Have you or any of your men had a chance to go through the files?"

Baker shook his head. "Why do you ask?"

"I'm just curious," Tricia said, hoping he hadn't noticed the slight quaver in her voice. When was Angelica going to get around to telling him what they'd found? "Was there anything else you wanted to say?" Tricia asked, keeping her tone neutral.

"Yeah, I thought . . . well, I know it's short notice, but I was wondering if you'd be free for dinner on Friday night?"

Tricia's heart sank. As always with Baker, it was too little, too late. "It *is* short notice. And I'm sorry, but I've already made plans."

Baker scowled. "I suppose you're having dinner with Christopher."

"You would suppose wrong," she said, keeping her tone even.

"Then, who—?"

"I don't have to answer that question."

"Come on, Tricia. How many times do I have to say I'm sorry?"

"You don't have to say it at all, Grant. We had some pleasant times together during the past couple of years, but the truth is we just didn't click—at least not on a permanent basis."

"You always knew that as a cop I was married to the job."

"I know that. And you're right, I've always known that."

"Couldn't we at least be friends?" he asked, and she could hear the strain in his voice.

"We *are* friends."

"Then won't you please consider having dinner with me on Friday?"

Tricia sighed. Why did he have to keep pushing? Why couldn't he understand that she needed so much more than he was willing—or capable—of giving? "I told you, I already have plans."

"Then how about some other night?"

"Maybe," she said, but she really wasn't sure she wanted to do so.

"That's the best answer you can give me?"

"Right now it is."

He looked down at his shoes. "I guess I deserve that," he said, sounding downhearted.

"You didn't mention lunch," Tricia said, feeling a bit sorry for him

"Would you like to go to lunch on Friday?" he asked hopefully.

"Valentine's Day is so loaded with expectations. Couldn't we go some other time? If I know you—and I think I do—you won't have time to go anywhere socially until you've wrapped up this case."

He sighed again. "You're right."

"Why don't I just take a rain check, and when you're free, we'll find a day that works for both of us."

"All right." Silence descended again. "I don't suppose you've heard anything else about Mrs. Dittmeyer since we last spoke," he said, bringing the conversation back to business.

Tricia pursed her lips; it was her turn to be silent.

"Tricia?" Baker prompted.

"I'm not sure."

"What does that mean?"

"It means . . . I may know something, but I'm not sure it's up to me to report it."

"If you know something, you *must* report it."

"Even hearsay? I'm not sure I want to do that."

"Can you at least tell me what it involves?"

"No. But . . . I will speak to someone who should report it and urge them to do so."

"Just tell me who to speak with and I'll go—"

"No," she said emphatically. "I promise you, you'll hear from someone today." *And it might well be me,* she did not add.

"I'll hold you to that," he said, drilling her with his green eyes, his secret weapon against her.

"I wouldn't expect any less."

"All right. But sooner would be better than later."

"I understand. Thank you for telling me about Betsy. I don't feel better for the knowledge, but . . . I appreciate the gesture."

"I'd better get back to work," Baker said. "I'll be waiting for a call."

"Okay. I'll talk to you later." Later being relative.

"Yeah. Bye."

As soon as the door closed on Baker's back, Tricia grabbed the heavy receiver on the old phone and dialed Angelica's number. It rang four times before voice mail picked up. She left a brief message, hung up, and tried Angelica's cell phone, with the same results. She left another message, and then tried the number for Booked for Lunch. It rang five times before a breathless Angelica answered.

"Booked for Lunch," she said in a singsong cadence. "We open at—"

"Ange, it's me. Grant just left my store."

"Has something new come to light about Betsy's death?"

"Yes. She didn't die from being crushed. Or, at least, that was just a contributing factor."

"What killed her?"

"She was nearly strangled before the bookcase toppled over on her."

"Strangled? Wow," Angelica said in a hushed tone. "Did you tell him Betsy was an embezzler?"

"No, I think that should come from you. It'll look suspicious if I tell him I was poking through the Chamber's computer files."

"You're probably right. I'm up to my ears in work. Bev called in sick and Tommy's leaving early for a dental appointment. I can't possibly call the chief until later this afternoon."

"I don't think it will matter all that much. After all, Betsy was stealing from the Chamber for quite a long time, and obviously nobody knew about it before last night."

"I could kick myself for not having someone look at the books before this," Angelica groused.

"For all we know, it might have been Bob who stole the money."

"I told you, Bob wouldn't do that."

"I don't know. Bob hasn't always walked the straight and narrow."

"Bob may be a lot of things, but he's not a thief," Angelica said, defending her former lover.

Tricia had never told Angelica about some of the things she'd caught Bob doing. Like smashing pumpkins all over town because he was jealous that the town of Milford had a successful festival and Stoneham didn't. Or that he'd rigged the raffle at the Sheer Comfort Inn, making sure Angelica won—hoping she'd invite him along to share the prize and rekindle their doomed relationship. Perhaps it was time to educate her sister on these and other things. First, she'd tell her about Bob's most recent transgression. "Ange, remember when Stan Berry's house was ransacked last fall? The state fingerprint lab finally came up with a match. They were Bob's prints."

"Why on earth would you say such a thing?"

"I didn't make it up. Grant told me about it yesterday."

"I don't believe it," Angelica protested.

"You can ask him yourself when you call him later."

"I certainly will," she said tartly.

Tricia gripped the receiver a little tighter. "I'm sorry, Ange. I didn't realize you still had feelings for Bob."

"I don't," she said emphatically, but it was obvious that she did—however buried she might have thought them.

Angelica sighed wearily. "I need to get the tuna and egg salads ready for my customers. I'll talk to you later," she said and ended the call.

Tricia replaced the receiver, feeling somewhat depressed. She'd never been fond of Bob, but finding out he'd stooped to vandalism to try to evict one of his tenants was really low. Then it occurred to Tricia what the fingerprint evidence meant: if his prints had been on file with the state, he must have already been accused—or perhaps even convicted—of a crime.

As though sensing her owner's blue mood, Miss Marple jumped down from her perch behind the cash desk and nuzzled Tricia's hand. She petted the cat. "It's disconcerting when you think you know someone, and then find out you don't."

"Brrrpt!" Miss Marple said, as though in agreement.

Tricia petted the cat and wondered if the next time she talked to her sister she ought to mention the possibility that Bob might be a felon. She sighed. If Angelica was still defending his character, she wouldn't like hearing that bit of news, either.

The shop door rattled, and this time it was an actual (hopefully) paying customer—an older woman dressed for the cold with heavy boots, a long camel-hair coat with a matching hat, and a knitted red scarf knotted at her neck.

"Good morning. Welcome to Haven't Got a Clue," Tricia said, trying to sound more cheerful than she felt. "Let any of us know if you could use some help."

The woman smiled and moseyed over to a set of book-shelves to browse.

Tricia turned her attention to the cash desk, which looked like it could use a bit of tidying. It took her all of a minute. She sighed. It would be a very long day.

During the rest of the morning, Tricia moped around the cash desk, waiting on the few customers who had braved the brisk wind and bone-chilling cold. Too often she found herself gazing out onto the quiet street, willing the winter to end and the spring to bring back the tourists.

It was nearly lunchtime when Mr. Everett approached the register. "Ms. Miles, I wonder if I might speak to you for a moment." He sounded so serious, and his expression was positively grim—a far cry from when he'd come into work that morning.

"Of course," she said.

"I am a terrible employee, and I feel like I've been taking money from you under false pretenses."

"I don't understand."

"We haven't had a customer in nearly an hour, and yet you've scheduled both Pixie and me to work today—and tomorrow. With business the way it is, I would prefer if you didn't pay me for my time this week."

"Oh, no, I couldn't do that," Tricia said. "We may not have had a lot of customers, but we're still in the black. And you not only provide our customers with good service, but you take care of the store, Miss Marple, Pixie, and me."

Mr. Everett was about to reply, when the phone rang. "Hang on," Tricia told him and picked up the receiver.

"Trish? It's Angelica. I need a favor. I'm not going to get

away from the café for hours yet. Could you go over to my place, get Sarge, and take him for a walk?"

"I'd be happy to," Tricia said, glad for an opportunity to end her conversation with Mr. Everett. She'd have to think of some way to allay his fears that he was driving her to the poorhouse, but that would take a bit of thought. "I'll go right now."

"Thanks. Tootles."

Tricia hung up the phone. "That was Angelica. She wants me to take her dog for a walk."

"I could do that," he volunteered, but Tricia shook her head. The sidewalk could be icy in places, and she hated the thought of him possibly falling and getting hurt. She told him so, and he bristled at the notion.

"I'm sorry," Tricia apologized. "The only job around here that needs doing is processing the Internet orders. I've got two of them up in the storeroom ready to be packaged right now."

"I could do that. Grace bought me a computer for Christmas. I'm getting quite good at using it. If you or Pixie could show me what needs to be done, I could take over processing all the electronic orders."

"That's a great idea. Why don't we do that as soon as I get back from walking Sarge?"

"While you're out, I could wrap the books that are already waiting. And I'll look forward to being trained on a new task," he said, smiling.

Tricia accompanied Mr. Everett to the back of the store. He entered the door marked PRIVATE leading to the stairs and the storeroom while Tricia grabbed her hat and coat. "Pixie, I've got to take Sarge for a walk. I should be back in about twenty minutes."

"Take your time," she said, once again fussing with Sarah

Jane in her carriage. The way she fretted over the doll was a bit unnerving. Had she had dolls as a child? If not, was this a way to placate her inner child?

Tricia was still pondering that thought as she left her store. The sky had cleared and the wind had done a good job of blowing the snow from Main Street's sidewalks. Tricia hurried the ten or so feet to the Cookery's door and entered. Frannie stood behind the cash desk with a novel open before her. She looked up.

"Hi, Frannie," Tricia said, pulling her gloves off and stuffing them into her coat pocket.

"What brings you into the Cookery on this not-so-fine day?" Frannie asked, smiling.

"I'm on my way up to collect Sarge to take him for a walk."

"It's been a while. His little legs are probably crossed by now. Angelica has had to put so much time in over at Booked for Lunch, she hasn't been around much during the day lately."

"That's why I'm here." Tricia took a step toward the back of the shop, but Frannie's voice stopped her.

"Have you heard anything new on poor Betsy's murder investigation?"

Tricia knew better than to share what she knew with Frannie, who was liable to repeat it to the next person who walked through the door. "No. How about you?"

She shook her head. "Not a damn thing. It's this prolonged cold spell. People have been holing up and keeping to themselves. The grapevine has shriveled to just about nothing. By now you've usually got things all figured out and have put our little police force to shame."

Tricia blinked, taken aback, and wasn't sure how to reply to that nugget.

Frannie laughed. "I meant that as a compliment." It hadn't sounded like it. She went on, "You usually make a fine suspect yourself, what with how you always manage to be involved in all the deaths that have happened these past few years."

Tricia didn't appreciate the comment. "Frannie, do you realize *you* could be considered a suspect in Betsy's death?"

Frannie waved a hand in dismissal. "No way. I barely knew the woman."

"That may be, but you went out of your way to irritate her every chance you got."

"Little old me?" Frannie asked, as though astounded by the news.

"You teased her every day she came to work in Angelica's storeroom."

"I was just making conversation," Frannie said, a note of defensiveness creeping into her voice.

"You made sure to let her know that leaving the Chamber was the best thing that could have happened to you. That you got all sorts of perks, like health insurance, and more money, when you came to work for Angelica, and hinted that though Betsy now worked for her via the Chamber, she had none of those things." Of course it turned out it didn't matter anyway; Betsy apparently had more money stashed away than all of them.

"Oh, Tricia, do you really think I'm that cruel?" Frannie asked. She wasn't kidding around now.

"I wouldn't say cruel, but in this instance, unkind, and that's not like you, Frannie."

Frannie stood taller. "Maybe I did tease her just a little. But you have to remember, I held the Chamber receptionist job for over ten years. Bob Kelly treated me like a slave and then fired me for helping a friend. I heard Bob hired Betsy for more than I ever got paid. And she got other perks, like more vacation, too." She let out a breath, her expression growing harder. "I guess maybe I was a little bitter, but I promise you I never wished Betsy any harm. I was just as shocked as everyone else when she died. And don't forget, I was with you and Angelica at the time of her death. I can't be blamed for her getting killed."

"No, not unless you paid someone to do it," Tricia suggested.

Frannie's mouth dropped open in shock. "Now you're really living in fantasyland. I save every penny I make for my retirement. A hundred thousand more and I'll be ready for the big move to Hawaii. I'd never waste a nickel on the likes of Betsy Dittmeyer, no matter how jealous of her I might have been."

"So you say," Tricia said diffidently.

Frannie frowned. "I'm really hurt that you could even say that, Tricia."

"I'm just playing devil's advocate," Tricia said evenly.

"You know, you really should leave the sleuthing to the professionals and not make accusations about innocent people." She sniffed. "Poor little Sarge is waiting for you," Frannie said in dismissal.

"You're right. I'll be back down in a minute or so."

Tricia felt Frannie's eyes on her as she made her way to the back of the store. She really shouldn't have laid it on so thick, but Frannie hadn't been kind to Betsy and she hadn't been all that kind to Tricia during their conversation. Still, Tricia ended up feeling like she was in the doghouse once again.

She opened the door to Angelica's apartment and Sarge came barreling out to greet her, just as happy as he'd been the night before. Unlike people, dogs, bless them, were all-forgiving.

Little Sarge really was a joy to walk. His former owner had trained him well. He sat at every corner, waiting for the signal that it was safe to cross the street, and he had learned where he should and should not do his business.

Since the Stoneham village square wasn't far from the Kelly Realty office, Tricia decided to pay Bob Kelly a visit. As she passed the petite log cabin that had been the Chamber's former home, she looked in through the window to the darkened interior. Bob hadn't put a FOR RENT sign on the door. The interior needed a thorough cleaning, as there were bags of trash and papers littering the floor. Bob apparently owned the couch and chairs that had made up the reception area, for they still stood in their accustomed spots, albeit looking shabbier than Tricia remembered.

Sarge had taken this pause to mean he should sit, and Tricia gave the leash a slight tug to let him know they were moving on. Kelly Realty was housed next door in a plain cement-block building painted a drab gray. Like its nearest neighbor it, too, was dark with a CLOSED sign hanging on the door. So much for talking with Bob. From the look of the mail stacked on the floor under the door's mail slot, he hadn't been there in several days. What did his clients think about his being inaccessible? It was unlike him, for Bob's greatest pleasure in life seemed to be making money. Curiouser and curiouser.

Tricia turned and Sarge willingly trotted along beside her. Did Bob have any real friends in Stoneham? Frannie might know, but now probably wasn't a good time to ask her. She'd ask Angelica later. Someone had to know how to contact him.

Tricia paused and Sarge dutifully sat down once again. Should she ask Baker if he'd tracked Bob down? Wouldn't he have mentioned it earlier that morning if he had? She turned, and looked up the street. Sarge stood at attention once again. The Stoneham police station was only another two blocks up the road. Then again, Baker might be out on patrol, or investigating, or snagging an early lunch at the Bookshelf Diner. Sarge sat back down.

Tricia stared down at the dog. "Are your joints beginning to ache from all that standing and sitting?"

Sarge yipped—obviously a yes.

"Come on. Let's go home," she said and Sarge was back on his feet and ready to return to the warmth of Angelica's kitchen and his comfy doggy bed. As they made their way down the sidewalk, Tricia resolved to corner Bob and make him talk. The problem was . . . if he wasn't answering his phones, or even visiting his office, how in the world was she going to pin him to the wall to talk?

This was going to take some thought and maybe a little investigation on her part. And since it was so dead at Haven't Got a Clue anyway, she had plenty of time to do both.

ELEVEN

Winter days in Stoneham tended to be so uneventful that one blended into the next without leaving any discernible memories. Much as she hated to wish her life away, and although she'd thoroughly enjoyed the camaraderie earlier that morning with Pixie and Mr. Everett, Tricia looked forward to warm summer nights, and days filled with happy customers. But if she was honest with herself, what she really longed for was a change of scenery.

Maybe it was time for a vacation. Pixie and Mr. Everett were more than capable of taking care of the store should she decide to take a few days' break, but the truth was she didn't want to go somewhere alone. Years before she would rather have gagged than contemplate a vacation with Angelica, but now the idea seemed pretty attractive. And where would they go? To West Palm Beach? Fort Lauderdale? Those places would be filled with tourists, and the idea of crowds of people was a definite turnoff. Still, if nothing else, the idea of a long vacation in some lovely sunny place was enjoyable to contemplate—especially on such a cold winter day. Of course the fact was that it wasn't likely Angelica would be willing— or able—to tear herself away from her three successful businesses.

Oh, well. It was a nice thought anyway.

With Mr. Everett and Pixie already gone for the day, Tricia vacuumed the rug and compared the relative merits of Costa Rica over the Bahamas as a pleasant place to relax and recuperate. That is, until the phone rang. Tricia turned off the Hoover and crossed the shop to answer it, even though Haven't Got a Clue had officially closed for the day some five minutes before. She caught it on the third ring.

"Haven't Got a Clue. This is Tricia. How may I help you?"

"By going out to dinner with me."

Tricia sighed. "Hello, Christopher."

"Hello, pretty lady of my dreams."

Dreams or delusions?

"What do you need?" Tricia asked.

"An answer. How about dinner on Friday?"

"This must be my lucky week. Yours is my third invitation for that night."

"Who got to you before me? Chief Baker, I suppose," Christopher said, sounding distinctly unhappy.

"Yes, but his was my second invitation."

"So who booked you in advance?"

"Why do you need to know?"

"Just curious. You had to know I was going to ask you out on Valentine's Day."

"Believe it or not, I don't hang around waiting for the phone to ring. I don't lift the receiver in anticipation that it's you or anybody else."

"But you *do* have feelings for me," he prodded.

"Of course I do, although they're not always positive."

"I know I hurt you, Trish. I've been trying to make it up to you."

"You don't need to. And I do wish you wouldn't spy on me all the time."

"I'm not spying on you."

"Then why is it every time I leave my shop I see you standing in your office window looking down at my shop."

"I told you, when I get stuck on a problem, I stand up and look out the window. It helps me think."

"And it's creeping me out."

"I don't see why."

"Because, it could be construed as stalking."

"Trish, I'd never do that to you. I love you."

"And that's exactly what all stalkers tell their victims."

For a long moment, there was only silence on the other end of the line. "I'm sorry, Trish. The last thing I want to do is frighten you. You know I'd never hurt you."

"I *don't* know that. You're not the man I married."

"I know. I've changed—and for the better. At least I like to think so."

"I'm glad if you're glad."

"Are you sure you can't have dinner with me on Friday?" he asked.

"Yes, I'm sure."

"Then how about some other night?"

"Maybe. Look, I have a lot of work to get done this evening. Can we talk about this some other time?"

"Just as long as we do talk about it."

"Now that we live in the same town again, it's inevitable that we'll bump into each other," Tricia pointed out.

"This sounds like a brush-off."

"Not at all. I'm just very busy, and I have a lot on my mind. And with so many new clients, your time should be just as booked—especially with people needing to stash their cash before April fifteenth."

"You're right about that. Still, I can't help it if I'm pre-occupied by thoughts of you."

"Stop looking out the window all the time. That might help."

"Okay, okay."

The "Ode to Joy" from Beethoven's Ninth Symphony sounded from Tricia's cell phone. She withdrew it from her pocket.

"Don't tell me you've still got the same ringtone after all these years," Christopher said.

"Yes, I do, and I need to answer it."

"Are you expecting a call from someone?" Christopher asked. "Chief Baker, perhaps?"

"No, and it's none of your business. Good night, Christopher." She hung up the receiver and pressed the answer button on her phone. "Hello."

"It's me," said Angelica. "Look out the window."

Tricia did so, and saw Angelica standing in the window of Booked for Lunch, waving at her. "Come on over and get some dinner. We had so many leftovers today and I hate to toss out food that I can't feed to customers."

"So you'll feed it to me instead?" Tricia asked, not sure if she should be offended.

"If you can eat a dinner made from food rescued from a Dumpster and not die from food poisoning, you can eat my leftovers and live to see another day."

She had a point. "Okay, I'll grab my coat and be right over."

Tricia gave Miss Marple some kitty snacks before grabbing her coat, hat, and scarf, and then locked the store behind her. She looked up and didn't see Christopher standing in his window, which was just as well. She'd just told him she had work to do and now she was on her way out. Then it occurred to her that she owed him no explanations, making her angry with herself.

The street was dry, but Tricia walked carefully in case there were patches of black ice, and in less than a minute she entered Booked for Lunch. A virtual smorgasbord of cold salads, sandwiches, and desserts wrapped in plastic had been spread across the café's counter, with two places set. "Take off your coat and help yourself," Angelica called from the kitchen.

Tricia wriggled out of the sleeves of her jacket and tossed it onto one of the seats of an empty booth. "Wow, you really do have a lot of leftovers."

Angelica emerged from the kitchen carrying a tray with two bowls of steaming soup. "Tommy took home a load of food, and even took some to Bev, although I told him not to breathe too deeply and catch whatever she's got. I can't afford to lose both of them to a virus right now. Although, come to think of it, business has been so bad I could probably take care of the café by myself if I had to. But I don't want to," she said, setting the bowls down on the paper place mats. "Dig in."

"Can't you give some of the surplus to the food pantry?"

Angelica shook her head, set the tray aside, and sat down

on one of the stools. "There are health department rules and regulations that prohibit it."

Tricia took the stool next to Angelica and picked up her spoon, stirring the soup: cream of tomato. Suddenly she had a hankering for a grilled cheese sandwich, but thought better of requesting one—not with the bonanza of leftovers in front of her. She placed a large spoonful each of tuna salad, egg salad, and chicken salad on the plate Angelica had provided, and helped herself to a packet of oyster crackers that sat before her.

"What a terrible week. First Betsy is killed, and then Bev gets sick," Angelica said and tested the soup, wincing at its heat. She helped herself to the salads, as well.

"Linda over at the Everett Foundation had an emergency appendectomy, too."

"That just proves my point," Angelica said.

They ate in companionable silence for a minute or so before Tricia spoke again. "What do you think about us taking a vacation sometime?"

"The two of us? Together?" Angelica asked, surprised.

"Why not?"

Angelica shrugged. "Why not, indeed? What were you thinking?"

Tricia shrugged. "Someplace warm, but not too crowded."

Angelica looked out the window onto the darkened street. "Right about now, that sounds like heaven. Of course, this is a terrible time for me, what with Betsy dying and the Chamber in chaos." She was quiet for a while. "I do wish I could say yes and jump on a plane tomorrow, but I can't. Are you terribly disappointed?"

Tricia shook her head. "It was just a pipe dream."

Angelica stirred her soup, which didn't need stirring at

all. "I'm sorry, but I'm terribly touched that you would even think of me as your travel mate."

"Maybe we could do something next winter."

"Yes, why don't we?"

The sisters looked at each other and smiled, but Angelica's eyes also glistened with unshed tears. It was time to change the subject.

"I tried to track down Bob today. I wanted to ask him about Betsy—what kind of employee she was, what he thought of her—but apparently he's still nowhere to be found," Tricia said, and popped one of the oyster crackers in her mouth.

"That's odd," Angelica said and sampled the egg salad, found it lacking, grabbed one of the shakers, and added a little pepper to it.

"I thought so, too." Tricia dipped her spoon into the soup, but blew on it several times before trying it. Just right. "Did you have a chance to talk to Grant about the Chamber files?"

"Damn. I completely forgot." She glanced at the clock. "Too late today."

"I'm sure he'd take the call, even if he is just tucking into his own dinner."

Angelica sighed. "I really don't want to get into it all with him. It would take hours and hours and, anyway, you were the one to actually come up with the blackmail angle. I think the news should come from you."

"I disagree."

"Then we can agree to disagree." Angelica took a bite of her salad, chewed, and swallowed.

"All right. I'll give him a call. Maybe tomorrow."

"Fine with me." Angelica changed the subject and opened a packet of crackers. "I'm looking forward to finding someone else to work with on Chamber business. Betsy was such an odd duck. She never let on what she was thinking or who she was as a person. And now she's dead and won't be missed. Isn't that just the saddest thing—to have lived half a century on the planet and no one to grieve for you?"

"Joelle was pretty upset about her death," Tricia said.

"Okay, then only *one* person to grieve for you."

"It certainly is sad," Tricia agreed. "I wonder how she lived when she wasn't at work for the Chamber. Did she have a nice house or did she live in an apartment? Did she secretly collect plates with clowns on them—"

"I think I could believe that," Angelica said, taking another bite of egg salad.

"—or did she grow orchids and cross-country ski? We'll never know."

Angelica's eyes suddenly widened. Tricia knew that mischievous look. "What are you thinking?"

"We could visit Betsy's house."

"A drive-by? What are we going to see when it's pitch-black out?"

"We could go in and take a peek," Angelica said with a devious lilt to her voice.

"That's breaking and entering. Not that that has stopped us before," Tricia admitted.

Angelica got up, retrieved her purse from under the counter, and took something from it, waving it in the air. "I have her keys."

"Where did you get them?" Tricia asked, aghast.

"The day she died, Betsy left them on my sales counter. I never had the chance to return them to her."

"And you never gave them to Chief Baker."

"Until just now, I'd almost forgotten I had them."

Tricia felt a smile tug at her lips. "Well, what are we waiting for? Let's finish eating and go!"

After taking Sarge for a short walk, the sisters jumped into Angelica's car and headed into Milford. No full moon illuminated the inky black sky as Angelica drove slowly down Vintage Road, while Tricia rode shotgun, looking for number 77.

"Most of these houses don't have visible house numbers," she commented. "Say they need to call 911 to report a fire or order an ambulance—how do they expect the good guys to find them?"

"Clairvoyance?" Angelica suggested. They'd reached the end of the street, so Angelica drove partway up one of the driveways, backed out, and started up the road once more, driving at a crawl.

"Stop!" Tricia said. "It's got to be this one."

"You think?"

"Number 79 is on the right and 75 is on the left. Process of elimination says this is the right one."

Angelica pressed the accelerator and drove on. "If we're going in, I don't want the neighbors to see my car and take down my license number."

"Where will you park?"

"That little strip mall on Nashua Street."

"Good idea. I'm glad I wore layers. It's at least a three-block walk and it's freezing out."

Angelica parked the car under one of the strip mall's tall lampposts. She groped under the driver's seat and came up with a big flashlight. "Will you take charge of this?"

"Sure thing," Tricia said, taking it from her.

They pulled on their gloves, got out of the car, locked it, and started off on foot.

After they'd gone a block, Angelica spoke. "Remind me again why we decided to move to such a cold place?"

"I wanted to open a bookstore. You arrived on my doorstep and never left. And you got here when the weather was perfect, and had no clue how nasty winter could be."

"I guess you're right. And I guess I love it too much to leave just because it's cold and miserable for five or six months of the year."

"Good."

Angelica stopped abruptly. "What did you say?"

Tricia stopped, too. "I said 'good.' Stay here with me forever."

Angelica smiled, her eyes filling with tears. When she spoke again, her voice cracked. "Okay, I will."

Tricia patted her back and then gave her a nudge, and they started off once more.

"I hope the wind has blown the snow off Betsy's driveway," Tricia said. "Otherwise we'll leave footprints."

"Good point," Angelica agreed. "Maybe we should have brought a shovel."

They walked the next block in silence. Would it look equally suspicious to Betsy's neighbors to see two strangers walking down their dead-end street on a cold winter's night?

"Have you got those keys handy?" Tricia whispered.

"Right in my pocket."

They turned up number 77's driveway. Betsy's house looked dark and forbidding with all its drapes drawn. The shaggy bushes that flanked the front steps helped reinforce an aura of neglect, but then most houses looked rather that way at night with no illumination to highlight their best attributes. Tricia and Angelica had already agreed to try the back door first in hopes of staying out of the neighbors' sight, and headed straight there.

Angelica fumbled with the keys while Tricia held the flashlight beam fixed on the door's lock. But something wasn't right. She moved the light to take in the doorframe. "Ange, I think this door has been kicked in—just like at your apartment."

"You mean someone's already been here and robbed Betsy? That's disgusting."

"Maybe we should just call the police," Tricia suggested.

"And tell them what? That we were about to enter a dead woman's house to snoop around and found that another crime had been committed before we even got here?"

"It doesn't sound good, but it's the right thing to do."

"We can do the right thing after we take a look." And with that, Angelica pushed open the back door and stepped inside. She fumbled for a switch, found it, and a light near the ceiling flashed on in what Tricia assumed would be the kitchen. "Oh, my God," Angelica murmured.

"What is it?" Tricia asked, trying to see beyond her sister, but Angelica's bulky parka made an effective barrier. "Move," she ordered.

"I can't. Wait a minute."

Angelica seemed to shuffle a foot or so forward, giving Tricia just enough room to enter. It was then Tricia's turn to mutter, "Oh, my God. Betsy was—"

"A hoarder," Angelica said in disgust. The entire kitchen was filled with mounds of big black trash bags, stacks of cartons, heaps of newspapers, dirty dishes with caked-on dried food, clothes, and heaven only knew what else.

"Well," Angelica said, sounding overwhelmed, "I never expected this."

"I don't suppose anyone does. Is there a trail you can follow?" Tricia asked and wrinkled her nose. The place didn't smell all that good, either.

Angelica shuffled forward, shoving stuff aside as she went. "I'm going to try to get into the next room. Are you game to follow?"

The truth was, no! But Tricia answered yes, anyway. She stepped farther into the kitchen and then shut the door as best she could and followed Angelica.

It took a good couple of minutes to navigate through the four-foot-high piles of garbage and junk before they made it into what must have been a living room, although if there was furniture, it was buried under more trash, clothes, un-opened Priority Mail boxes, sagging cartons, and bulging plastic storage containers. Angelica hit a light switch and the dusty light fixture in the middle of the ceiling flashed on.

"Good grief," Tricia cried in awe as she took in the decorations lined up on the wall. "I was only kidding when I said Betsy collected clown plates." There must have been twenty or more of them hanging about a foot above the trash heaps, each of them encrusted with greasy dust and cobwebs. "If someone broke in to rob Betsy, how would the police know if anything was missing?"

"That's a good question." Angelica shuffled forward again, then halted and let out a strangled squeak.

"What's wrong?" Tricia asked, concerned.

"Eew. There's a dead mouse on this pile of crap," Angelica wailed.

"Better it's dead than alive," Tricia said.

"How could Betsy live like this? I always thought she had

a screw loose, but I never anticipated this," Angelica said in exasperation.

"It beats me how someone so organized at work could be so disorganized at home," Tricia said. She thought of something she'd heard some months before. "Last fall, after Joelle and Stan Berry broke up, Frannie told me that Joelle used to come here to stay with Betsy so as not to sully her reputation. But I can't imagine anyone in her right mind wanting to stay in this hovel."

"Unless Joelle is a hoarder, too. Then she probably wouldn't blink an eye at a mess like this."

"Maybe."

Angelica gazed around the room. "What should we be looking for—and more important—are we ever likely to *find* what we're looking for?"

"You got me." Tricia thought about her sister's question. "Keep an eye out for bank statements, insurance forms, and stock certificates—you know, financial papers."

"A lot of that stuff is now delivered via e-mail. Do you see any sign of a computer?"

Tricia looked around the room. "Maybe we should try to find her bedroom. She might have stored all her important stuff in one place."

"I think the trail veers to the left," Angelica said and started shuffling forward again.

Tricia kept her eye out for anything that looked important—but it all appeared to be trash littered with mouse droppings and spiderwebs, and around the floors and on every picture or knickknack hanging on the walls was a thick layer of greasy dust. And worse, she suspected under all the rubbish was likely to be black mold. After all, packed in tightly as it was, the junk curtailed the circulation of air. Tricia shuddered at the thought, and couldn't wait to get home to throw her clothes—jacket and all—into the washer, and then jump in the shower with water as hot as she could stand.

Angelica had stopped moving and stood before the opening to a hall, grimacing. "Oooh, it's the bathroom, and it's even nastier than a gas station restroom."

It took a few moments for Tricia to reach the open door to the bathroom. The hall before her was stacked with cartons and draped with yet more piles of clothes. She looked into the bathroom and felt distinctly queasy. The toilet had no seat, and the bowl was caked with . . . she didn't want to speculate. The tub was piled so high with clothes and towels that there was no way Betsy could bathe in it. "No wonder Betsy spent so much time in the Cookery's washroom. Her own was unusable."

Angelica made no comment and continued picking her way through the accumulated trash once again. She opened a door. "It's a bedroom . . . I think. This could have been a child's room. It's painted lilac—favorite little-girl color."

"Joelle mentioned Betsy had a daughter who died. Can you get in?" Tricia asked.

Angelica shook her head. "I don't think so. I can't see a bed, or any toys or books, just more piles of crap."

Tricia caught up with her and looked inside. Other than the color of the wall, there was no indication the room had ever belonged to a child. It was filled with more of what they'd found in the rest of the house. "Do you think Betsy was trying to replace her dead child and the husband who left her with piles and piles of rubbish as some weird way of filling the voids in her life?"

"It doesn't make sense to me, but after the death of a child, heaven only knows how deep her grief ran." Angelica craned her neck. "There's another door across the way." She sidled past more boxes and stood before an open doorway. "This might be it." She reached inside the room, found and flipped a switch. Yet another dusty bulb illuminated the littered space.

Angelica waited for Tricia to catch up before she entered the room. At least this space wasn't quite as cluttered. A small area had been cleared and Tricia saw a dirty Berber carpet covered with coffee and food stains. A computer desk piled high with papers, dirty coffee cups, and a thick layer of dust was crammed into a corner next to a double bed. Half the bed was piled with clothes, leaving only a narrow sleeping area with grimy sheets and blankets.

Tricia swallowed hard, disgusted. What a difference from her lovely, uncluttered home—where she fervently wished she was at that moment. "How could anyone live like this?"

"It's a disease," Angelica said with sadness. "Poor Betsy couldn't relate well to people, so she must have spent her free time collecting stuff that comforted her. I'll bet she valued all this rubbish over the people who remained in her life."

"And maybe her hoarding was responsible for her failed marriage," Tricia said. "Joelle mentioned how she and her husband fought over their assets. Maybe she couldn't find them in all this junk to satisfy a judgment."

Angelica picked through the stack of papers on the computer desk. "Looks like mostly old bills. I'll bet she paid them electronically."

"That would save on stamps," Tricia agreed.

"And maybe she paid them as they came in so they wouldn't get lost." Angelica hit the computer's power button and they waited for it to boot up. Unfortunately, the first screen up demanded a password. "What do you think Betsy would use?" she asked.

"I have no idea. Maybe her maiden name?" Tricia suggested. "What if it's her mother's maiden name? That's what the banks always seem to want as a security check."

"Do you have to be such a pill?" Angelica accused. She turned back for the keyboard. "Lowercase? Initial caps? All caps? We've only got three tries before we're locked out."

"We're as good as locked out now," Tricia pointed out.

Angelica sat on the grubby office chair, stared at the dust-covered, grimy keyboard for a long moment, and then removed her gloves.

"You'll leave fingerprints," Tricia warned.

"I can't type with them on. And I can always dust the keyboard off when I'm done. It certainly needs it." She rested her fingers on the home-row keys, but paused. "What's Betsy's unmarried sister's last name?"

"Morrison."

"I'll try initial caps." Angelica tapped the keys and got a warning message to try again. She tried all lowercase letters and got the same warning. "One last time," she said, hit the caps lock key, and tried again. Sure enough, the sign-on screen morphed into the desktop display, which was as littered with files as the room was cluttered with junk. "Oh, boy. Where do we start?"

Tricia noticed an open container of recordable CDs peeking out from under a soiled towel. "Copy all the files onto these CDs and we can peruse them at our leisure."

"Who has time for leisure?" Angelica asked, but she accepted an empty disk from Tricia and proceeded to copy all the desktop files. After that, she dug deeper into the documents file and copied everything there before starting on a third disk.

The task took a good twenty minutes, and as each minute

passed Tricia's anxiety level rose. "That's got to be enough," she said. "We've got to get out of here before someone finds us here."

Angelica popped the final CD from the read/write drawer and added it to the others in her pocket. Then she pulled out a pocket container of hand sanitizer and squirted some into her palms, working it in before she pulled her gloves on again. She grabbed a towel from the pile overhead, squirted sanitizer on it, and wiped down the keyboard.

Tricia began to make her way through the house, aiming for the kitchen with Angelica following, switching off lights as she went.

A loud bang reverberated through the house and Tricia stopped dead.

"What was that?" Angelica whispered.

"There's someone else in the house!" Tricia practically squealed.

"Hide!" Angelica said.

"Where?"

But they had no time, because a voice from the kitchen doorway demanded, "What the hell are you doing here?"

TWELVE

Tricia felt her mouth go dry, but managed a nervous laugh. "Hi, Joelle. What a surprise to see you here."

"It's an even bigger surprise to find the two of you in my sister's house. Did you kick in the back door?" she demanded.

"No, we found it that way," Tricia said.

"We were going to use Betsy's keys," Angelica said and pulled them out of her jacket pocket, dangling them for Joelle to see.

"You have no right to be here. I'm going to call the cops," she said, and began to dig into the purse hanging from her shoulder.

"Wait—please don't," Tricia said. "We came here tonight to try to figure out why Betsy was killed."

"That's a job for the police," Joelle said.

"Did you know that Tricia has assisted the Sheriff's Department and the Stoneham Police Department in solving several local murders?" Angelica said.

"Yes," Joelle grudgingly admitted. "After Stan was killed."

"You *do* want your sister's murderer to be found sooner rather than later, don't you?" Angelica asked. "I know I would."

Tricia shot her an annoyed glance. "All we want to do is help. I assure you, we had no intention of taking any of your sister's things." *Except for three CDs' worth of data from her computer,* she silently amended.

Joelle waved a hand before her, taking in the mess. "As you can see, Betsy really had nothing worth stealing."

"When did she start hoarding?" Tricia asked.

"Betsy never was a neatnik, but she didn't start collecting papers, clothes, and other junk until after her daughter, Amy, died. That was ten years ago. In the last five years—since her husband, Jerry, left—she became much, much worse."

"She accumulated all this in only five years?" Angelica asked.

Joelle nodded. "For the most part. Her collections, as she called them, became more important to her than any of the people in her life. She lost all of her friends, and her husband, because of them. I was the only one left who'd have anything to do with her, and sometimes she was so mean to me, I think she deliberately tried to drive me away."

"So you two were no longer close?" Tricia asked.

Again Joelle nodded. "I guess I tried one too many times to get her some help, but she just got angry. She told me she was going to change her will. I had been her beneficiary since the divorce, but she said she knew I'd throw all her treasures in the trash before her body was cold." She looked around the dump that had been Betsy's living room. "She had that right."

"Do you have any idea who might have wanted her dead or why someone would have kicked in her door?"

Joelle shook her head. "She kept to herself these past five years. She worked, she shopped, and she stayed home alone. It wasn't much of a life."

"And someone took even that from her," Angelica commented sadly.

"What made you decide to come here tonight?" Tricia asked.

"I . . . um . . . came to look for a nice outfit for her to be buried in."

"Then you've heard that the medical examiner ruled on the cause of death?" Tricia asked.

"She was crushed," Joelle said with a shrug.

She hadn't heard. And why hadn't Grant Baker contacted her to tell her the official cause?

"You said you came here tonight to look for something that would help you figure out who killed Betsy. And?" Joelle demanded.

"And?" Tricia repeated dully.

"What have you discovered?"

Tricia threw Angelica a guilty look.

"That the motive wasn't robbery," Angelica said.

Tricia's head snapped around to glare at her sister and could have cheerfully kicked her. "Sadly, nothing," she told Joelle.

Joelle scowled. "You're supposed to be so smart when it comes to mysteries. You haven't been able to come up with anything else?"

Tricia shrugged. "Not so far."

Joelle scowled. "Then I assume your reputation as an amateur sleuth has been greatly exaggerated."

"I've always thought so," Angelica muttered.

Tricia gave her sister another annoyed glare, but Angelica seemed oblivious.

"Look, it's getting late. You two had better go," Joelle said firmly. "If you give me Betsy's keys and leave right now, I won't call the police and report you."

"We were just about to leave when you got here," Angelica said.

"Yes. It's getting late," Tricia agreed, and she made her way through the piles in the living room and squeezed past Joelle to head for the back door.

Angelica handed Joelle the set of keys as she passed. "Please let us know what you decide to do about the funeral. We'd like to come."

Speak for yourself, Tricia was tempted to say. "Good night," she called as she went out the back door.

"Good night," Angelica echoed and tried to close the door behind her. It wouldn't catch, and after a few tries she gave up.

Tricia breathed in the crisp clean air. The odor in Betsy's house had been so penetrating she felt as if she could taste it. She waited until Angelica flanked her, and then the sisters started down the driveway. "Do you notice what's missing?" Tricia asked.

Angelica looked all around her. "No, what?"

"Joelle's car."

"What are you saying—that she was sneaking around the same as us?"

"It did take her a moment or two to come up with the burial-clothes excuse."

"So why do you think she really came here tonight?"

"I have no idea. But if she'd been disinherited, then just like us, she really had no right to be there. Was she going to sift through the trash to find hidden treasure before the house is sealed for probate?"

"If so, naughty Joelle."

They turned the corner and walked along Nashua Street, heading back toward the strip mall and Angelica's car. Angelica raised her arm to sniff her jacket sleeve. "I think I'm going to have to fumigate my clothes. Either that or burn them."

"Mine, too."

"Do you think the smell will transfer to my car seats?"

"Not if you leave a window open overnight—and pray it doesn't snow."

"Great idea."

"What do you want to do about the CDs?" Tricia asked and ducked her head, wishing the wind weren't so strong.

"You have more free time than I do. You can have them, look them over, and then let me know what you find—if you find anything at all, that is," Angelica said, reaching into her pocket and withdrawing the CDs, and then handing them to Tricia.

"It might be that Betsy only chronicled the junk she collected."

"And if that's the case, I think you should look at the disks and then destroy them. As it is, we're violating her privacy," Angelica said.

"But now she's dead and beyond caring. And you can tell an awful lot about a person by the junk they collect on their hard drive."

"Which makes me want to purge my computer the minute I get home. That and change all my passwords. It really was far too easy for us to get into Betsy's computer."

"And thank goodness it was," Tricia said.

"But only if something good turns up. I have a feeling you'll find rummaging through her files to be a complete waste of time."

Tricia did, too. And if she didn't, how on earth was she going to use the information without incriminating herself and Angelica?

It wasn't something she wanted to contemplate.

Yet.

It was almost ten by the time Tricia had thrown her clothes into the washer and emerged lobster red from her shower, much too late to call Chief Baker. He was an "early to bed, early to rise" kind of guy, and she didn't want to annoy him by waking him.

Instead, she sat down in front of her computer with Miss Marple on her lap and went through the first of the three CDs. Not only did Betsy collect physical junk, she collected a lot of pictures. One of the files contained her user IDs and passwords to all her online accounts. Her Pinterest account had over forty thousand pictures spread over 252 boards. They ranged from recipes to vintage Christmas cards to do-it-yourself projects, and she had copied many of them to her hard drive.

Tricia felt like a voyeur pawing through the dead woman's virtual closetful of secrets, and like her home, nothing seemed to be of any real value.

The buzzer on the washer sounded and Miss Marple jumped down from her lap, allowing Tricia to get up and put the clothes in the dryer. She'd have to stay up and take the clothes out when the cycle finished, or she'd be spending the next night or so ironing everything, which was a chore she absolutely loathed.

With the dryer drum happily turning, Tricia wandered back to the computer, but this time Miss Marple did not join her. Tricia considered logging on to Betsy's account at the Bank of Stoneham but figured the police might subpoena the computer records and possibly trace the inquiry to her home computer. She wanted to find Betsy's killer, but not if she had to go to jail to do it.

Tricia scrolled through a number of files, but nothing seemed relevant to Betsy's death, and as Angelica suggested, she felt like a voyeur violating Betsy's privacy. Finally a glance at the time listed at the bottom-right corner of her computer monitor told her that the dry cycle would soon be finished. She'd started closing screens when she noticed a Word document with the title of DIET RECIPES. Since she worked so hard at maintaining her own weight, she found herself double-clicking on the icon. The software loaded and the document opened. Sure enough, a recipe for makeover chocolate muffins appeared. Instead of oil, the recipe called for prune paste or applesauce. Instead of cane sugar, the recipe called for an artificial sweetener. Tricia was all for lowering calories, but she preferred food to be made of real ingredients, not something from a test tube in some chemical company's laboratory.

She scrolled down to the next page, and the next. More and more interesting makeover recipes appeared, including a low-cal version of Waldorf salad—something she'd always enjoyed. She hit the print button, specifying that page, and wondered if she could get Angelica or her short-order cook to make it for her. She was about to close the file, wishing Betsy had included a table of contents, when she stopped scrolling. Her heart began to pound when columns of names, cities, and numbers filled the screen. What did it mean? Did Betsy have bank accounts spread out all across the nation with money hidden in other names? How could she have accomplished it?

Tricia sat back in her chair and pondered the implications. Had Bob looked into her background before he hired her, or had he offered employment to the first warm body he could find to fill Frannie's empty chair? Was it possible the Chamber still had her employment application? Would that give a clue to the woman's work background and her last several employers? If asked, would they give truthful answers, or would they fall back on the standard, "we can't give out that information" and only reveal Betsy's employment dates?

Tricia sat back in her chair and considered her options. If she said nothing, would Grant Baker—or one of his officers— find the information buried in a word processing document containing recipes, or should she tell him what she'd found— or have Angelica, as Chamber president, do it?

She glanced at the clock and realized just how tired she felt. It had been a long day and she was in no condition to make such a decision. She closed the files and shut down the computer. "Bedtime. Come along, Miss Marple."

The cat opened her sleepy eyes, got up, and stretched, then jumped down from the couch.

Tricia grabbed a book from her living room shelves, and headed for her bedroom. She got undressed, climbed into bed, and opened Josephine Tey's *The Daughter of Time,* but soon found she couldn't concentrate on the words. She had far too much on her mind. She lay awake in the dark for a long time, trying to make sense of all the various threads of information she'd gathered that day, but it was no use. None of the pieces to the puzzle seemed to fit properly, and it was only exhaustion that finally took her to dreamland.

THIRTEEN

Tricia awoke late the next morning and only had time to take a quick shower, feed her cat, and grab some yogurt from the refrigerator before she made it downstairs to open her store for the day. On days like this, her exercise regimen was the first thing eliminated from her to-do list.

Haven't Got a Clue's first visitor of the day wasn't a customer, but Charlie the mailman, bundled up for the cold, his cheeks red from the vicious wind. "Hey, Charlie. You look frozen stiff. I'm just about to make a pot of coffee. Would you like to join me?"

He sorted through the contents of his leather mailbag and came up with an assortment of circulars and bills. "I wish I could, but I really don't have time for . . ." His words drifted off, and Tricia noticed the lines around his eyes seemed more deeply defined than they had the last time she'd spoken to him.

"Is something wrong? Can I help?" she asked sincerely.

"I've got a lot hanging over my head, Tricia," Charlie said and sighed. He set the mail on the counter.

"Why don't you tell me about it?" she asked.

Again Charlie sighed, his gaze focused on the floor. "It's the police. They seem to think I might have had something to do with Betsy Dittmeyer's death—and all because I happened to be in the Cookery just before it occurred." He straightened and met her gaze. "What they failed to understand is that I'm there five days a week—and almost always at the same time."

"Chief Baker is only doing his job, although I can tell you from personal experience that it's no picnic to be the object of his scrutiny."

"I'll say."

"Why would the chief think you had some connection to Betsy?"

"Because," he said, his gaze turning downward once again, "I do."

Tricia's eyes widened. "You and Betsy had a relationship?" she asked, taken aback.

Charlie looked absolutely horrified. "Me? And Betsy? Oh, please."

"Then what?"

Charlie sighed, still not looking Tricia in the eye. "Part of the twelve steps are that you don't talk about it."

Oh, dear. "You and Betsy were alcoholics?"

"Not 'were.' Once an alcoholic, always an alcoholic."

That made sense. Betsy had a compulsion to hoard. Perhaps that had driven her to drink, as well. And what had compelled her to steal?

"Where did the two of you meet?" Tricia asked.

"At a meeting in Milford, although I hadn't run into her at one for some time. I did see her on a regular basis when the Chamber of Commerce was located up the street."

"Does anyone else know she was an alcoholic?"

"Just her immediate family and the others who frequent our meetings. But they're not likely to talk about it, either. That's one of the reasons they call it Alcoholics Anonymous."

"I hope you won't think I'm nosy, but I can't imagine you as . . ."

"A drunk?" He laughed. "It's okay to say it. I always did."

"Then how did you start drinking?"

"Like most kids—stealing my parents' liquor. Then finding friends and helping them steal their parents' liquor. I worked, I earned money, I spent it on beer or whiskey. It was a vicious cycle. I was engaged, but my girl told me if I didn't sober up, she would leave me. That did it. I joined AA and the rest is history."

"How many years ago was that?"

"Thirty-five. And we've been happily married the whole time."

Tricia smiled. "Do you still go to meetings?"

He nodded. "Several times a week. It's part of our philosophy to help others get off the alcohol treadmill and regain their sobriety."

"Have you ever fallen off the wagon?" Tricia asked.

"A couple of times," he said sheepishly. "I've haven't had a drink in almost eighteen years now."

"Good for you, Charlie."

"Honest, Tricia. I didn't kill Betsy. I admit, I might be

able to understand it if others had reason to do so—she had a heartless manner. I'm not sure she ever really embraced our philosophy, but as far as I know, she went to her grave stone-cold sober."

Someone had helped Betsy to her grave, and in quite a horrific manner. And one of the tenets of the twelve-step program was to ask forgiveness of those you'd wronged. Betsy was so busy stealing from her employer and goodness knows how many other people, she apparently had no time or inclination to do so.

"I don't suppose you know how I could get in touch with Betsy's ex-husband."

"Jerry the welder?" he asked.

"I didn't know his name—or where he worked," Tricia said.

"Try Black's Village Smithy. Do you know the place? It's up on the highway."

"I know about it," she said. More important, she knew the owner—although the last time they'd spoken they hadn't been on good terms. In fact, they'd *never* been on good terms. "Thanks for the tip. I'll see if I can track him down."

"Seems to me Betsy mentioned it to me the last time I spoke to her. She was angry that he'd be working so close to her. I guess their divorce was pretty bitter."

"So I've heard."

Charlie looked down at his bulging leather mail pouch. "I'd better get going. My boss wasn't happy when I got hauled off to the police station during my rounds—and he won't like it if it happens again."

"I'm sure the chief will soon clear you."

"From your lips to God's ears," Charlie said with what sounded like a forced laugh. He gave a wave and headed out the shop door.

No sooner had he gone when Tricia called directory assistance. "Yes, could you please give me the number for Black's Village Smithy?"

Pixie was late—by more than half an hour—when she finally showed up at Haven't Got a Clue. "Didn't I tell you I should get some new tires for my old boat?" she asked. "When I got down to the car, it had a flat. I got the Triple A to come and put on the spare, but I'm going to have to get a new tire any day now. Ya think I could leave early one of these nights?"

"Not one of these nights," Tricia said, "you'll do it tonight. I don't want you to have an accident. Meanwhile, I have an appointment this morning. Do you think you could mind the store?"

"Piece of cake," she said with a dismissive wave of her hand, and went to the back of the shop to hang up her coat and hat and retrieve Tricia's before heading back to the front of the store.

"Thanks," Tricia said, donning the coat. Wasting no more time, she flew out the door. A minute later, she was in her car and heading north toward the highway.

Tricia hated to admit it, but she actually felt nervous as she pulled into the small gravel parking lot outside of Black's Village Smithy. The proprietor had been the husband of her friend Deborah Black, the former owner of the Happy Domestic. She'd died the summer before when a plane crashed into the Stoneham gazebo on Founders' Day. Tricia and David Black had never gotten along, and she hoped she wouldn't run into him at what was now his art studio. An astute businessman, Black also hired welders to take in commercial jobs to keep the business afloat while he worked on his metal sculptures.

Tricia entered the front office, which looked like it could have doubled for a doctor's waiting room. "May I help you?" asked a pretty young woman from behind a circular desk. She was dressed in a turquoise sweater set and dark slacks, not unlike what Tricia usually wore when working at Haven't Got a Clue. Her long hair and pretty smile reminded Tricia of her late friend. Had David hired her because of that resemblance, and could he be bedding her, too? He hadn't been faithful to Deborah, but then she hadn't been faithful to him, either.

Tricia stepped up to the desk. "I'm here to see Jerry Dittmeyer. He said he'd be taking his morning break about now."

"Sure. I'll page him." She picked up the receiver, pressed a button on the phone, and spoke into the mouthpiece, calling him to the office.

Tricia stepped back and looked around the small reception area while she waited. Although Black's Village Smithy had only been in business for about six months, they seemed to be doing very well. A stand on the counter featured a glossy brochure of Black's sculptures, with information on how to commission a piece. A window on the west wall overlooked the studio, where Black was fabricating a huge metal abstract work.

Despite the heavy padded clothing and the welder's mask that covered the face, Tricia could tell by the man's stance that it *was* Black himself wielding a torch. A waterfall of blue-white sparks flowed around him as he joined two large pieces of metal. Tricia hated to admit it, but she rather liked his artistry and had even considered hiring him to do some ornamental metalwork for the front of Haven't Got a Clue. Since her store was already reminiscent of 221B Baker Street in London, glossy painted iron railings were all she'd need to complete the transformation.

The door to the welding shop opened and a burly man with salt-and-pepper hair and a few days' worth of stubble poked his head inside. "You called?" he asked the receptionist.

Tricia stepped forward. "Mr. Dittmeyer? Hi, I'm Tricia Miles. We spoke on the phone. I knew your ex-wife."

"Too bad for you," he said with scorn.

"Can we talk for a few minutes?"

Dittmeyer glanced at the receptionist as though looking for permission.

"Why don't I give you two a little privacy. I need to get another cup of coffee anyway," she said, grabbed her empty cup from the desk, and went out the door to the shop beyond.

"Look, Ms. Miles, I don't know why you'd want to talk to me. I didn't kill Betsy, if that's what you want to know. I haven't even seen or heard from the bitch in over a year. If I was going to kill her, it would've been five years ago when she started turning our house into a pigpen. When she refused to clean it or get rid of any of her crap. When she took us both to the cleaners by refusing to abide by the judge's order and give me my half of our assets," he said bitterly.

"Was there an outstanding judgment against her?"

He shook his head. "She finally paid me off about a year ago. I got a check in the mail—it even included interest. I guess she figured if she didn't give it to me that I might come after her for more."

"What do you think made her finally pay you after all that time?"

He shrugged. "I don't know—and I don't care."

"You must have loved her at one time," Tricia said kindly.

"Lady, back in the day I woulda moved heaven and earth for my Betts. But then she changed. I don't know for sure what caused it; maybe losing our daughter, Amy . . . but Betts would never talk about it with a shrink or even me. That's when she became obsessed with just about everything. Money, collecting all that junk." He shook his head once again, his gaze seeming to wander until it fixed vacantly on the floor. "I'll never know for sure why she decided to give up on everyone she loved for a load of crap."

Tricia got the feeling that at one time he *did* want to know, and he really did care.

"I've moved on with my life. I got me a new girl, and we're starting a family. I'm sorry Betsy's dead, but I've put the life we shared out of my mind."

Tricia admitted defeat. He wasn't going to tell her anything more; she might as well leave.

The door from the shop opened once again, but instead of the receptionist it was David Black who stood in the doorway. "What are you doing here?" he practically spat, glaring at Tricia.

"Hello, David. I came to speak with Mr. Dittmeyer."

Black faced his employee. "Jerry, you don't have to talk to this bitch. She always goes snooping around whenever anyone in the area dies. She likes to harass them—pry into people's business and question the quality of their grief. If she's harassing you, I'd be glad to call the cops and have them arrest her."

"It's okay, Dave. She's not hassling me. And we were done talking, anyway," Dittmeyer said with a glance back to Tricia.

"Thank you for speaking with me. I'm sorry to have bothered you, Mr. Dittmeyer."

"Once upon a time, Betsy really was a dynamite gal," Dittmeyer said rather wistfully.

Tricia gave him what she hoped was a warm smile. "Yes, I'm sure she was. Good-bye." She turned for the door, but David Black's voice stopped her.

"Good riddance."

Tricia stood there for a long moment, then reached for the door and exited the building. As she walked to her car, she decided that if she ever did decide to get the glossy black railings for Haven't Got a Clue's façade, she wouldn't have them built by Black's Village Smithy. And as she started her car and pulled out of the lot, she also realized that Jerry Dittmeyer made a terrible suspect in his ex-wife's death.

Was she really back to square one?

Since she was already halfway to Milford, Tricia decided to pay another visit to Betsy's house, just to see how it looked in broad daylight. This time she didn't bother with subterfuge and parked her car right in Betsy's driveway. She switched off the engine and sat for a moment, listening to the creaks and crackles of her engine as it cooled off, staring at the forlorn little house, which didn't look any better in daylight than it had the night before.

Should she canvass the area asking the other homeowners about their murdered neighbor? What if they were gainfully employed and weren't available during the day? Should she come back later? Which neighbor's fence had infringed on Betsy's property? Both lots on either side of hers had fenced-in yards. It was too hard to tell which fence was newer. And what if the fence dispute had happened a decade before and not in the recent past? How long could a neighbor hold a grudge?

Deciding that even being there was yet another hare-brained idea, Tricia was about to start the car again when the front door of the house on the left opened. An older woman with short-cropped gray hair stepped onto her front step and waved. Tricia rolled down her window.

"Can I help you?" the woman called. She wore a heavy sweater over dark slacks, and wrapped her arms around herself to ward off the cold.

Tricia wasn't exactly sure what to say. Before she could open her mouth, the woman called out again, "Mrs. Dittmeyer died late last week, you know."

Tricia closed her window, grabbed her keys, and got out of the car. "So I heard." She walked a few steps up the drive until she was facing the woman.

"Are you a friend?"

"I thought so. Now . . . I'm not so sure," Tricia said.

"It's freezing out here. Would you like to come in and talk?"

"Yes," Tricia said, a bit startled by the invitation. She quickly walked down Betsy's drive and hurried up the neighbor's front walk. She was ushered inside the neat home's small foyer, and the woman closed the door.

"I'm Margaret Westbrook. I was Mrs. Dittmeyer's neighbor for over twelve years."

"I'm Tricia Miles. I own the mystery bookstore in Stoneham. Betsy worked as the receptionist for the Chamber of Commerce there. My sister is the president."

Margaret nodded. "Her death shocked the whole neighborhood. Although I must say she wasn't the most friendly person to live next to. To tell you the truth, I didn't think the old—" She caught herself, and Tricia wondered what uncomplimentary descriptor Margaret had been about to utter. She cleared her throat. "I didn't think Mrs. Dittmeyer had *any* friends," Margaret finished.

"Perhaps *acquaintance* would be a better descriptor," Tricia agreed.

"I heard she worked in one of the outlying towns. I must admit we were hoping she'd move there."

"Oh?"

"Since her husband moved out, Mrs. Dittmeyer hasn't been diligent about trash removal. We've all had a devil of a time with mice. The exterminators come at least once a month to keep our traps filled with bait, otherwise we'd be overrun with them." Tricia remembered the dead mouse she'd seen while in Betsy's house, and shuddered. "I hope whoever takes care of her estate will get the place cleaned out before summer and we're beset by flies again, too."

"She really wasn't a good neighbor," Tricia said and, as expected, Margaret nodded.

"She made Pete and Donna Anderson tear down their fence three years ago because it was inches over her property line. She could have just signed a paper saying she knew it was on her property and didn't dispute it, but instead she threatened them with a lawsuit and made them tear it down. It cost them a couple of thousand dollars to make things right."

"I take it you weren't on friendly enough terms to call each other by first names."

"It wasn't my choice," Margaret said ruefully. "Her husband, Jerry, would at least acknowledge us if we were out in the yard, but Mrs. Dittmeyer would pretend she hadn't seen us when she'd get out of her car or come out to get her mail."

So far, Tricia had learned nothing more about Betsy than

she knew when she'd first driven up. Did Margaret really know anything about the woman, or was she just a lonely person who wanted someone to talk to, and should Tricia say anything that would give her more fodder for gossip?

"I haven't heard anything about a funeral service being planned," Tricia tried instead.

"I don't suppose there will even be one. I think Mrs. Dittmeyer alienated just about everyone she knew."

"I understand she has a sister," Tricia said.

Margaret nodded. "She was over to the house just a couple of hours ago. She's been coming and going for the past couple of days. She introduced herself to me the day after Mrs. Dittmeyer died."

Had she? "Is she emptying the house?"

"Oh, no. At least I don't think so. I haven't seen her carrying anything to her car." She hesitated. "Although . . . she always seems to have a different purse when she leaves."

Betsy probably had a bunch of them. You could stuff a lot of small collectibles into a big purse. Then again, Christopher said Betsy had a lot of money. Was there a chance she'd been liquidating her assets and hiding the money in her house? But why?

Margaret shook her head. "I never did understand that woman, and now I guess I never will. At least I have hope that the next person who moves in will keep up the property and get rid of all the trash. And maybe he or she will be a lot friendlier, too."

Tricia nodded. There didn't seem to be much else to add. "Thank you for speaking with me, Margaret. I think I'll try to get hold of Betsy's sister to ask about the funeral arrangements."

"Would you like me to tell her you dropped by the next time I see her?"

That wouldn't be a good idea at all. It would tip Joelle off that Tricia was still snooping around. She wished she hadn't given her name, although even if she hadn't Tricia was sure Margaret would have given Joelle a thorough description and might even have taken down her license plate number. "That won't be necessary. We're acquainted," she said simply and left it at that. "I'd better go now. Thank you so much for speaking with me."

"Come back anytime," Margaret said and followed Tricia out onto her stoop.

Tricia went straight back to her car. Since Margaret hadn't known much about Betsy, it was likely none of the other neighbors would, either. And she knew Margaret would report back to Joelle if she did any further snooping around Betsy's property. And what else was she looking for that she hadn't already seen when she'd been inside the house?

Margaret waved as Tricia pulled out of the driveway. As she drove down the street she looked up at her rearview mirror and saw that she was still being watched. Rats. She was sure to hear from Joelle before the day was through.

An uneasy feeling settled in the pit of Tricia's stomach. Did Joelle, who'd been disinherited, have a compelling motive for murder? And if she had killed her sister . . . was there a possibility she might kill again?

FOURTEEN

Tricia parked her car in its usual spot in the Stoneham municipal parking lot. The wind was still wicked as she cut across the lot to reach the sidewalk. She paused for a moment, looking over at the *Stoneham Weekly News*. She hadn't spoken to Russ Smith in several weeks. Perhaps she ought to visit and offer her congratulations on the new arrival and maybe bend his ear about Betsy Dittmeyer's death. Russ often had information that Tricia wasn't privy to, although six months before he'd told her that after sharing an important piece of information that she owed him a big favor, and that one day he would collect. It had sounded ominous. She hoped today wouldn't be the day.

She crossed the street and entered the newspaper's office. Patty Perkins sat behind a counter staring intently at her computer screen. She looked up and smiled brightly. "Hey, Tricia. I haven't seen you around here in quite a while."

"'Tis the season. I feel like I've been hibernating in my store. There sure haven't been many customers since the Christmas rush ended."

Patty nodded. "Yeah, our display ad revenues are way behind last year at this time. I'm going to have to start calling our regulars and see what we can do about that. But that's not why you're here today. Did you want to talk to Russ?"

Tricia looked toward Russ's closed office door. "If he's available."

She grimaced. "He's going over the accounts. I'm sure he'd welcome any interruption about now. Go right on in."

"Thanks."

Tricia stepped around the counter and rapped her knuckles against the hollow-core door. She opened the door a crack and stuck her head inside. "Hi, Russ. Are you terribly busy?"

Russ looked up from his computer screen. "Yeah. But these spreadsheets are depressing the hell out of me. Come on in and sit down—and try to cheer me up, will you?"

Tricia stepped inside the office and closed the door. She tugged off her coat, hanging it on the back of Russ's guest chair, and took the empty seat in the shabby little office she had come to know so well. She and Russ had once been lovers but that had ended when he'd dumped her, thinking he was going to find a job with a large-circulation paper in a bigger city. That hadn't worked out and he'd tried to get back together with her. When that hadn't worked, he'd stalked her. That ended when he'd gone for counseling and started dating Nikki. Until she'd spoken to Nikki a few days before, Tricia had assumed they were quite happy.

"Nikki shared your big announcement with me. Congratulations, Daddy," she said with a smile.

Russ shrugged and his expression was anything but happy. "If you say so."

"Oh, come on, Russ. This is wonderful news."

The man looked positively depressed. "It would have been . . . if we had *your* money."

"Hey, the two of you have two successful businesses. Okay, this is the leanest part of the retail year, but things will pick up—and soon. I'm sure of it."

"From your lips to our cash registers." He shook his head and looked sadder yet. "The truth is, ever since I had the misfortune of buying this rag I haven't had a pot to piss in. Nikki owes so much the Patisserie that we're really struggling—and I don't see things getting better anytime soon."

"Surely you can hang on until the tourists return in a couple of months," Tricia said.

"Barely. That won't help my bottom line—or hers."

"You can't take it out on the poor baby," Tricia chided.

"Tricia, I'm forty-five. When my kid graduates from high school I'll almost be eligible for Social Security. And besides that, will I still be able to throw the kid a baseball?"

"You might have a little ballerina on your hands," she said.

"Whatever it is, it's going to need clothes, shoes, and a college education. We can't afford a kid, and Nikki's got her heart set on staying home with it. That just isn't going to happen. We've been arguing about it for days."

"Stop being so negative," she chided, frowning, and thought of her mother and how her negativity had shaped Tricia's life. "I can tell you from experience that what you say and do in front of your child will have a lasting effect that will stay with him or her for their entire life."

"What kind of experience? Are you talking about your mother?" Russ pushed.

She nodded. When they'd been dating, she'd told him all about her stormy relationship with her mother. "Angelica finally spilled the beans on why I've been persona non grata my entire life."

He raised an eyebrow. "Are you going to share it with me?"

Tricia thought about it for a moment. Russ's opinion of her mother wasn't likely to be improved, but then he wasn't ever likely to meet her, either.

"It turns out I had a twin brother who died at two months. It seems my mother has held it against me my entire life." There. She'd said it aloud. She'd said it without rancor. She was getting used to the whole idea and while it didn't feel good, she thought she was near acceptance.

"And you never knew?" Russ asked, surprised.

She shook her head.

"Are you going to bring it up the next time you talk to her?"

Tricia shook her head once again. "What's the point? Nothing I say will change her mind. She'll always blame me for what happened."

"But you were a baby."

She managed an ironic laugh. "Yeah, go figure."

Russ's expression darkened. "I'm sorry you had to go through that, Trish."

"Me, too. That's why I want you to promise me that you'll give yourself a chance to fall head-over-heels in love with your child. I have a feeling you're going to think that having this baby was the best thing that ever happened to you and Nikki."

"I sure hope so." He sat back in his chair, signaling it was time to move on from that subject. "What else is on your mind? Or should I even bother asking. Betsy Dittmeyer's death, right?"

Tricia nodded, and unhappily so.

"If I know you, you've been poking your nose into things. What have you found out?"

"The face Betsy showed the world was far different than the way she lived in secret."

He smiled and his eyes opened wide as he leaned forward, eager for her to spill what she knew. "For instance?"

"She was a hoarder."

Russ winced. "I've seen a couple of TV shows on the subject. It's pretty nasty business."

"It sure is."

"Can I assume that you—and probably Angelica—visited Betsy's home to learn that piece of news in person?"

"I'm not admitting to anything," Tricia said. "I can tell you that from what I've discovered, Betsy wasn't a very nice woman, and she had a lot of money—from multiple sources, not all of them aboveboard."

"Did you come here thinking I might have some inside information on her?"

"You do seem to be able to dig up dirt the rest of us would never have access to."

Russ shrugged. "I admit, I have spoken to a few people about her."

"Are you willing to share?" Tricia asked.

He shrugged. "Since I'm only going to be doing an obit,

I might as well. Although I'll probably skew it to the sunnier side of her life."

"You're not going to run a straightforward news story?" Tricia asked, surprised.

"Whatever I've got will be old news by the time the next issue comes out."

"Not necessarily. Will the Nashua and Manchester papers even care about her death two weeks down the line?"

Again he shrugged. "You've got a point. Okay, I'll share. Betsy was an alcoholic."

"I knew that."

"She had a bitter divorce."

"Knew that, too."

"She had a daughter who died young. I guess it crushed her spirit."

"I heard that, too."

Russ scowled. "Then why don't you tell me something about her that *I* haven't heard."

Tricia wrestled with her conscience. "All right, I'll share the biggie. Betsy was embezzling money from the Chamber of Commerce."

Russ's eyes widened in surprised. "That's a biggie, all right. What do Bob and Angelica think about that?"

"I'm pretty sure Bob doesn't know. Angelica was appalled and she's arranging to have the books audited. She'll probably have to sue Betsy's estate to get the funds back. Betsy's Chamber files also contained a dossier of members that was highly uncomplimentary."

"Am I on the list?" he asked warily.

"*Everybody* is on the list, and none of it is complimentary. I wondered if she might be using it for blackmail purposes, but I haven't found any evidence to support it—yet."

"Who's going to admit it and paint themselves as a suspect? That said, it could explain where she got some of her money."

Tricia thought about the file she'd opened the night before. "I wonder if she kept lists like that on her previous employers and fellow employees. Over the years she might have collected a lot of cash. I know she had a lot of investments."

"How much is a lot?" he asked.

"Millions."

"That's a lot," Russ agreed.

"And she recently disinherited her younger sister. Joelle Morrison said it was because she nagged Betsy to get counseling, but I'm not sure I swallow that excuse."

"Have you narrowed down the list of suspects?" Russ asked.

Tricia shook her head. "I'm stumped. There are plenty of people with an ax to grind, but their motives just aren't strong enough to warrant a murder charge and a long jail sentence."

"People do stupid things in the heat of passion, and from what I learned from your police chief friend, someone strangled the old witch before pulling a bookshelf onto her."

Tricia nodded. She and Russ stared at each other for a long minute, and for the first time in a long time she realized she once again saw him as a friend. The anger at his rejection of her and then from stalking her was suddenly gone. He'd changed since meeting Nikki—and for the better. She'd brought out his more noble qualities and Tricia hoped they could reach a compromise about their new arrival. "I don't have much else to go on. When will you write Betsy's obituary?"

"The paper goes to bed on Friday afternoon. Do you think you'll find out anything else before then?"

Tricia shrugged. "I don't know. This one's a puzzler. If

the people on Betsy's unflattering list knew about the information she'd collected on them they'd be angry—but I don't think there's anything on the list worth killing for."

"Good. Then count me out," Russ said with a laugh.

Tricia stood, grabbed her coat, and put it on. "I've got to get back to my store."

"And I've got to get back to my spreadsheets. Promise you'll share whatever else you find out?"

"Only if you do, too."

He gave her a wink. "You got it."

"And think about what I said about your new arrival. I have faith that you and Nikki are going to be wonderful parents, and when that baby arrives, you'll wonder how you ever lived without him or her."

He still looked skeptical. "I sure hope you're right."

"Have you ever known me to be wrong?"

Russ shook his head and smiled. "Never."

Tricia returned his smile, glad she and Russ no longer had to be at odds. "I'll see you later."

Tricia was chagrined to find just how late it was when she finally returned to Haven't Got a Clue. She found Pixie sitting in the empty store's readers' nook with stacks of catalogs piled on the large square coffee table before her, her reading glasses resting on the tip of her nose and a big yellow highlighter in hand. Miss Marple was curled up on the chair across from her, while a Sinatra CD played quietly on the store's stereo. "Oh, you're back," Pixie called in greeting, and even Miss Marple opened a sleepy eye to acknowledge Tricia's presence.

"Angelica called wondering where you were for lunch."

"I was so busy I never got around to it. I'm sorry I wasn't here for you and Mr. Everett to go out together," she said, and shrugged out of her coat.

"That's okay, he went to the diner and got us sandwiches to go."

"Have we had many customers since I've been gone?" Tricia asked, folding the coat over her left arm.

Pixie shook her head sadly. "Not a one. But Miss Marple and I have been studying catalogs, and I fielded a number of calls. We got another invitation to look over a book collection—leftovers from an estate sale. I told them you'd call back."

"Thank you."

"How did your errands go? Did you learn anything new?" Pixie asked rather hungrily. And why not? Except for Mr. Everett, the poor woman had been cut off from human contact for a good chunk of the day.

"Not as much as I'd hoped." Tricia left it at that.

She was about to head to the back of the store to hang up her coat when she remembered that she'd promised Angelica she'd ask Grace about her attending Mr. Everett's surprise birthday party on Friday. She made an about-face, set her coat on the back of one of the nook's comfortable chairs, and headed to the cash desk to make the call.

"Hi, Linda. It's Tricia Miles. Is there a chance I could talk to Grace?"

"I'm sorry," said an unfamiliar voice, "but Mrs. Harris-Everett has stepped away from her desk." Tricia winced. How could she have forgotten that Grace had said that her assistant, Linda, was out following an emergency appendectomy? The person who answered was no doubt the temp she'd mentioned she'd hired.

"Oh, dear. I was hoping to speak to her before this afternoon. Could you please have her call me?"

"Of course. Although if you want to catch her, she said she was going to stop by the Dog-Eared Page. Perhaps you might see her there."

Tricia couldn't help but smile. Grace really must have enjoyed that sherry the other day. "Thanks. I'll do that."

"Have a good evening," the temp said and ended the call.

Tricia set down the receiver and picked up her coat once more.

"Going somewhere else?" Pixie asked.

"Um, yes. I need to run across the street for a minute or two. I shouldn't be gone long."

"Take your time," Pixie said, and went back to studying the catalogs. "Me and Miss Marple have got nothing *but* time to kill."

Pixie killing time during working hours was not terribly efficient, but it was convenient to have her there when Tricia wanted to run errands. She donned her coat and headed out the door once more.

Tricia opened the door to the Dog-Eared Page and found it quiet, with only three or four customers. Shawn, the daytime bartender, was waiting on several early-evening customers, while the pub's manager, Michele Fowler, sat at one of the back tables with Grace. Tricia paused. She could hardly ask Grace to invite Angelica to Mr. Everett's birthday celebration with Michele there.

She was about to turn and leave when Grace saw her, waving a hand for Tricia to come and join them. She pasted on a smile and threaded her way between the tables, heading toward the back of the room.

"Tricia, what brings you here at this time of day?" Grace asked, smiling.

"The woman in your office told me I might find you here."

"Oh?"

"It's about Friday night," she said, lowering her voice.

"William's birthday?" Michele asked with a grin. "Grace was just telling me about it. Sounds like it will be a jolly good time."

"Yes, it does," Tricia agreed warily.

"The thing I miss most about working days is joining friends for dinner. I'm missing out on all the fun," Michele said with a pout.

"What was it you wanted to ask?" Grace asked Tricia.

There was no other way to get around it. "It seems Angelica would like to be included in Mr. Everett's birthday bash. She was going to call you herself, but I didn't want her to put you on the spot."

"Nonsense. I'm sure William would love to have her join us. That is, he would if he knew about the party, especially as she's included us in so many of her own celebrations. I feel ashamed that I didn't think to include her from the start." She turned to Michele. "Now you are sworn to secrecy," she chided.

Michele laughed, and for a moment held her index finger to her lips. "I shan't tell a soul. But should you want to continue the celebration after dinner, I hope you'll come back to the pub. We'll have live music, lots of drink specials, and the first round is on me."

Grace beamed. "Perhaps we shall."

Tricia felt awkward standing there. "I'd better get going. I'm so looking forward to Friday. See you then."

Grace lifted her glass as though in a toast, and Tricia waved before she turned to leave.

The sky was a washed-out gray and the wind was fierce when Tricia stepped out of the Dog-Eared Page. She waited for several cars to pass before she crossed the street and saw a man with a week's worth of stubble on his cheeks bundled in a ragged camouflage coat, a matching hunting cap, and a scarf wrapped around his face, who stood in the space between By Hook or By Book and the Outer Limits Sci-Fi and Comics shop. The man had wrapped his arms around himself and looked half frozen. Were there actually homeless people tramping the streets of Stoneham?

The man seemed to notice Tricia staring, and turned and hurried down the street. There was something familiar about his gait. And then Tricia realized just who it was she'd been studying. "Bob! Bob Kelly! Wait!" Her calls only made the man break into a run.

Tricia frowned, checked traffic once again, and crossed the street for her shop.

The bell over the door jangled cheerfully, but Tricia felt anything but cheerful as she entered. Still seated in the readers' nook, Pixie looked up from the catalog she'd been perusing. "Is something wrong?"

"Did you see a man in a camo jacket outside just a few minutes ago?"

Pixie nodded. "Yeah, I did. Looked like some old rummy. Not the kind of guy you usually see hanging around the village."

"I think it was Bob Kelly."

"Shut up!" Pixie said, rising from her seat and moving to join Tricia.

"I'm serious."

They both looked south out the big display window. "I've never seen that guy without his green sport coat," Pixie said with a shrug. "Has he come on hard times?"

"He seems to have been hiding for the past couple of days—maybe as long as a week."

Again Pixie shrugged. "Has he got a *reason* to hide?"

Tricia sighed. Yes, he did. But she wasn't sure she should be talking to Pixie about it.

Pixie looked at the clock on the wall. "Holy cow, it's about time for me to hit the road."

"Oh, I'm sorry. I didn't mean to be gone so long and for most of the day, especially since you said you needed to get a new tire for your car."

"Don't worry about it. Tomorrow I'll just set my alarm for an hour earlier and see if I can get that tire before I come in to work. I might have to wait, though, so don't panic if I'm a few minutes late."

"I won't." Pixie took Tricia's coat and went to the back of the store to fetch her own.

"I really appreciate all the boring hours you've put in this winter."

"Are you kidding? I haven't been bored for one second of the time I've spent here at Haven't Got a Clue. You want boredom? Spend a couple of years in stir. That's almost as bad as a death sentence. And thanks to your giving me this job, I'm never going to jail again."

For a moment Tricia thought Pixie might burst into tears. "I'm glad you feel that way, Pixie. Now, shoo! Go get that new tire for your car."

"Thanks, boss. See you tomorrow."

As Pixie went out the door, Angelica entered, carrying a large pizza box. "Anybody hungry?" she called cheerfully.

"I'll say. I missed lunch today."

"And don't I know it," Angelica said. "Your tuna plate is still sitting in my undercounter fridge."

Miss Marple raised her sleepy head and looked at Angelica as she unfastened her coat, shrugged out of it, and tossed it onto the cash desk. "Let's eat this in the readers' nook."

"No soda?" Tricia asked.

"Rats. Sorry. I forgot. Have you got any wine?"

"By the time I run upstairs to get it and some glasses, the pizza will be cold. Would you like some coffee?"

"Coffee dregs and pizza?" Angelica asked, appalled. "No thanks."

No longer drowsy, a hopeful Miss Marple sat primly in her chair, watching Tricia's every move as she grabbed a wad of paper napkins from the beverage station and joined Angelica in the nook.

Angelica opened the box, letting out a burst of steam, and selected a slice before shoving the pie toward Tricia. "Oh, good, veggies," Tricia said.

"Yes, if you put enough on"—and she had: onions, peppers, mushrooms, and broccoli—"you can almost convince yourself that it's a healthy meal."

They both took a bite. De-lish!

Tricia chewed and swallowed. "Have you heard anything from Karen Johnson?" she asked, eyeing the cat, who'd not only been known to sniff but take a taste of pizza on more than one occasion.

Angelica wiped her mouth with a napkin. "As a matter of fact, yes. I invited her to speak to the Chamber at the next breakfast and she agreed. I figured it would be a nice way for her to get to know everyone."

"I meant in regard to finding a place for the Chamber to rent."

"As a matter of fact, yes on that count, too," Angelica said and practically squealed with delight. "NRA Realty has found the Chamber potential office space."

"Where?"

"Across from the bank." She took another bite of her pizza.

Tricia had to think about it for a moment. "I don't remember any office space near there."

Angelica finished chewing and swallowed. "Think again. The little run-down white house with the shutters falling off."

Tricia frowned. "You've got to be kidding."

"No. Apparently Antonio has been working on it for a while. Several months ago Billie Burke at the bank alerted him that the owner might be willing to sell."

"Bypassing Kelly Realty?" Tricia asked. "What gives?"

"I have no idea. But Antonio finished negotiating a month or so ago and Nigela Ricita Associates took possession of it just today. It's Karen's first property to lease and she's eager to have me look at it. Would you like to come with me?"

"Sure," Tricia said. After all, she had nothing better to do. "When?"

"This evening."

"Is that a good time to look at a potential home for the Chamber—in the dark?"

"Why not?"

"You might miss all its flaws and then get stuck with it."

"I don't think Antonio would let the Chamber get involved if he didn't think it was a good prospect."

"Promise me you won't make up your mind until after

you've seen it," Tricia advised and noticed Miss Marple inching closer to the open pizza box.

"I won't," Angelica said.

Tricia ate another bite of her pizza and continued to keep an eye on the cat before speaking again. "I still don't get it. For years Bob's had all the property sewn up on Main Street. How come he never got his hands on that little house?"

"Apparently he annoyed the little old lady who owned it by continually badgering her to sell. She was so irritated she refused to deal with him. When Antonio found out about it, he took it upon himself to track down and meet the owner. Apparently she found him irresistible and he sweet-talked her into the deal."

"He is rather lovable," Tricia agreed as Miss Marple raised a paw to bat the pizza box. "No, no," Tricia admonished and the cat sat back down, looking dutifully chastised. "If I'm not mistaken, that property has been empty the entire time I've lived here in Stoneham. And you're talking about a house—not office space."

"Karen feels it can easily be converted to office space," Angelica explained.

"Who owned it?"

"A widow. She moved in with her daughter in Manchester several years back. Apparently the place needs a little work, but NRA Realty is going to refurbish it for us."

"What are they going to charge the Chamber?" Tricia asked, still finding herself speaking as the voice of doom.

"Oh, dear. I didn't think to ask." Angelica bit her lip. "Maybe I shouldn't have sounded so eager when I spoke to Karen. What if she jacks up the price?"

"You don't have to take it," Tricia said.

"My storeroom isn't exactly handicapped accessible, and

that little house already has a ramp. We need to move some-place and fast."

"First you need to hire someone to take on the Chamber's day-to-day duties."

Angelica nodded and sighed. "That I do." She took an-other bite of pizza, chewed, and swallowed. "That's all my news for the day. What trouble did you get into today?"

"Hardly trouble. I spoke to Jerry Dittmeyer," Tricia said.

"Oh?" Angelica said, sounding interested.

She nodded. "Did you know he works for David Black?"

"No," Angelica replied, distinctly uninterested. "Betsy called David when he first opened his business and asked him to join the Chamber. He said no, of course. Said he didn't want to have to run into either of us if he could help it. Now that I think of it, Betsy reported that little piece of information with a tinge of glee." She sighed. "I'm sorry she's dead, but I'm aw-fully glad I won't be stuck with her for the remainder of my term as Chamber president. Speaking of which, I spoke to Libby Hirt." Libby ran the local job bank, along with the Stoneham Food Shelf. "She's got several people looking for secretarial work. She's going to send me their résumés. In fact, they're probably already in my e-mail in-box. I just haven't had a chance to log on in the past couple of hours."

"I thought you were going to wait until after Betsy's fu-neral."

"Well, no one has said anything about plans, and I do have to keep up with things. I simply can't juggle my own businesses *and* keep the Chamber on track without help."

Finally figuring out that she wasn't going to be offered a bit of cheese, Miss Marple got up and sauntered away, head-ing for the back of the store. "Have you thought about hiring a virtual assistant for yourself?" Tricia asked Angelica.

"A virtual assistant? What could someone like that do for me?"

"I had a long conversation about it with the last author who came to sign at Haven't Got a Clue. They do all kinds of things for authors—like posting on various social media sites, and sending out bookmarks and such to fans."

"This sounds intriguing. I'll have to look into it." She sighed. "But my first priority must be the Chamber. Dear Antonio has offered to have one of his staff take care of the Chamber's March breakfast, but I still have to give him an estimate of how many are coming. And then there's the monthly newsletter . . ."

"Virtual assistants do newsletters, too. I'll bet if you found one for yourself, they could also do Chamber work, too."

"I don't know. I'd have to think about it. The Chamber really needs to have a real person who can deal with problems that arise. I think my best option is still to find a small office to rent and replace Betsy as soon as possible."

Tricia nodded. "Let me know if you change your mind and I'll put out some feelers."

"Thank you. Now, did Betsy's ex have anything juicy to say about her?"

Tricia shook her head. "You know, he was angry when we first started talking, but the more he spoke about her, the more he seemed . . . I don't know, regretful? He said at one time she was a dynamite lady." Tricia sobered. "Somehow I just can't imagine Betsy as a real spitfire, but . . . I suppose anything's possible. Or was when she was younger."

"Do you want another slice of pizza?" Angelica asked, taking one for herself.

Tricia shook her head. "I also went back to Betsy's house and managed to talk to one of her neighbors."

"Did you learn anything of interest?"

"Only that, thanks to Betsy, the neighbors have a terrible mouse problem. She said after Jerry left, Betsy didn't bother with proper maintenance. She corroborated some of the things Joelle told me on Saturday. And, speaking of Joelle, the neighbor also said she's been back again and again, but she doesn't leave with anything other than her purse. Or at least *a* purse."

"So what's she been doing there?" Angelica asked.

"Tidying?" Tricia suggested. "If the neighbor hadn't been watching me like a hawk, I might have walked around back to see if Joelle had lifted any of the blinds." Tricia ate her last bite of pizza. "I have one piece of happy news for you." Angelica's eyes lit up. "You are now officially on the guest list for Mr. Everett's surprise birthday party."

"Oh, good. If I can't be out on a date with a rich, handsome, and kind man, then I'd just as soon be among my friends—and you, dear Tricia."

"Thank you." Tricia wiped her mouth with one of the paper napkins. "What time do we have to meet Karen?"

Angelica bit into her pizza and looked at the clock. She chewed and swallowed before answering. "In about fifteen minutes."

"That soon?"

"Why, have you got something else planned for tonight?"

"Hardly," Tricia said without enthusiasm. She noticed Miss Marple patiently waiting by the stairs that led to her loft apartment. "I've got to feed Miss Marple. By the time I'm finished, it should be time to leave."

"No rush," Angelica said and reached for a third slice of pizza.

Tricia got up from her chair, shaking her head. No doubt

Angelica would soon be complaining about her weight again and Tricia would have no sympathy for her. And what if the little house proved unsuitable as office space? Would Angelica find solace in junk food and eat even more?

Tricia wasn't going to speculate.

Instead, she opened the door marked PRIVATE and headed up the stairs with Miss Marple trotting along beside her. If the house did meet Angelica's standards, and she indeed rented it for the Chamber of Commerce, it would no doubt annoy the hell out of Bob Kelly, and that at least made Tricia smile.

Since the rental house was only two blocks up the street, Tricia and Angelica elected to walk the short distance. They saw a car parked at the curb. As they approached, the engine died, and Karen Johnson got out. "Good evening, ladies."

"Hi," Tricia called.

"I hope you don't mind me bringing Tricia along," Angelica said, and pulled her scarf just a little bit higher on her neck.

"Not at all. The more the merrier." Karen joined the sisters on the sidewalk. She held a large flashlight in one hand, and picked through a set of keys with another.

"Oh, dear. Will we have to see the inside of the place by flashlight?" Angelica asked.

"Oh, no. Antonio called the power company and had all the utilities turned on. He came over earlier and got the furnace working so there should be heat and light, but I imagine it might take a few days for the house to warm up and thoroughly dry out."

"Was there water damage?" Angelica asked, concerned.

"No, but Antonio said it felt damp. It's been shuttered for over a year. Overall he felt the property was in pretty good shape."

"So you haven't seen it yet, either?" Tricia asked.

Karen shook her head. "Antonio told me there are still some boxes inside. The former owner had rented out the building for storage for the last couple of years, but the last tenant hadn't paid the rent in some time. They were contacted several times and asked to collect their belongings before the sale went through, but the owner never heard from her tenant again."

"So who has to clean the place out?" Tricia asked.

"Tell us when we get inside," Angelica complained. "I'm cold!"

"Follow me. The steps are icy. We'll use the ramp," Karen said and led them around to the side of the building and the wooden ramp that had been cleared of snow. She unlocked the door, reached inside, and flipped a couple of light switches before allowing Tricia and Angelica to enter before her.

Karen hadn't been kidding when she'd said there were some boxes inside. The descriptor *some* was certainly an understatement. What must have once been a living room was stacked floor to ceiling with cartons.

"Now would be a good time to answer Tricia's question," Angelica said, sounding apprehensive. "Who's going to empty this place?"

"Of course, NRA will clean the place before the Chamber takes possession. Antonio has already ordered a Dumpster to be delivered tomorrow. We'll take care of clearing the place out, and we'll also paint, and either replace the carpet or put down a new floor. It depends on what we find when we rip up the old stuff."

Tricia gave her sister a skeptical look. "You can't be serious about renting this place."

"I'm more than serious, I'm desperate," Angelica said. She turned back to Karen. "Let's see the rest of the place."

A short hall linked the living room to a bathroom, a closet, and a small bedroom. At the back of the house was a tiny kitchen, which was only big enough for a bistro table and four undersized chairs. The former tenant must have left them, but all the appliances were missing.

"There are two small bedrooms upstairs that could be used for storage," Karen said hopefully.

"How much is it a month, and how long a lease does the Chamber need to sign?" Angelica asked.

"We'd like a year's lease. We can talk about the price when we get to my office."

"Can you throw in a fridge and a microwave?" Angelica asked hopefully.

"We can talk about it," Karen said, still sounding hopeful.

"That bathroom looks like it's in terrible shape," Tricia said, trying to be helpful.

"We won't be bathing," Angelica said.

"We'll make sure the plumbing works before you take possession," Karen promised.

"Do you have the paperwork with you?" Angelica asked.

"As a matter of fact, I do."

"Then let's not bother to go back to the Brookview. We can hash it out right here."

"Very good," Karen said, sounding delighted.

Tricia gave her sister a penetrating glare. "I thought you weren't going to rush into signing a lease."

"Once the place is cleared out, it should be adequate as a

short-term solution." She held her arm out, gesturing for Karen to sit.

Tricia shrugged. "While you negotiate, I'll just wander around the place. Maybe check out the upstairs bedrooms."

Angelica wasn't listening. She grabbed a wad of paper towel from the roll that hung under the cabinet near the sink, dusted off one of the chairs, and sat down.

Tricia climbed the narrow stairway up to the darkened second floor. She fumbled for a light switch, found it, and flipped it. A dim bulb glowed at the top of the stairs. Like the floor below, the bedrooms were stacked with boxes and the floor was covered in dust. The ceiling sloped on both sides, which might have been perfect if the occupants had been children with twin beds. Had a happy family once dwelled within these walls? Tricia's bedroom in her parents' home had been the size of this house's entire second floor, and had been beautifully furnished and decorated. Still, she would have traded that to have felt loved and cherished by her mother.

Don't start down that road again, Tricia warned herself. She hadn't dwelled on thoughts of her dead twin in days. She didn't want to think about the life he'd never had—depriving her of a happy childhood as well.

Between the bedrooms was a tiny, and dingy, bathroom with a miniscule triangular shower. In a house this small it must have seemed like a luxury to the previous inhabitants.

Turning off the light, Tricia headed back downstairs. Angelica and Karen were deep into negotiations by then, and Tricia wandered into the downstairs bedroom, found the light switch, and flipped it. The ceiling globe was missing, leaving a bare bulb in a socket. Whoever had lived in the house must have been a cheapskate. The bulb couldn't have been more than forty watts. Someone had left a metal crucifix hanging on the wall above where a bed might have gone and where there were now boxes and boxes of stuff stacked.

Tricia wandered back into the living room. The cartons weren't taped; they'd merely had their top flaps folded so that they interleaved. If the contents were going to be trashed anyway, Tricia figured she might as well open one of the boxes to see what was inside. She chose the top box of the shortest pile and pulled open the flaps. The carton was filled with old magazines, newspaper articles, and recipes clipped from food boxes and jars. She pawed through the contents and found an envelope that seemed to be stuffed with old receipts. She pulled out the wad of folded papers, shuffled through them, and froze when she saw the name of the recipient on the power company's monthly bill: Elizabeth Dittmeyer.

FIFTEEN

Tricia stared at the name on the utility bill, unsure what she should do next. After a few moments
it became obvious—look for more evidence that it
was actually Betsy who'd been renting the house to store her
treasures.

Tricia shuffled through the bills. Yes, all of them were for
Betsy at her Milford address, and they were only two years
old—long after the breakup of her marriage—so it wasn't
surprising they were all in her name and not that of her ex.

So what happened? Had Betsy simply run out of space to
store her junk and, since she had worked in Stoneham,
approached the house's former owner about using it as a
storage facility? Why hadn't she just rented a conventional
self-store unit? There were plenty of them around. Or did

she want her trash to be close to her workplace so she could visit it as need be? And why had she stopped paying the rent? From what Tricia had seen on her financial statements, Betsy had had plenty of money.

Tricia set the bills down and investigated the rest of the box. Paper, paper, and more paper. She closed the lid and moved the box to the floor, looking into the carton directly below it. It was filled with dirty stuffed animals. Had Betsy frequented tag sales in the area during her lunch hours and bought them all for small change? What had she intended to do with them? Clean them, find them loving homes with disadvantaged children during the holidays, or just keep them in case she needed the love and adoration of an inanimate object? It all seemed so sad and pointless.

Tricia opened a third box. Sitting on top of more magazines and newspaper clippings was a sealed fat #10 envelope with an equally fat red rubber band around it. It had probably come off a large bunch of celery from the Milford Shaw's grocery store. She edged her thumbnail under the loose end of the flap and ripped it open a couple of inches, then gasped and stared at the sight of the stack of bills inside. She ripped the envelope a little more and flipped through the money— all well-used fifty-dollar bills. There had to be at least a hundred of them.

Footsteps heralded Angelica and Karen's arrival into the home's overstuffed living room, and Tricia shoved the envelope into her coat pocket, trying not to look guilty.

"We've struck a deal," Karen said, smiling broadly.

"Yes," Angelia said with what sounded like resignation, "we have. The Chamber can move in as soon as the property is cleaned up. A week, two at the most." She narrowed her gaze, studying Tricia's face. "And what have you been up to?"

"Nothing much. Just looking through some of these boxes." She reached for the envelope of old receipts. "It seems Betsy Dittmeyer was the person renting storage space in the house."

"Oh, no," Angelica groaned. "Don't tell me you're going to report this to Chief Baker and that they'll impound the house."

"I don't see how they can," Karen said, sounding not quite sure of herself. "Our company bought the house and its contents." She looked down at the briefcase in her hand. "Oh, darn. I left my purse in the kitchen. Excuse me, will you?"

"Of course," Angelica said.

Tricia waited until Karen was out of earshot before speaking. "There's more, but I don't want to go into it with Karen here. We've got to get rid of her."

Angelica shrugged. "I'll take care of it," she whispered, and cleared her throat as Karen reappeared from the kitchen. "Wouldn't you agree, Trish?"

Tricia blinked, startled, then caught on. "Yes. Completely."

Angelica turned to Karen. "Tricia has some marvelous ideas about how we should set up the Chamber offices. Do you mind if we hang around for a few minutes and discuss it? We've kept you here far too long, but if you'll leave the keys with me, I promise I'll get them back to you first thing in the morning," Angelica said sweetly.

Karen looked unsure of herself, but then forced a smile. After all, the customer was always right. "Of course." She fastened the buttons on her coat, and then fumbled in her pocket for the house keys, handing them to Angelica. "I'll say good night, then."

"Good night," the sisters chorused.

Angelica watched as Karen headed for the door. "I was thinking, perhaps I should have the Chamber's file cabinets spray-painted a nice shade of mauve."

"Oh, that sounds wonderful," Tricia agreed enthusiastically.

The door closed and Angelica sobered. "This had better be good."

"Not only did I find Betsy's old utility receipts, but I found this." Tricia withdrew the envelope from her pocket and brandished it in front of Angelica.

"Good heavens," Angelica cried and snatched the envelope. She flipped through the money. "There has to be at least five grand in here. Do you think Betsy was a counterfeiter?"

"Not a chance. Those aren't new bills. We know she was a hoarder. Looks like she hoarded her money, too—in cash."

Angelica's eyes narrowed and her smile widened. "This will go a long way toward repaying the money Betsy stole from the Chamber."

"You can't take that," Tricia protested.

"You heard Karen. These boxes are considered trash. They're going to throw them in a Dumpster. You finding this envelope is no different than the Dumpster diving you did with Ginny and her friends a couple of years ago."

"These boxes haven't yet been thrown out as trash. As of this moment, they still belong to Nigela Ricita Associates."

Angelica opened her mouth to protest, but must have thought better of it. She sighed. "What do you suggest we do?"

"Call Antonio. He's the NRA representative here in Stoneham."

"Of course, you're right." Angelica opened her purse and took out her cell phone, hit the speed dial, and waited. "Antonio? It's Angelica." She paused. "Angelica Miles. Head of the Chamber of Commerce. Owner of the Cookery—" She paused again. "Yes, that Angelica. You're hysterical, you know that?" she deadpanned.

While she explained the situation, Tricia dug through the box, looking for more cash. What could Betsy have been thinking when she stashed the money in the box? Had she forgotten she'd done so when she'd decided not to pay the rent on the house? Was it possible there was even more cash to be found?

Finally Angelica hung up. "He'll be here in ten minutes."

It was almost seven o'clock. "I'll bet Ginny won't be thrilled by that."

"It's in his company's best interests," Angelica pointed out. "What should we do in the meantime?"

"Start looking through the rest of the boxes. Who knows what we might find."

Angelica's expression soured. "I wish I'd brought a big bottle of hand sanitizer. If this stuff is as dirty as the crap in Betsy's house, we'll probably catch some dreadful—and lethal—disease." She shrugged out of her coat. "Hand me your coat and hat and I'll put them in the kitchen. At least it's cleaner there than in here."

Tricia handed over her coat and went back to work emptying the box.

A knock at the door came some ten or so minutes later, and Angelica opened it to admit not only Antonio, but Ginny, too. "Welcome to the treasure hunt," Angelica said, sounding anything but enthusiastic.

"May I see the envelope of cash?" Antonio asked.

With reluctance, Angelica surrendered the envelope. The three women watched as Antonio counted the cash. "Five thousand dollars exactly," he said, sounding astonished.

"There could be a lot more," Tricia said.

"Or there could be nothing," Ginny said, sounding discouraged as she took in the room and those beyond, all filled with boxes. "What are we going to do?"

"Betsy Dittmeyer stole from the Chamber of Commerce. They deserve to be the recipient of this windfall," Angelica said.

"And what would Nigela Ricita have to say about that?" Tricia asked.

Antonio looked uncomfortable. He looked down at the cash in his hand, and then back to Angelica. "I will have to ask her. And that is the first thing I intend to do tomorrow morning."

"And what do we do in the meantime?" Tricia asked.

Antonio sighed. "I think it would be prudent for us to go through all the boxes."

"Us who?" Ginny asked, sounding appalled.

"I don't think we should tell anyone about this until we know what we're dealing with," Angelica advised.

"The first thing you should probably do is talk to a lawyer. If nothing else, there might be some tax liability," Tricia advised.

"I am not worried about paying taxes on a paltry five thousand dollars," Antonio said, "though I agree in principle. But first, I will talk with Ms. Ricita."

"I hope you were kidding about us going through all these boxes," Ginny said, sounding resolute.

"No, I was not," Antonio said. "There may be other valuables that can be sold. The cost of renovation will not be cheap. And Ms. Ricita has not decided what to do with the property yet."

"She's renting it to me," Angelica said firmly. "I just signed a one-year lease."

"Yes," Antonio said, nodding, "the plan was to leave it as is—with a few enhancements—for a short time, but ultimately the house will be razed and we will rebuild in much the same way we did for the Dog-Eared Page. In the long run, it will be a much more substantial investment."

"Do I have to be part of this project?" Ginny asked resentfully.

"You *are* a member of the NRA team," Angelica pointed out. After all, Nigela Ricita Associates owned the store Ginny managed.

Antonio's smile was beguiling. "I am sure our employer will reward you handsomely."

"She'd better," Ginny groused, then let out a resigned sigh. "Okay, what's the plan of attack?"

They all looked at Tricia for guidance.

"There's no way we can make a dent in this tonight—"

"I still think we should try," Angelica said.

Ginny sighed. "We can't just dump it all on the floor. That would make sorting too difficult."

"I could retrieve my car and go to the convenience store up by the highway and buy out all their heavy-duty trash bags," Angelica said.

Antonio shook his head. "I would not feel comfortable letting you go on your own at this time of night."

It wasn't all that late, Tricia reflected.

"If you ladies don't mind starting the work, I will get the trash bags and be back in fifteen minutes. With four of us going through the boxes, we may be able to clear out at least this living room tonight." He looked hopefully at Tricia. "Are we in agreement?"

Never one to turn down a chance to dig for clues, and this time literally, she nodded.

Antonio kissed Ginny good-bye and took off.

"Where do we start?" Angelica asked.

"Let's section off the room," Tricia said, taking charge.

"And how do we do that?" Ginny asked.

"We'll each work in a corner and dump an entire box. That would seem the easiest approach. Then we'll refill the boxes with whatever looks like salvageable material. Perhaps we can even donate some of it to various charities—like the Clothes Closet."

Angelica and Ginny nodded, chose a corner, and set off to work.

Unfortunately, soon the piles of trash far outweighed the salvageable materials. As an irrational hoarder, Betsy collected the oddest array of what seemed to Tricia to be nothing more than junk—most of which was absolutely worthless. They soon came up with a system: stuff to be tossed, stuff that could be used again, and paper to be recycled.

Angelica was the first to come up with another envelope full of cash. This time it was only a hundred one-dollar bills—no more, no less. Did Betsy only save money in one-hundred-bill increments? Was the number one hundred somehow sacred to her?

By the time Antonio returned from the convenience store, the women had found envelopes full of fives and tens—again, each with one hundred bills.

"We have to keep looking," Tricia said as Antonio scooped trash into the bags. Ginny used Angelica's author signing pen to mark the boxes with what to keep, sell, and recycle.

They worked silently—each of them concentrating on the task at hand. By midnight, they'd found $44,600 in cash and had nearly filled a large peanut butter jar (which Angelica had found under the kitchen sink) with loose change. And to think they'd only gone through what amounted to about a quarter of the boxes in the house.

Antonio leaned against one of the piles of boxes, his face

drawn. "I can ask the employees at the Brookview Inn to volunteer to help us go through the rest of these boxes tomorrow," he offered, but the women voted him down.

"It's not that I don't trust them," Ginny said, "but why lead them to temptation?"

"I agree," Angelica said. "It might take the four of us the rest of the week, but I think we can do this more efficiently. That is, if the Dumpster Antonio ordered is delivered by tomorrow."

"And who takes charge of the money?" Tricia asked.

"Me," Antonio said adamantly. "Under the terms of the sale of this property, all of this now belongs to my employer."

"I thought she was your stepmother," Tricia said.

"She is the only mother I have left. And everything in this house now belongs to her," Antonio stressed. "I will take care of it for her."

"Of course you will," Angelica said and stepped up to rest a hand on Antonio's shoulder. He turned and gave her a wan smile.

"Then it's agreed. We'll meet here again tomorrow night to continue searching," Tricia said.

The others nodded.

"I will call the waste management company and see to it that they deliver a recycling container, as well," Antonio said.

"Can we borrow the inn's shredder? There are financial papers here that really should be shredded," Tricia said.

"That's a real time sink. We could box up everything of that nature and send it to a commercial shredder. The money we found will more than take care of that," Angelica said.

"How could Betsy have just walked away from all that money?" an exasperated Ginny asked.

Tricia shook her head. "Talk about being absentminded."

"That wasn't how I'd have described Betsy," Angelica said. "The woman had a mind like a steel trap."

"With all the junk she collected over a lifetime, she probably mislaid it."

"If we find as much cash upstairs, NRA will have acquired the property for free," Antonio remarked with irony.

"Please don't make me empty any more boxes tonight," Ginny pleaded.

"Take your tired wife and go home," Angelica said in a voice that meant business. "We can finish this tomorrow night."

Ginny needed no further prodding. She struggled to her feet and headed for the kitchen, where they'd all stashed their coats on the backs of the kitchen chairs.

"I would ask you ladies not to speak of what we've found here tonight," Antonio said.

"My lips are sealed," Angelica said, and to prove it she turned an imaginary key in front of her mouth.

"What are you going to tell Karen?" Tricia asked.

"Nothing. At least for now. Now that the property is rented, she doesn't need to concern herself with it. It is up to me to have the house cleaned and painted," Antonio said.

"Are you going to call Chief Baker and tell him what we've found?" Tricia asked.

Antonio shook his head. "I see no reason to do so. When NRA bought the house, it was stipulated that it came as is with all contents. The former owner was adamant—she did not want to go to the trouble or expense to empty it."

"Couldn't Betsy's heirs press for a share?" Angelica asked.

"I do not think so. The former owner presented copies of receipts of several registered and certified letters demanding the tenant clear the property. They were signed as having been received. Notice was given. Notice was ignored—much to NRA's good fortune, it now turns out. However, for your peace of mind, I will consult with our attorney," he said.

"I think that's prudent," Angelica agreed.

Ginny arrived, her arms laden with their coats, hats, scarves, and purses. She passed them out and then they all headed for the door, where Angelica surrendered the keys to Antonio. He locked the door behind them.

"I told Karen she'd have those keys back first thing in the morning."

"As I said, I will keep them, and let her know that I have them."

"What time will we meet here tomorrow night?" Tricia asked.

"If you come just after five, I will supply a gourmet take-out dinner from the Brookview Inn," Antonio promised.

That seemed like a perfectly reasonable offer.

"Good night," Tricia called, and she and Angelica started back down the sidewalk toward their shops and homes.

"Well, this entire evening was totally unexpected," Angelica said.

"It sure was. I never really knew Betsy, but from what we've found out about her since she died, she was even stranger than I'd given her credit for."

"You and me both," Angelica agreed.

They crossed the street and continued down the sidewalk. "I don't understand her. Why would Betsy walk away from thousands of dollars in cash?"

"Do you think maybe she was ill? Early onset of Alzheimer's disease or something?" Angelica asked.

"Not that I noticed. And anyway, you'd have had a better handle on that."

"Yes, I suppose I would. It could just be that she mixed up the boxes she sent for storage at the rental house and the stuff she kept at home. The boxes sure looked the same to me, and none of them were marked."

"Or do you think there was something in the rental house she didn't want found and she was willing to part with everything so that it would never be found?"

"I'm not sure that makes sense, but in retrospect, nothing Betsy did makes sense."

They reached the Cookery and Angelica dug in her pocket for the keys. "Want to come up for a nightcap?"

"Are you kidding? It's hours past my bedtime."

"Mine, too. And I've still got to take Sarge out for one last walk."

"Do you want me to hang around until you do?"

Angelica shook her head. "You aren't here most other nights, why should this one be different?"

"Because there's been yet another death in the village. In your own building," Tricia reminded her.

"Yes, but if whoever killed Betsy wanted to come after me, I'm pretty sure they would have already done so," Angelica said reasonably.

That didn't make Tricia feel any better. "I'll talk to you tomorrow."

"Good night," Angelica said, opened the shop door, and went inside, locking it behind her.

Tricia walked the ten or so feet to her own store and let herself in. She had a feeling that with all she'd learned that evening, she'd have a hard time drifting off to sleep.

Damn Betsy Dittmeyer for being such a strange duck. Damn her to hell.

SIXTEEN

Tricia dreamed about cash. Piles and piles of it, in every denomination. So much cash she was buried to her waist. Like a child tossing confetti into the air, she joyfully tossed fistfuls of bills, laughing with merriment. That is, until an angry Betsy Dittmeyer appeared, demanding Tricia give her back her money, and not until she'd counted it out in hundred-bill increments. But Tricia had no envelopes or rubber bands to keep the cash together. Betsy was not pleased and berated her, her voice growing shriller and shriller, threating to pummel her until . . .

Tricia awoke with a start, breathless and sweating, and realized the phone was ringing. She grabbed it.

"You asked me to keep you posted," said a man's familiar voice.

"Posted?" she repeated dully.

"If anything broke on the Dittmeyer case."

"And?" she demanded, finally recognizing the voice as Russ's.

"I just heard on the police scanner that her house is on fire."

"Fire?" Tricia repeated, this time in shock.

"Fully engulfed. Do you want to have a look? There's nothing like a good fire," he said eagerly.

"I can be dressed in two minutes."

"Make it three, and I'll pick you up."

"But what—" She didn't get to finish her sentence, as Russ had already hung up.

What was Nikki going to think about him taking her to a fire at—she glanced at her bedside clock—two in the morning? She'd no doubt find out later.

Throwing back the covers, and disturbing a perturbed-looking Miss Marple, Tricia jumped out of bed and raced to get dressed, putting on four layers of clothes. She had a feeling they might be standing in the cold for several hours and was determined to be prepared.

Tricia was bundled up in her heaviest coat and warmest hat and gloves, her feet encased in two pairs of heavy socks and boots, waiting on the sidewalk outside of Haven't Got a Clue when Russ's battered pickup truck pulled up to the curb. She hopped in and Russ took off with tires spinning.

"What were you doing listening to the police scanner at this time of night?" Tricia asked as she fastened her seat belt.

"Unlike you, Nikki finds it rather soothing to fall asleep to."

Tricia frowned in disbelief. "I don't think Nikki would be happy to hear you're comparing us in quite that way. And, in fact, isn't she going to be annoyed when she finds out you took me to a fire?"

"Hey, she suggested it."

Tricia raised an eyebrow. "As I recall, in the not-so-distant past she was jealous of any time you spent with me—including talking on the phone."

"I guess she finally got it through her head that you and I are a thing of the past."

That was certainly true, although his replacement—Grant Baker—sometimes didn't seem to get it. *Don't think like that,* she chided herself. Angelica was right. Her list of life goals didn't necessarily include a man. She missed the kind of intimacy she'd shared with Christopher, but neither Russ nor Baker had been a real contender when it came to comparisons to him. She wasn't sure she wanted to dwell on that thought, either.

"Although," Russ offered after a long pause, "she probably hasn't heard that you and Chief Baker are on the outs."

"Who says we are?"

"Word on the street is that you turned down his Valentine's Day invitation."

"Oh, that," she said, hoping to make light of the subject. "It's Mr. Everett's birthday and Grace is throwing him a surprise party."

"And you couldn't bring a date?" Russ asked.

"Grant's working on the Dittmeyer case."

"He couldn't take an evening off to be with you?" Russ pushed.

Tricia shrugged.

"It sounds like you're making excuses for him."

Tricia shrugged again. "I've had enough dates canceled not to expect much," she said and hoped he'd drop the subject. She stared straight ahead, watching the portion of road revealed by the truck's headlights speed by.

Not only were the streets of Stoneham devoid of traffic, but Milford was just as quiet, which made the muffler on

Russ's pickup sound even more obnoxious. That is, until they approached Vintage Road, which had been closed off at Nashua Street, with the police refusing to let them enter—even on foot. But Russ was an old newshound. After parking the truck at the same strip mall Angelica had days earlier, he led Tricia down the block, where they turned and hurried to the cross street. The smell of smoke was thick and they could see flames reaching into the sky.

"It must be one hell of a fire," Russ said as they neared, joining neighbors who had clustered to rubberneck along the police barricade. Tricia recognized one of them: Betsy's next-door neighbor, Margaret Westbrook.

"Margaret! Margaret!" she called. The older woman looked around, spied Tricia, and waved. Tricia wormed her way through the others until she was standing next to the woman.

"Tricia! What on earth are you doing here at this time of night?"

"I was—" Tricia's mind raced. "On a date," she fibbed, just as Russ arrived at her side. "This is my friend Russ. Russ, this is Margaret Westbrook, Betsy's next-door neighbor."

Russ's eyebrows shot into his thinning hairline, and his grin of pleasure was positively creepy at their stroke of luck. Tricia fought the urge to give him a dig in the ribs with her elbow and holler, *Down boy!*

"What happened?" Russ asked and for once he didn't have his usual steno pad at hand.

"One of the neighbors was awakened by her dog. When she went to let him out, she smelled the smoke and saw the fire. Soon after, the police were knocking on my door and told me I had to evacuate." She turned her worried eyes back to the fire. "Isn't this awful? What if I lose my home? Everything I own is inside. All my photos of my dead parents and husband, my jewelry, and—oh, just everything!" Her bottom lip trembled and Tricia put an arm around the woman's shoulder, hoping she felt less alone . . . as foolish as that sounded, for she barely knew Tricia.

"I'm sure the firefighters will do their best to save it." The words seemed terribly inadequate in the face of what might lie ahead for poor Margaret.

"They say it might be arson. Poor Mrs. Dittmeyer was murdered and now someone has set her house on fire? What is this world coming to?" Margaret pleaded.

Russ tapped Tricia's arm. "You stay with her. I'll see if I can find out anything."

Tricia nodded.

"Oh, thank you!" Margaret called to Russ's quickly retreating back. Russ probably knew all the firefighters and Milford cops and Tricia knew he'd bug anyone he thought had information until he found out what was going on.

Tricia watched a team of firefighters who stood in Betsy's driveway battling the fire, wrestling with a long hose that trailed behind them to a hydrant somewhere down the street. They aimed a fierce stream of water at the flames, which seemed to finally be calming down, but it seemed to cause the smoke to become even thicker.

Silent tears traced a line down Margaret's weathered cheeks and every few seconds she let out quavering breaths. It nearly broke Tricia's heart to have to witness her distress, and all they could do was stand there and watch Betsy Dittmeyer's pitiful treasures feed the fire until there was very little left.

It was after five when Russ dropped Tricia off at Haven't Got a Clue. She found a worried Miss Marple sitting behind the loft's door. The cat immediately rose to her feet, scolding Tricia for leaving her alone in the middle of the night and disrupting her regular routine. But when Tricia slipped between the cool sheets of her bed, Miss Marple attached herself to Tricia's chest like a barnacle, purring so loudly Tricia was sure she'd never fall back to sleep. But sleep she did, and heavily. And when the alarm went off at its usual time she felt logy, wishing she had another couple of hours before she had to face the new day.

There was no way Tricia was going to run four miles on her treadmill, and she spent the extra time washing and rewashing her hair, which had picked up an unpleasant smoky odor. She tossed the clothes she'd worn the night before in the washer, too. That particular jacket was getting quite a workout that week.

Once dressed, Tricia fed Miss Marple and remembered that days before she'd promised Nikki she'd patronize the Patisserie. It might also be a good time to find out if Nikki actually had encouraged Russ to take her along to see the fire. Tricia locked her apartment door and she and Miss Marple went down to the shop. Tricia grabbed her coat and hat and headed for the bakery.

As before, there were no other customers when Tricia entered the shop. The door buzzed, and seconds later Nikki appeared from the back room. There were dark circles under her eyes, and she seemed to droop as she walked. Was her exhaustion caused by her pregnancy or from arguing with Russ about the baby?

"Oh, Tricia, it's you. Thanks for stopping by."

"It feels like a Danish type of morning. Do you have any out back?" Tricia asked, noting the refrigerated case had very few pastries on display.

Nikki frowned and shook her head. "There hasn't been much call for them lately. I'm trying to stock only what sells. I've got chocolate cupcakes and blueberry muffins."

"I'll take a couple of muffins. And how about a dozen thumbprint cookies?"

"Sorry. I've only got chocolate chip."

"I'll take of dozen of them," Tricia said, knowing Pixie would be ready and willing to polish off at least half of them.

"I really appreciate you stopping by," Nikki said again as she bagged Tricia's order.

"I hope you weren't angry that Russ invited me to the fire last night."

Nikki shrugged. "You wouldn't believe how many times he rushes out after hearing something on that damn police scanner. But I guess that's what you get when you marry a newsman."

Tricia nodded. "It was terrible. I'd never seen a working fire before—except on TV. Betsy Dittmeyer's next-door neighbor was beside herself with worry. Luckily she only lost a few of her shrubs to the fire. It could have been so much worse."

"Russ said Betsy was a hoarder, and that there was a lot of combustible stuff in her house."

"And that the cause was most certainly arson," Tricia added.

"Who would do such a thing?" Nikki asked, setting the bakery bags on top of the counter.

Tricia had a couple of ideas but didn't think it would be prudent to discuss them with Nikki. "Are you feeling better?" she asked instead.

"Physically or emotionally?" Nikki asked. She sounded like at any moment she might burst into tears.

"Both."

"I haven't had morning sickness these past few days, but

Russ and I still can't see eye to eye on my not working after the baby comes."

"Deborah Black used to bring little Davey into work with her."

"She didn't have dangerous machinery in her back room," Nikki said.

Tricia hadn't thought of that. "I'm sure everything will work out."

"I sure hope you're right." Nikki rang up the sale.

Tricia paid and picked up the bags. "I'll see you soon," she said as she headed out the door.

Again she crossed the street for the Coffee Bean, bought two coffees, and stopped at the Happy Domestic. Ginny was seated at a stool behind the main counter, tagging merchandise. She looked up when Tricia knocked.

"Didn't I see you not ten hours ago?" Ginny asked when she opened the door.

"You did," Tricia said, settling her purchases on the cash desk. "And it feels like it was a million years ago."

Ginny eyed her friend. "You look really tired. We could go sit in the back," Ginny offered, but Tricia shook her head.

"I'm fine standing." She passed the decaf coffee to Ginny. "Did you hear Betsy Dittmeyer's house burned last night?"

"No," Ginny said, sounding shocked.

Tricia nodded grimly. "It looks like it was arson."

"Wow. Do you think whoever killed her burned her house, too?"

Tricia shrugged. "It could just be a coincidence."

"But you don't think so."

Tricia shook her head and took a sip of her coffee. "I'm sorry we didn't get to talk much last night."

"Digging through boxes of junk wasn't my idea of a fun

evening. But if I hadn't gone along with Antonio I'd have been miserable at home without him."

"I love hearing that you two are so happy," Tricia said, wishing Nikki and Russ would experience a little more joy in their marriage. "I take it you still haven't told him about the baby." She opened the bakery bag, taking out the muffins.

Ginny shook her head. "The timing hasn't been right. I thought I'd wait until the weekend to tell him."

"Speaking of the weekend, have you spoken to Grace about Friday night?"

"No, why?" Ginny asked, removing the paper from her muffin.

"It seems Mr. Everett has never had a real birthday party, and she'd like to give him one on Friday night."

"That sounds wonderful."

"I'm surprised Antonio hasn't mentioned it to you. I believe Grace spoke to him about the reservation at the Brookview."

"He's had so much on his mind lately, I'm not surprised he forgot. Who's invited?"

"You, Antonio, Pixie, and me."

"Gee, that's an awfully small party."

"She thought we could all go to dinner and celebrate."

Ginny's brow furrowed. "Isn't Friday Valentine's Day?"

"That *is* Mr. Everett's birthday."

Ginny frowned and paused in her work. "Oh. I was kind of looking forward to a romantic evening with Antonio. After all, it might be our last. I've heard romance is a thing of the past once kids enter the picture. I sort of decided Valentine's Day might be the best time to tell him the good news." She sounded anything but happy about the announcement.

"I hadn't thought about the romantic aspect of the day, probably because I had no plans and I doubt Pixie does, either. Would you like me to ask Grace to postpone the dinner until Saturday?"

"Oh, no. That wouldn't be fair to Mr. Everett. At his age, who knows how many more birthdays he'll have. I'll call Antonio later this morning and run it by him. I'm sure he won't mind. We can have our dinner a day later. By then a heart-shaped box of chocolates will sell for half price. Maybe he'll even buy me two of them," she added hopefully.

Tricia smiled. Trust Ginny to look at the bright side of things.

"You didn't mention Angelica as being on Grace's guest list. Is there a reason she isn't invited to Mr. Everett's party?"

Tricia shrugged, removing the paper wrapper from her muffin. "Sorry. She wasn't on the original list, but she had me ask if she could come and, of course, Grace was happy to include her. Now that she and Bob are history, I don't think Angelica was looking forward to being alone on Valentine's Day."

"Bob certainly left her with a mess with the Chamber of Commerce," Ginny said and took a bite of her muffin.

"That he did. And it seems Bob's been among the missing lately. I've been trying to track him down to ask what he knows about Betsy Dittmeyer. After all, he worked with her for two years."

"I never got the sense that she shared much with anybody. And let's face it, unless there's some kind of financial angle, Bob isn't much interested in being friendly to people in general, either. At least that's the impression I always got. To tell you the truth, I could never figure out what Angelica saw in him."

"I hear you," Tricia agreed.

"Although I must say Bob's been nicer to me since I started managing the Happy Domestic," Ginny said.

"Paying your rent on time probably has a lot to do with

that," Tricia agreed. "I'm not sure Deborah always did." She sipped her coffee. "Are you looking forward to tonight?"

Ginny shook her head and sighed. "I can't say pawing through a dead woman's junk is all that interesting."

"But what about all that money?" Tricia asked.

"I'd probably be more interested if I got to keep it, but Antonio was absolutely thrilled. He couldn't wait to talk to his stepmother about it this morning. I guess NRA paid more than market value for the house, so finding that money takes the sting out of it."

"I still can't understand why Betsy didn't pay the rent she owed and reclaim the boxes that held the money. How does one forget forty-four thousand dollars?" Tricia sampled her muffin. *Good!* No doubt about it, Nikki made one heck of a good product—no matter what she baked.

"And where on earth did Betsy get that kind of money? And while it looks like she had it, she sure didn't flaunt it. Not the way she dressed, or the car she drove."

"I agree." Betsy seemed to favor big ugly sweaters and matronly dresses. And Tricia never saw her wear anything but scuffed penny loafers.

Ginny looked pensive. "Don't you think all that cash had to be ill-gotten gain?"

"Are you thinking she sold drugs or something?" Tricia asked.

"Dealers do run a cash-only operation," Ginny pointed out. "I wonder if Antonio should get it tested for cocaine residue."

"You've been reading too many police procedurals," Tricia said.

"Well, you were my bad influence in that respect."

Tricia broke off another piece of muffin and shook her head. "I can't see Betsy involved in the drug trade. Someone would have noticed people hanging around her home. I spoke with one of her neighbors and was told she pretty much kept to herself."

"Blackmail?" Ginny guessed.

"I wouldn't put it past her," Tricia said, but didn't go into why.

Ginny lifted her cup, taking another sip. "But who would Betsy try to blackmail—and with what?"

Tricia shrugged, thinking about the Chamber MEMBERS file that currently sat on her computer's desktop, and remembered she hadn't called Grant Baker to discuss it. That would have to be next on her list of things to do.

Ginny polished off the last of her muffin and looked hopefully toward the shop door. "I wonder what time my first customer will arrive. Yesterday it was after one."

"We've done better than that over at Haven't Got a Clue, but not by much," Tricia said.

"At least it's given me a chance to plan my Saint Paddy's Day displays," Ginny said.

"We didn't even decorate for Valentine's Day," Tricia admitted. "Except for Pixie changing that weird doll's outfit every other day."

"That often?" Ginny asked skeptically.

Tricia shrugged. "Maybe it just seems that way." She drank the last of her coffee. "I should get back to my store. I have some things that need to be attended to."

"I'm glad you stopped by," Ginny said, getting up from her stool. "It gets pretty lonely here sometimes."

Tricia pulled on her coat and hat. "I'll see you tonight at the rental house."

"I'll be there," Ginny said with resignation, and walked Tricia to the door.

"Bye."

Since there was no traffic coming, Tricia jaywalked across

the street. Pixie would be showing up soon and she wanted to make a list of items she should talk about with Chief Baker. And she wondered how annoyed he'd be to know she'd been keeping possibly pertinent information from him. She decided it might be better to visit at the police station. It felt awkward to talk to him—whether on business or personal matters—at her store with Pixie listening to every word.

There were some things Tricia didn't want to share with her employee. Talking about Betsy Dittmeyer's death was one of them. The fact that Baker always managed to steer their conversations to their personal lives made it even more uncomfortable.

Most of all, Tricia wasn't up to being scolded in front of an audience.

Tricia sat in the police station's small, drafty waiting room for more than half an hour, glad she hadn't hung her coat on the rack near the door. Was Baker punishing her or was it his sharp-eyed receptionist/dispatcher? Polly Burgess was probably in her seventies, with thinning, snow-white hair worn in a bun. That day she wore a blue wool suit that had probably served her well over the years when she'd had an office job at St. Joseph Hospital in Nashua. Here in Stoneham it looked a bit prim and proper. But that was Polly, who probably wouldn't take guff from anyone—she'd sure put the fear of God in Tricia. Every so often she'd look out from her receptionist's station behind a half wall with a window, probably to make sure Tricia hadn't lifted a few of the well-thumbed ancient magazines that sat on one of the small tables between the six uncomfortable folding chairs.

Tricia sighed, exasperated for having forgotten to bring a

book along, and stared at the walls, noting how in just a few short months the newly opened station already had a rather shabby feel to it. She'd visited a few times before, but felt she'd never warm to the place.

Tricia noticed Polly's gaze drift to the clock on the wall outside her cubby. Suddenly she sat up, pulled back the window, and announced, "You can go in now."

Tricia grabbed her purse and stood. "Thank you." She stepped across the small lobby and reached for the door handle that led to the station's inner sanctum.

Baker's door was open. He didn't seem to be expecting her, for when he saw her, his eyes lit up and he smiled. "Tricia. This is a surprise."

"I've been sitting waiting in your reception room for the past forty-five minutes."

"Oh? I wonder why Polly didn't say something."

Tricia forced a smile. "Perhaps she's overworked."

"Well, you're here now. What's new?"

Tricia closed the door and sat on yet another uncomfortable folding chair. "I'm sure you probably already know about the fire at Betsy Dittmeyer's house."

Baker frowned, distinctly unhappy. "Did you see it on the news?"

Tricia shook her head. "I was there. Russ Smith heard it on his police scanner, called me, and the two of us went to have a look."

"I thought you were done with him a long time ago," Baker said, glowering, and sounding very much like a jealous ex-boyfriend.

"I was. And as you recall, he's married."

"And as I recall his wife is jealous of you," he said much louder than he needed to. Had his voice penetrated the thin walls? Was Polly listening? Was she as big a gossip as Frannie? If so, she must run in another circle.

"Not so much, these days," Tricia admitted and changed the subject. "Have the Milford firemen ascertained the exact cause of the fire?"

He shook his head. "Only that it was arson. They'll have a preliminary report to me as soon as they know."

"How soon is soon?"

"Could be a day or two. Could be a week. Could be longer."

That certainly sounded open-ended.

"That wasn't what brought you to my office," Baker said.

"You're right. Have you had a chance to look at the files on the Chamber's computer?"

He shook his head and she told him about what she'd found when digging through the files. As predicted, the chief was not happy. His eyes narrowed and his brow furrowed. "Why didn't you tell me all this when we talked yesterday?"

Tricia sighed and looked away, taking in Baker's immaculate office. There wasn't a paper or a book out of order, and the floor looked like it had recently been polished. His many awards hung on the cheap paneled wall behind his desk in precise rows, along with pictures of him taken with other officers and local politicians during his time with the Hillsborough Sheriff's Department. "I knew you'd be annoyed, because honestly it should have been Angelica who reported this to you."

"*You* had the files. *You* did the snooping. *You* should have told me about this as soon as you knew. And when was that?"

"Um . . ."

"This is Wednesday," he said, eyes blazing, as angry as she'd ever seen him.

"Well, I'm telling you now. And the thing is you've had the information since Saturday afternoon when you confiscated the Chamber's computer. It's not my fault you haven't looked at any of the files. I'm just bringing your attention to what you've already got."

"We're a small department. I don't have the benefit of passing those kinds of responsibilities off to an investigator. *I'm* the investigator."

Tricia handed him her flash drive. "After you copy the files, I'd like to have this returned."

Baker turned toward the monitor on the wing of his desk, inserted the flash drive, and opened it. "It's the file called MEMBERS. And don't forget to study the spreadsheets. I showed them to Christopher, and he's on tap to find someone to go over the books for the Chamber."

"You've talked to Christopher about this?" Baker asked angrily.

"I needed corroboration that there was something wrong with the files."

"Why am I always the last to know?" Baker groused.

"Because your force is too small to deal with murder cases?" she suggested.

"Are you intimating that we, a force of seven officers and a receptionist, aren't capable of solving this murder, but you—a solitary civilian—are?"

"Not at all," Tricia answered, but she had been reading murder mysteries since the tender age of ten, whereas Baker had only been an officer of the law for some twenty-odd years.

"Who else knows about these files?" Baker demanded.

"Just Angelica and Christopher."

"Keeping it all in the family, eh?" he said with a bit of a sneer.

"Christopher isn't part of my family."

"But he was for ten years."

"What's that got to do with anything?"

"You called *him*, not *me*, to look at these files."

"He's a financial expert. Betsy had been stealing from the Chamber. I wanted him to verify it before I brought it to anyone's attention."

"Why don't you take out an ad in the *Stoneham Weekly News* and tell everyone in the village? And don't tell me, let me guess, you've also compared notes with Russ Smith on this subject, too."

"I congratulated him on his impending fatherhood the other day. Betsy's death may have come up during the conversation."

"You know damn well it did," he accused.

Tricia sat back in her chair. She'd known he was going to be upset, but she had no idea *how* upset. "I could have just kept this information to myself, you know."

"No, you couldn't."

Was he implying *she* was a gossip? She preferred not to think about it.

"I'd advise you to look at every single file on the Chamber hard drive. Betsy hid what could be important information mixed in with things like recipes."

"Do you have an example?"

"Uh . . . no."

"Then how do you—?" He stopped, turning his piercing gaze on her. "Please tell me you haven't been poking around in other places you shouldn't."

"I don't know what you're referring to," she bluffed.

"I think you do."

Tricia didn't look away. Should she admit Angelica had copied files from Betsy's home computer and given them to her? The computer had no doubt been destroyed in the fire; only she and Angelica had an inkling of what information it contained.

"I'm just giving you a friendly piece of advice," she told him.

Baker studied her face. "There's more you're not telling me."

"I don't know what that could be," she fibbed. Should she mention the cartons in the rental house? She didn't see how that could be relevant. The money they'd found the previous evening could have been collected from people Betsy had been blackmailing, or it could have been earned honestly from items she'd sold on eBay or found in people's trash. The latter were unlikely, but possibilities nonetheless.

"Is there anything else you want to ask me?" Tricia said.

Baker frowned. "I have thousands of questions for you, but nothing at this moment that pertains to the case. I presume you'll be available if and when I do have further questions?"

"Absolutely."

"Then you may as well go back to your store. I'll call you if I need you."

"Yes, sir," Tricia said and saluted.

Baker didn't seem to appreciate her levity. "I'm only going to say this once: I want you and Angelica to stop playing sister sleuths. I don't want you poking your noses into stuff that doesn't concern you. I want to keep you both safe. Do I make myself clear?"

Again Tricia saluted. Baker turned back to his computer monitor.

Tricia stood, picked up her purse, and waited for Baker to say something else, but he didn't. "I'll talk to you later," she said, turned, and opened his office door, waiting for a reply.

Baker didn't look up. So, he was going to punish her with silence. Well, two could play at that game.

She walked out of the dreary little office and she didn't say good-bye.

SEVENTEEN

Tricia returned to Haven't Got a Clue and found Pixie behind the cash desk waving a Post-it note in the air. "Your sister called. She said she'll meet you here at five to walk over to the new Chamber office. She said to wear your old clothes. Does that mean you're going to help her clean?"

"Something like that," Tricia said and unfastened the buttons on her coat. Why had Angelica even bothered to call when she knew Tricia would be seeing her at lunchtime? She hung up her coat and settled on the stool behind the cash desk that Pixie had so recently abandoned, hoping for, but not expecting, many well-heeled customers with long lists of vintage mysteries they were eager to buy.

Pixie sidled up to the cash desk, looking expectant. "Did you notice Sarah Jane has another new outfit?"

Tricia turned her gaze to the vintage doll carriage that sat along the side wall, partially blocking books by authors whose last names began with the letters *T* through *Z*. Maybe it was Sarah Jane's forever frozen startled expression that creeped Tricia out. At least this latest ensemble included a matching frilly bonnet to cover the doll's hairless vinyl head. The dress, hat, and patent leather shoes had probably cost some proud grandmother a small fortune, but when the lucky owner had outgrown the outfit—or more likely had never had the opportunity to wear it, except perhaps inside a photo studio—it had found its way to Pixie's favorite thrift shop, where it had probably been purchased for a song.

"It's very nice," Tricia had to agree.

"She's wearing real vintage Curity diapers, rubber panties, and a taffeta slip under the dress. I thought since we sell authentic vintage mysteries, Sarah Jane should be wearing authentic vintage undies."

Tricia wasn't sure what to make of that leap of logic and instead found herself simply nodding in agreement.

"Hey, I had the tube on before I came into work this morning," Pixie said, changing the subject. "I saw some fire footage on the news. They said it was the dead dame's house. Did you hear?"

"Yes, I did," Tricia said.

"They said it could be arson," Pixie continued, her voice rising as though to elicit a greater response.

"Did they really?" Tricia asked.

Pixie nodded. "The broad lived less than a mile from me, but I never heard any sirens. The truth is, I sleep like the dead. You could play reveille full blast on a bugle right next to my ear but until I've had my full eight hours of shut-eye, nothing wakes me up."

"How interesting," Tricia said, and repositioned the stapler that sat on the cash desk. "Did you have a chance to make the coffee?" she asked Pixie. "I'm afraid I don't sleep quite as well as you. I was awake half of last night and got a late start this morning." She didn't explain why.

"Can't you smell it?" Pixie asked. "That Colombian blend you've been buying lately smells like heaven to me. You wouldn't believe the swill that passes for coffee I had to drink when I was in stir. Would you like me to get you a cup?"

"That would be lovely, thank you." She got up from her perch and joined Pixie at the beverage station. Pixie poured the brew into Tricia's usual ceramic cup, doctoring it just the way she liked it. Watching her go through the motions with such an obvious desire to please made Tricia feel terribly guilty. Pixie might have a few rough edges—eavesdropping being her worst habit—but all in all she'd become an exceptional employee, which Tricia had been happy to report to her parole officer the times he'd checked up on her.

Pixie handed her the cup and a paper napkin. "Careful, it's hot."

Tricia inhaled the aroma and took a tentative sip. "Thank you, Pixie. I don't know what I'd do without you."

Pixie's cheeks blushed under her pancake makeup and she positively beamed with delight. "Since Mr. E won't be here until later, would it be okay if I went upstairs and unpacked and sorted that big box of books you bought off eBay? Did I mention it arrived while you were out yesterday?"

"No, but it would be very helpful if you'd take care of it. Thank you, Pixie."

"Just doing my job," she said with pride, pivoted, and

headed for the back of the store and the door marked PRI-VATE. Miss Marple jumped down from her perch and scampered off to follow her.

Tricia sighed, held the cup in both hands, and let its warmth seep into her. It was barely ten thirty and already she felt like she'd put in a full day's work. She hoped the coffee helped her get her second wind, and if not . . . considered heading for the Coffee Bean and a cup of espresso. There was more than one way to stay awake on the job.

Though he wasn't scheduled to begin work until two o'clock, Mr. Everett showed up at precisely one to join Pixie for lunch. It pleased Tricia that two people with such diverse backgrounds had become fast friends thanks to Haven't Got a Clue.

She had already collected her coat and was ready to leave for her own lunch when they returned from the Bookshelf Diner at 1:59. But when Tricia visited Booked for Lunch, she found an anxious Tommy—the short-order cook, ready to leave for the day—with a message that Angelica had already taken off to run an errand. Tricia's usual tuna plate had been transferred to a foam take-out box. Tricia hadn't called Angelica to talk about the fire, figuring she'd probably already heard about it, but she'd been eager to discuss it with her sister nonetheless.

After returning to her store, Tricia climbed the steps to her loft apartment and ate her lunch at her kitchen island, picking up where she'd left off in *The Daughter of Time* with only Miss Marple for company. Much as she loved her cat, Tricia found she much preferred eating her midday meal at the counter in Angelica's homey little café with her sister for company. They'd come a long way in just over four years.

The rest of the day dragged. Mr. Everett and Pixie retreated to the storeroom above, with Pixie acting as instructor, teaching him how to fill the Internet orders. It was slow going, but Mr. Everett seemed to be picking up the whole book-fulfillment process, and Pixie predicted that they'd be caught up on all orders before the weekend. While they'd worked upstairs, Tricia and Miss Marple held the fort in the shop—a shop with absolutely no customers. Sometimes Tricia wondered if it was worth even opening the store during the winter. She glanced at the calendar and crossed her fingers, hoping Punxsutawney Phil's prediction for an early spring would come to pass. Thank goodness the promise of warmer weather grew with every passing day and the sky remained lighter just a little longer each evening. Winter's back might be broken, but they had five more weeks of winter to endure until the spring equinox.

As promised, Angelica strode into Haven't Got a Clue at precisely 4:59. Her idea of old clothes didn't match Tricia's, for she was dressed in what looked like a brand-new pair of freshly ironed jeans, with a crease so sharp it could have drawn blood, and under her short ski jacket she had on a pretty lilac-colored sweatshirt that also looked like it had only just had the sales tag snipped. She also held her big pink purse, which could only mean that she had brought Sarge along for the evening's entertainment.

"Why did you bring Sarge?" Tricia asked.

"You couldn't say, 'Hello, darling sister, I'm so happy to see you'?"

"Hello, darling sister, I'm so happy to see you. Why did you bring Sarge?"

At hearing his name, the little white dog's head popped over the top of the purse and he yipped cheerfully, which caused Miss Marple to spring to her feet, jump to the top of the sales counter, and hiss.

"Miss Marple," Tricia admonished.

"Sarge doesn't like to be alone for so much of the day and then the evening, too. He won't be any trouble," Angelica promised. Sarge yipped again as though in agreement.

"Well, I hate to break up this happy reunion, but it's time for Mr. E and me to head out for the night," Pixie said. "See you in the morning, Tricia. Bye, Angelica. And bye to you, too, Sarge."

"Good night," Mr. Everett called as he followed Pixie out the door.

Once her employees had left for the day, Tricia heaved a sigh. "Good, now we can talk. Where were you this afternoon? I had to eat lunch all by myself."

"Aw, you missed me," Angelica said with a grin. "If you must know, I went out to buy Mr. Everett a birthday card. I must say, the pickings over at the Happy Domestic are awfully slim—at least if you're trying to buy a card for a man. I was going to give Ginny a few suggestions on her card selection, but only her little assistant was there. I must remember to bring it up tonight when we see her. Anyway, I ended up at the convenience store. After that, I had a meeting with Marina over at the Sheer Comfort Inn." She babbled on—much more information than Tricia really wanted to hear—but before she could get a word in edgewise, Angelica continued, "I do love to be the point person for that little venture, although I wish I could be more hands-on at the inn. Don't you think it would be fun to entertain people on a daily basis?"

"No," Tricia said. She let out an exasperated breath. "By now I'm sure you've already heard all about the fire."

Angelica looked at her blankly. "What fire?"

"Betsy Dittmeyer's home was a target of arson."

"Arson?" Angelica repeated in disbelief.

Tricia nodded. "Good grief. It was filled with all that paper and trash—it looked like a gigantic bonfire."

"Bonfire? It sounds like you witnessed it."

"I did." She filled Angelica in on her adventures with Russ Smith during the wee hours of the night.

"Was anything salvageable?" Angelica asked.

"You mean the computer?" Tricia asked.

"Yes."

"I don't know. I spoke to Grant earlier today and hinted about what we found in Betsy's files, but I didn't dare implicate myself."

"Arson," Angelica repeated and shook her head, preoccupied. "Why would someone set the place on fire? Do you think it could have been the same person who killed her?"

Tricia nodded. "And probably kicked the door in, too."

The fine lines on Angelica's face suddenly seemed deeper. "What if the killer was trying to get rid of something he or she didn't want anyone else to find?"

"That was my thought, too."

"Then we'd better finish cleaning out the Chamber's new home before it gets out that the junk inside belonged to Betsy, otherwise whoever torched her place might set fire to it, too." Angelica turned and peered out the shop's big display window. "Antonio's car just passed by. We can finish this conversation on the way over to the rental house, or have you learned something else about this mess you wouldn't want to say in front of Antonio or Ginny?"

"No. Let me get my coat and I'll be right with you."

A minute later Tricia locked the door to Haven't Got a Clue and the sisters started off down the sidewalk heading north. Angelica spoke first. "This morning I interviewed four candidates for the Chamber receptionist job and I think I may have found the right person," Angelica said.

"Anyone local?"

"Yes, one of the villagers. She's an empty nester and looking for a part-time job to fill part of her day."

"So you've made up your mind that Betsy's job should go part-time?" Tricia asked.

"Actually, the more I think about it, the more I may actually want to hire more people. As it is, our Chamber does very little for its members. I've been networking with other Chamber presidents and it seems like Bob never did much except toot his own horn."

"What kinds of perks were you thinking of?" Tricia asked.

"Special deals with big-box office supply stores, for one. Our members would get a discount with every purchase. We could get deals on checks, credit card processing, and for the larger businesses, like the dialysis center, payroll discounts."

"That all sounds nice," Tricia admitted. "What else?"

"We could hold classes on leadership, small business counseling, and how to prepare better promotional mailers. We could do a lot more networking events. Do you realize we only have fifty-six members in our Chamber, but there are over one hundred businesses in and around Stoneham that would qualify for membership?"

"That many?" Tricia asked, surprised.

Angelica nodded. "Of course, if so many of our members weren't found dead on a regular basis, it might help recruitment."

Tricia frowned. Since she seemed to have an uncanny knack for finding the dead; she was usually initially (and unfairly) blamed for their demise. She decided to change the subject. "As I mentioned, I spoke to Grant today. Needless to say he was upset—very upset—that we hadn't brought Betsy's dubious Chamber files to his attention before now."

"He's had them since Saturday. That means he never even bothered to look at them."

"I did point that out to him."

"So why was he so annoyed?"

"He doesn't like to be kept out of the loop. He threatened to talk to you, too."

"Then I guess I won't be checking my phone messages for the next couple of days. I hope you didn't tell him we'd gone snooping in Betsy's house."

"Not a word," she replied.

"Good," Angelica said as they approached the house. The trunk lid was up on Antonio's car and he had his head buried in it.

"Do you need some help?" Tricia offered.

Antonio straightened. "You are just in time, lovely ladies. If one of you would take the keys—"

"I will," Angelica said, appropriating them from him, and quickly marched toward the front door, leaving Tricia and Antonio to carry in the stack of foam take-out boxes that were packed with food.

"Looks like you brought enough to feed an army," Tricia said as he handed her one of the stacks.

"A well-fed workforce is a happy workforce," he said, snagging a bottle of wine and tucking it under his arm before he grabbed a large paper sack. "I will come back for the rest of it." He slammed the lid and they started for the steps, which someone—probably Antonio—had thoughtfully salted earlier that day.

"I came by this afternoon," Antonio admitted, as though reading Tricia's mind. "I wanted to make sure the Dumpsters had arrived." They had, and now took up the entire length of the home's driveway.

Angelica stood in front of the front door and called to them. "Good. We've got to get this place emptied out tonight—even if it *takes* all night," Angelica said.

"I don't understand."

"We can discuss it while we eat," Angelica said, turned, and unlocked the door.

"Where's Ginny?" Tricia asked Antonio.

"She will be here soon. I called her just before I left the Brookview Inn. She said she would be changing her clothes and would be here as soon as she could."

Angelica had already set Sarge free by the time Tricia and Antonio made it inside. They walked through the stacks of cartons and into the kitchen, putting down their boxes. Angelica had peeled off her coat, but as Tricia went to unfasten the buttons on her own, Angelica stopped her.

"Since the Dumpsters are already out there, why don't you two start taking stuff out to them so we can have more room to work."

"Why don't *you* carry the stuff out?" Tricia asked, annoyed.

"Because someone needs to take charge, and as I am a natural-born leader, I have taken on the burden of command." Funny, everyone had looked to Tricia to take charge the night before.

"Marvelous idea," Antonio said. "I will take out the first bag of trash and then bring in the rest of our dinner."

"Get to it. Tricia, you know where all the trash is stacked," Angelica said and turned back for the kitchen.

Tricia ignored her last comment. "What exactly does the burden of command entail?"

"I'll set up our dinner while the two of you tackle some of those bags of trash. When Ginny gets here, we can eat and then the real work will begin."

Though unhappy with her assignment, Tricia nonetheless headed back to the living room and began taking the bags of trash out to the Dumpster.

Ginny arrived ten minutes later, breathless and full of apologies but ready to start work. With three worker bees now in attendance they set up a kind of bucket brigade, with Tricia tossing bags out the side door to Ginny, who tossed them to Antonio, who tossed them in the Dumpster. It took only ten minutes to clear out the mess from the evening before, so they could start making a new mess.

Angelica had impeccable timing, announcing that dinner was served just as the last bag landed inside the Dumpster. Tricia had been ready with a snarky quip, but had to eat her words when she saw that while the three of them were on garbage patrol, Angelica had been scrubbing the kitchen. The table, sink, and counters were certainly cleaner than they had been the night before, and she'd spread out the food, buffet style. Sarge trotted around the table looking hopeful, but Angelica admonished them not to feed the bichon frise. "He's already had his dinner. You don't want him to get fat and have to go on a doggy diet, do you?" But it was hard to eat such delicious chicken, beef, and pâté with Sarge's little brown eyes following every bite.

Antonio poured wine for all of them, but Tricia noted that Ginny didn't touch hers. Apparently she still hadn't shared the news of her pregnancy with her husband.

"Antonio, I'm sure you heard about the fire at Betsy Ditt-meyer's house overnight," Tricia said.

"I did. Everyone at the inn was talking about it."

"And that it was arson?" Angelica asked.

He nodded.

"I'm afraid if we don't finish tonight, someone might find out that Betsy's garbage had been housed here for the past couple of years and do the same. That's why we must get the house emptied. I'm not going to lose the Chamber's only viable home to an arsonist."

Antonio looked unhappy but nodded in agreement.

"Does this place have any outside lights? If it's lit up like a Christmas tree, it might discourage anyone from coming nearby," Angelica continued.

"Do you think we should call Grant or maybe Fire Chief Farrar?" Tricia asked.

"It probably wouldn't hurt. Once we're finished, I think I'll do just that," Angelica said.

The temptation to linger over their lovely meal was thwarted when Antonio suddenly became businesslike and announced that it was time to get back to work. "I'm hope-ful, but not anticipating, that we will finish our work here tonight. And that will not happen unless we get started."

"Shall I clean up here?" Ginny asked, looking hopeful, and before Angelica could volunteer for that lighter duty.

"Yes. The rest of us will begin clearing out the upstairs," Antonio said.

"I'll make my calls first," Angelica said, and turned to grab her purse and her cell phone.

"Why don't we do the same thing we did outside: someone toss the boxes downstairs and we open them here. That'll save us lugging all the trash down the stairs," Tricia volunteered, but Antonio shook his head.

"The Dumpster sits directly under one of the upstairs windows. We can simply toss the trash bags into it."

"Good idea," Tricia agreed, and the two of them started for the stairs to the second floor, leaving Ginny to tidy the kitchen and Angelica with her phone.

Sarge seemed to think they were competing in a race, and zoomed on ahead of them, excitedly barking for them to join him at the top of the landing.

Tricia started working in the smaller of the bedrooms, dumping boxes and methodically going through the accumulated mess. Sarge thought it was some kind of game and sniffed at the items. He'd pick one up, carry it around the upstairs, showing off his new toy before dropping it and grabbing something else.

Soon Ginny joined them, but rather than stand over her emptied boxes, she sat on the floor sorting the wheat from the chaff, while Angelica and Antonio worked in the other room.

The pickings weren't anywhere near as good as they had been the night before, and soon Antonio opened the window on the south side of the house and began tossing the trash into the Dumpster.

Before the end of the first hour, Tricia's back ached. By the end of the second hour, her legs were sore. By the end of the third hour, she loathed the sight of boxes and newspaper clippings, and hated Betsy enough to have done her in—that is, if someone hadn't already beaten her to it.

Finally Ginny called out, "This is boring! How much longer until we can go home?"

Tricia surveyed the bedroom. "We've got only two more boxes to go; how many do you guys have?"

Angelica didn't answer right away, presumably counting the boxes before answering. "Nine."

"Why don't I go help them while you finish up in here," Ginny said.

"Okay," Tricia agreed, and lifted the interleaved flaps on the next-to-last carton. She looked inside. More papers. Betsy collected the most useless stuff. But mixed among the newspaper clippings and recipes torn from magazines were a handful of lovely old postcards. The stamps were old. If the cards themselves weren't worth anything, maybe the stamps were. She set them aside, and tossed the rest of the papers into a trash bag.

As she went to lift the flaps on the last carton, she noticed a wet spot on the side of the box and suddenly realized Sarge had been missing for quite some time. Had he relieved himself on the box, known he'd done something naughty, and decided to lay low before anyone noticed? She shook her head and opened the box, glad she hadn't tried to lift it. It was full of old books, with wads of yellowed crumpled newspaper to cushion them and fill out the box. Lifting them one at a time, she inspected the titles. Nothing special at all: a couple of cookbooks, a few dog-eared paperbacks, and several little blue books from Alcoholics Anonymous. The copies of the *Nashua Telegraph* were at least ten years old. Had Betsy saved them and then decided to use them for packing, or had the box been sitting somewhere like a garage for a long time and she decided to move them to the house to make room for more junk in her own home?

At the bottom of the box was a very old and large—at least fifteen inches in length—Bible clad in cracked brown leather. Tricia carefully lifted the old book out of the box and set it on the edge of the empty box beside its former home. She opened the cover and looked for some kind of copyright date without finding one. Well, the text was at least two thousand years old, but she wondered if there was some other way of dating it. Sure enough, at the center of the book was a genealogy chart that began in 1847 leading up and into the twentieth century. The last entry was for a John Morrison—Betsy and Joelle's father? The date would be about right. So, it was the family Bible. This might be something that should be given to Joelle.

Tricia closed the cover and left it to concentrate on tidying the room. She scooped up the rest of the trash, placed it in the last of the plastic garbage bags, tied the end in a knot, and tossed it into the hall. Then she set the Bible on the floor, flattened the boxes, and carried them out into the hall.

Angelica, Ginny, and Antonio had made fast work of the remaining boxes and were finishing up as Tricia entered the room. "Hey, looks like we're just about done."

"Thank goodness," Ginny breathed, looking exhausted, and suddenly Tricia wondered if she should even be doing all this heavy lifting and carrying in her condition.

"Did you find anything interesting?" Angelica asked, as she used her hand to sweep more litter into one of the trash bags.

"Just an old family Bible, and not in very good condition. But I'm sure Joelle would probably like to have it."

Angelica straightened, and Tricia noted there were cobwebs in her hair. "If she'd been cut out of the will, should you even contemplate giving it to her? And how are you going to explain where you got it?"

Those were two very good questions, but Tricia was too tired to think about the answer just then.

"I have had enough," Antonio said and offered Ginny a hand, helping her to her feet. "We have found nothing of real value tonight, but the job is done. I have spoken to my contractor, and he will meet me here tomorrow to decide what to do with the floors and other renovations so that the Chamber may move in as soon as possible."

"Hallelujah!" Angelica crowed. "I'll call my new receptionist and see how soon she can start. Maybe I can have her trained and ready to help us move in by next week," she said hopefully.

Tricia hefted the Bible. "Do you mind if I take this home and have a better look at it?" she asked Antonio.

"Do as you wish. If you want to sell it, you may do that, too."

"I don't know about that," Tricia said.

"It is no good to me or my employer. If you don't wish to sell it, perhaps you can donate it to a worthy soul."

Tricia nodded. "I'll find it a good home—one way or another." And probably with Joelle. Now all she had to figure out was a way to tell her about it without revealing that Betsy had rented the little house and filled it with tons and tons of trash.

Antonio closed the upstairs window for the last time, locking it, and they started down the stairs with Angelica turning out the lights as she went.

Once back on the first floor, Antonio paused to take in the now spacious living room. "Ladies, you have done very fine work these past two nights. I'm sure my employer will be very pleased by your industry."

"Yes, and please be sure to remind her that Tricia is not a member of the happy Nigela Ricita empire. Perhaps she should be given some kind of honorarium," Angelica said.

"That is an excellent suggestion," Antonio agreed.

"Oh, no—I don't need anything. I'm just happy I could

help out. The Chamber needs its new home—and the faster they can move in, the better."

"You have a good heart," Antonio said.

Tricia felt a flush rise from her neck to color her cheeks. "Besides, you've already graced me with this Bible." She hefted it. "That's all the reward I need."

"I don't know about you, but I would've asked for a piece of that forty-four grand," Ginny grumbled.

"My employer would not be *that* grateful," Antonio said, and they all laughed.

While Antonio moved the few boxes of useful items to his car, Angelica found Sarge asleep on one of the heat grates, nudged him awake, and clipped his leash onto his collar.

As Angelica had suggested, Antonio left the outside lights on, and left one burning in the living room so that anyone walking nearby would see the house had been emptied. Now they just had to hope Betsy's arsonist wouldn't set the contents of the Dumpsters on fire.

Ginny and Antonio got into his car and took off for home, and Tricia walked along with Angelica and Sarge in silence on their usual route through the village square. The ebony sky was filled with stars. Tricia held tight to Betsy's family Bible, wondering why she'd squirreled it away with so much other useless junk.

It was just another question for which she'd probably never have the answer.

"I wasn't kidding when I suggested Ms. Ricita repay you for your efforts these past two nights," Angelica said as they paused under the glow of a lamp to let Sarge do his worst.

Tricia shook her head. "There's very little I need these days, and after seeing how Betsy lived, I feel like I should clean out a closet or two of my own."

Angelica smiled. "Me, too."

Tricia hefted the Bible. "Now that her house has burned and we've gone through all the boxes, I'll bet the killer goes into deep cover. He—or she—didn't leave many clues. There's a good chance we may never figure out who killed Betsy."

"I hope you're wrong. My home and business were violated. I want closure," Angelica insisted.

But if the killer didn't resurface, closure was something she—and Joelle Morrison—might never see.

EIGHTEEN

 If Tricia had known she was destined for another night of vivid dreams she might have decided not to go to bed after spending a second evening emptying boxes containing Betsy Dittmeyer's so-called treasures. This time she ended up surrounded by piles and piles of trash pressing upon her, and the sensation that invisible insects and mice crawled on and all around her. And from far across the warehouselike room, a candle dripped wax—threatening to set the place on fire.

She awoke early and immediately jumped in the shower. It took a lot of scrubbing before she felt clean once again.

After a leisurely breakfast that included perusing the *Nashua Telegraph*—which, as she'd predicted to Russ Smith, had done no follow-up story on Betsy's murder—Tricia went down to her store to start the workday with Miss Marple bringing up the rear.

"Good morning," Pixie called, arriving right on time. She saw the Bible sitting on the cash desk, where Tricia had left it the night before, and zeroed right in on it. "Hey, whatcha got there?"

"A Bible."

"I can see that. Man, it's older than both of us put together," Pixie said and lifted the cover to look at the title page.

Tricia fought the urge to shoo her away. "It was a gift from Antonio Barbero."

"Are you giving up bookselling to join a nunnery or something?" Pixie asked and laughed.

"Heavens, no."

"Thank goodness. I like this job and don't want to see it end," Pixie said and headed for the back of the store to hang up her coat.

Once Pixie was settled in she pondered what title Sarah Jane should hold that day to entice customers, while Tricia planned to spend an hour or more studying Betsy's Bible and the papers that were stuffed within its cover. Then the phone rang. Tricia picked up the receiver. "Haven't Got a Clue. This is—"

"Tricia? It's Billie Burke at the Bank of Stoneham. I tried to get hold of Antonio Barbero and Angelica, but haven't had any luck."

"Sorry I can't help you there."

"Oh, but you can. There's a crowd of people crawling all over the Dumpsters at the house across the street. If one of them gets hurt—"

"What can I do about it?"

"Call the Stoneham police."

"Not to be a pain, but why don't you call them?"

"Officially, it's none of my business. But as you're Angelica's sister—"

"Gotcha. I'll do it now. Thanks for calling." Tricia pressed down on the old phone's switch hook and waited for a dial tone and, since the situation wasn't an emergency, she dialed the station's regular phone number. She relayed the problem, but Polly couldn't promise that the patrolling officer would arrive anytime soon. "How about Chief Baker?" Tricia asked.

"I'm not going to bother the chief with something so trivial," Polly scolded.

If someone broke his or her neck while trespassing, the result would be anything but trivial.

"Thank you," Tricia said and hung up. She considered calling Baker's private cell phone number and decided to go for it, but only succeeded in reaching his voice mail. Still, she left a message.

"Pixie!" Tricia called.

Pixie scurried across the store. "What's up?"

"I have to run yet another errand."

"No problem. I serve at your pleasure, Madam President of Haven't Got a Clue."

Tricia smiled at such enthusiasm and retrieved her coat, hat, gloves, and scarf, and left her store, hurrying down the sidewalk toward what would soon be the Chamber of Commerce's new home.

As Billie had said, there were at least five people inside and outside the Dumpster, picking through its contents.

"Excuse me," Tricia called, but no one turned to look at her. "Excuse me!" she tried even louder, and still none of the men or women looked up. "Police raid!" she hollered in desperation.

That did it. Everyone looked up.

"You people have to leave right now. You're trespassing."

"Says who?" replied a brawny man of about fifty, bundled in a grubby Carhartt work jacket and pants, with at least a week's worth of beard stubbling his cheeks.

"Says me. I represent the new leaseholder. You're trespassing on private property. The police have been called and will be here any minute."

"Sorry, but we don't believe you," said another man dressed in the same heavy-duty—and just as filthy—clothes as the first.

"I've been through everything that got tossed in the Dumpster, and there's definitely nothing of value left."

"We'll be the judge of that," the first man said smugly, and went back to tearing open the garbage bags and dumping the contents.

Tricia sidled past the big metal garbage bin to the smaller recycling bin, where two older women sifted through the ton or more of worthless paper.

"Excuse me, but you're trespassing," she tried again.

Neither of the women looked up. "Our bad," one of them said and continued to work.

Frustrated, Tricia retraced her steps until she was again standing in front of the large Dumpster. She was about to pull out her phone when she saw Chief Baker hurrying toward her on the sidewalk.

"I take it you got my message," she said, relieved.

"Yeah. Hey, guys," Baker called and got no response from the pickers. He put his thumb and index finger between his lips and blew a loud wolf whistle. That got their attention. "Bernie, what the hell are you doing in there?"

Grumpy Guy Number One looked up. "Looking for treasure, what else?"

"You're breaking half a dozen laws. If you don't want me to arrest you and your people, you'll have to leave right now."

"Come on, Grant. A guy's gotta make a living."

"Well, find some other line of work—or else."

Bernie frowned, but he and his cohort grudgingly climbed over the edge of the Dumpster and dropped to the ground. Another man held a large plastic trash bag filled with their spoils.

"Toss your bag of goodies into the Dumpster," Baker ordered.

"Aw, come on. It's no good to the owner. We heard she died earlier in the week." And who besides Ginny, Antonio, Angelica, and Tricia knew that fact?

"Be that as it may," Baker said, "clear out."

"Wait," Tricia said. "Let me have a look." She moved to stand next to the third man, who held out a clear plastic bag. Something sparkly caught her eye and Tricia yanked off her gloves, stuffing them into her coat pockets before she reached into the bag to pull out what looked like a solitaire diamond ring. She glanced at Bernie, who quietly fumed.

Tricia examined the ring. It wasn't a particularly large diamond, but it had to be worth something. How had they missed it the previous evening? She poked through the rest of the stuff, deciding nothing was of any real value—at least to her. She faced Baker. "They can have the rest."

By then, the women had joined the group. In their bag were pieces of ephemera: old playing cards, greeting cards, a couple of calendars from before World War II, and some vintage postcards. Ginny must have gone through the boxes that contained this stuff, not knowing old paper could be worth something. Still, Tricia figured if she let the pickers keep what they'd found, they might not come back for more—or would it just entice them to return when nobody was around?

"They can keep this stuff, too," she said. Nobody said thank you and instead glared at Tricia for ending their treasure hunt.

With much swearing and grumbling the men and women took off on foot. Tricia and Baker watched until they'd turned the corner, presumably to retrieve their transportation. "Do you think they'll be back?" she asked.

Baker nodded. "The minute we leave."

"I don't care about the stuff they found; I'm more concerned with liability issues."

"Let me see that ring," Baker said and Tricia handed it over. "It looks like the real thing to me."

"And me," Tricia agreed. She held out her hand to take it from him, but Baker took hold of it and slipped the ring over her finger.

"What do you know? We're engaged," Baker said and laughed.

"We are not." But when Tricia tried to take the ring off, it stubbornly remained stuck below her knuckle. "Now look what you've done," she said irritably.

"It was just a joke. Soap it up and it'll come right off."

"It had better. It belongs to Nigela Ricita Associates. And what are we going to do to keep those people away? We can hardly stand guard out here in the cold for any length of time."

Baker had no time to answer, because a car pulled up to the curb and Antonio stepped out. "*Boungiorno!* Hello, Tricia. To what do I owe the pleasure, Chief Baker?"

"Dumpster divers," Baker said. "We just chased them away, but unless you get rid of this hunk of steel full of garbage today, they'll be back."

"It's already arranged," Antonio assured them. "They should be here within the hour."

"Good. Look what we missed last night." Tricia held out her hand, showing him the ring.

Antonio's eyes lit up and he smiled. "Ah, who is the lucky man?"

Tricia glared at Baker. "Nobody. The scavengers found it, but it looks like this ring now belongs to your boss, too. I'll give it to you as soon as I can get it off."

A battered Ford pickup pulled up to the curb and a lanky man in his fifties got out. "Ah, this is my contractor, Jim Stark."

"We've met," Tricia said with delight. How could she forget the man who had converted Haven't Got a Clue from a ruin to a showplace—and performed the same magic on her loft conversion? "Jim's company has done a lot of work for me. Good to see you again, Jim."

"Same here," Stark said, shaking her hand. He was a good-looking man with a full head of gray hair and a wicked mustache. He reminded Tricia of the actor Sam Elliott. His grin was positively infectious.

"Would you like to come inside, Tricia? Perhaps if you warm up, the ring will come off. And you can listen to Jim's recommendations and relay them to your sister."

Tricia immediately brightened. "I'd love to." She turned back to Baker. "Thanks for showing up and chasing those guys away. I really appreciate it, and I know Angelica will, too."

"My pleasure. I'll see you later, Tricia," Baker said and tipped his hat.

"Bye," she called and watched as he turned and headed back

down the sidewalk toward the police station. Baker was a genuinely nice man and she really *did* like him. A piece of her heart ached because she was sure they weren't destined to be together.

Antonio wasted no more time. He pulled the house keys from his pocket and led Tricia and the contractor to the front door.

Tricia spent the next hour watching and listening as the men discussed the repairs and cosmetic changes that were to be made to convert the home into office space. She wished she had a pad and pen to take it all down, surprised at how much work Nigela Ricita Associates was prepared to do for the Chamber of Commerce—especially as the lease was only good for a year and they intended to raze the building. She was sure Angelica would be eager to hear all about it.

Before she left the house, Tricia visited the kitchen and found a bar of soap. She worked up a good lather and the diamond ring slipped right off. She studied it, deciding it probably was worth at least a thousand dollars. Maybe selling it would cover the cost of refinishing some of the floors. The diamond sparkled. Although it was just a simple setting, seeing it brought back feelings of regret that the engagement ring Christopher had given her, and she'd worn for nearly eleven years, now resided in her jewelry box.

Tricia dried her hands and went back to the living room, where Antonio and Stark stood talking.

She handed the ring to Antonio.

"*Grazie.* It's good you got it off—otherwise the village would be buzzing with rumors about your impending nuptials." And no doubt the person who'd be most interested was none other than Joelle Morrison, who'd call to once again offer her wedding planning services.

A big flatbed truck rumbled up to the curb outside the

house. "Ah, good. They are here to pick up the first of the Dumpsters," Antonio said and peered out the front window.

Tricia joined him. "I'd sure like to know who let it out that we'd found buried treasure in all those boxes of junk," Tricia said.

"I assure you it was not Ginny or me. I know it was not you. That means it must have been Angelica."

"Never," Tricia protested.

"Then perhaps she told one of her employees," Antonio suggested.

Tommy didn't seem a likely suspect, nor did Bev, the waitress, who'd been out sick with the flu. That only left one person.

Frannie. The village gossip.

Rats!

Antonio offered to drive Tricia back to Haven't Got a Clue, but since it was only a couple of blocks away she thanked him and opted to walk. As she neared the space between the buildings that housed the Have a Heart bookstore and the Patisserie, she saw the toes of a scuffed pair of boots protruding and had a feeling she knew who they belonged to.

"Bob, is that you?" Tricia called.

"Quiet!" Bob ordered. "I can't be seen."

Tricia looked around the village's empty main street. "Who's going to see you?"

"Your boyfriend is after me. He's going to arrest me," Bob said with what sounded like panic.

"I know. Bob, why don't you just face up to it? Stoneham is a very small town, and you can't hide out forever."

"Would you let me stay with you . . . just for a couple of days while I figure things out?" The poor man seemed absolutely desperate.

Tricia frowned, wishing she could see Bob's face, which was hidden in shadow. "You know I can't. That would be harboring a fugitive. What's the worst that could happen if you gave yourself up? They'll charge you with a misdemeanor. Big deal."

"It's not the vandalism charge I'm afraid of," Bob hissed.

"Then what?"

Bob practically squirmed.

"Come on, Bob, what is it you're *really* hiding from?" Tricia demanded.

"It's none of your business," he said tersely, huddling deeper into his jacket.

Tricia nodded. "Okay, then let's talk about something else. You are aware that Betsy Dittmeyer was murdered at the Cookery on Saturday, right?"

"It's all everyone is talking about—not that I've spoken to anyone lately," he hedged.

"Were you also aware that Betsy was skimming Chamber funds?"

Bob moved into the light, his eyes wide-open in alarm. "I hope you're kidding."

Tricia shook her head.

"That thieving cow," Bob growled, his gloved fists clenching. "If I had known, I'd have fired her on the spot. And called the cops on her in a heartbeat." But that would have had to have been before they were after him for goodness knows what former transgression.

"Angelica is going to ask for an audit of the books from an independent source."

"As she should. In fact, I should have done it on a more regular basis."

"How often were the books checked in the past?"

Bob shrugged. "Every two or three years. I know, I know—it should have been every year. And now I feel like a fool for trusting Betsy. But she seemed so competent at everything she did." He was quiet for a moment. "You don't suppose I could get in trouble over that as well, do you?"

"Maybe, but you've got more problems than just that. Did you know Betsy kept a dossier on all the Chamber members?"

"Oh?" he said, but the inflection in his voice was all wrong. Bob really was a terrible actor, and Tricia could tell by his expression that he knew all about the file.

"Yes. It's filled with the dirt on every Chamber member. I would almost say the information was worthy of blackmail."

"You don't say," he said, his voice rising unnaturally.

"I do. There was one notable exception. *Your* name was missing from the roster."

"It was?" he asked, feigning surprise.

"Don't play dumb with me, Bob. You instigated the compiling of that list."

"I did not," he protested.

"Then you *do* know about it."

Bob pursed his lips and frowned. "It was Betsy's idea, and yes, she did show it to me. I told her to delete it. The people on that list were my friends, and what she did was despicable."

"And it didn't give you a clue about her character?"

"She had impeccable references, she showed up for work every day on time, she completed every task I gave her without a lot of instruction, and she didn't spend half her day gossiping with anybody who'd listen." That last remark was referring to Frannie.

"Did you ever actually check her references?" Tricia pressed.

Bob shrank farther back into the shadows. "I think so. I don't really remember."

Probably just pure laziness on his part. And how odd was it that Bob considered the people on Betsy's blackmail list to be his friends? Tricia doubted many of the Chamber members thought of Bob as any more than an acquaintance, and those who rented storefronts from him knew they'd be hounded if they didn't pay up on time, which hardly contributed to a feeling of goodwill. Chauncey Porter, owner of the Armchair Tourist, immediately came to mind. Bob had pestered him on a daily basis when he'd gotten behind on his rent. That gave Tricia an idea.

"Bob, have you been sleeping at the back of the Armchair Tourist?"

Bob looked up sharply, his face draining of color. "Of course not."

Aha! A blatant lie. Tricia knew Chauncey had a cot in the back of his store. He'd lived there for a while during a lull when business was bad and he'd had to give up his apartment. She had no doubt Chauncey would have let Bob hide out there for a reduction in rent—and the longer the better.

"What does Betsy's list have to do with Chauncey Porter?" Bob demanded.

"Nothing. I'm just putting pieces of the puzzle together. And what do you think Chief Baker is going to think when he sees that list?"

"What do you mean?"

"After Betsy's death, the chief confiscated the Chamber's computer as evidence."

Bob looked positively horrified.

"As I said," Tricia continued, "one might think Betsy—or you—collected that information as blackmail material."

Bob's eyes widened with indignation. "I never asked her to draw up that list. I told her to delete it, and she assured me she had."

"But you never bothered to check," Tricia stated.

Bob's expression darkened. "No. I trusted her to follow my orders—that's what she was paid for."

"It seems like Betsy commanded far too much of your trust."

"Well, what do you expect me to do about it now? I'm not the Chamber president and Betsy is dead."

"I'm sorry, Bob, but you picked the wrong time to drop out of sight. It looks very suspicious."

"I had no reason to kill Betsy," he declared, his voice rising once again.

"And you apparently have no alibi, either," Tricia bluffed.

Bob looked away. "Betsy Dittmeyer worked for the Chamber for over two years. I didn't know her well and I hadn't spoken to her in at least a month before she died. There's no way Chief Baker can tie me to her death—and neither can you."

"You're right. *Perhaps* you're right, but there's more."

"More?" Bob asked, confused.

"Did you know Kelly Realty now has competition here in Stoneham?"

"What do you mean?" he demanded. The threat to his wallet made his eyes bulge most unattractively.

"Nigela Ricita Associates has opened a real estate office here in Stoneham."

"That's impossible," he nearly shouted.

"It's entirely possible. Right now they're operating out of

a bungalow behind the Brookview Inn, but as soon as they can scare up some office space—and probably from one of your disgruntled clients—they intend to be the number one real estate agency in the area." Okay, Karen hadn't exactly said that, but Tricia considered it a true statement, since that's how Nigela Ricita Associates had operated so far. In the short time they'd been investing in the area, they'd had no business failures.

Bob let out a shaky breath and for a moment Tricia thought he might cry. "It's all falling apart. My entire life is falling apart," he practically whimpered.

"Bob, what event from your past is so heinous that you would ignore your business and live on the street? From what I've seen, it's what you love most in life."

"For the past twelve years, I've worked damn hard to turn this village around. I brought in the booksellers. I got the Board of Selectmen to improve the infrastructure. I strived to make it a tourist mecca, with people coming from all over the eastern seaboard, and now your sister has ruined it."

"Ruined Stoneham?" Tricia echoed in disbelief.

"No, my life. She *stole* the Chamber presidency from me."

"Bob, the members took it away from you—not Angelica," Tricia said reasonably, but she could tell he wasn't listening. "And you still haven't answered my question. What are you going to do about NRA Realty?"

Bob huddled deeper into his coat. "I've got to go." He turned and inched his bulk down the space between the buildings, turned left at the alley, and then disappeared.

Tricia didn't bother to follow him and instead turned and headed back to her store. Bob was a fool, but then she'd always known that. No way had he been involved in Betsy's death, but evidently he had plenty of other things to hide, and the fact that he'd been dodging Chief Baker for the better part of a week was suspicious indeed. But for some reason Tricia didn't feel she should talk to Baker about him. At least, not yet. There was still so much about the various goings-on in Stoneham that she didn't know. She'd just have to keep on asking questions.

After all, it seemed to be what she did best.

NINETEEN

As usual, Tricia crossed the street to join Angelica at Booked for Lunch just after the café officially closed for the day. But when she opened the door she didn't see her sister. Was she destined to eat another lonely lunch from a foam box? "Ange?"

"In the kitchen. Be right there."

Relieved, Tricia slipped out of her coat and set it on one of the booth seats, then walked around the counter to find her tuna plate in the little fridge under the counter. She'd just sat down when Angelica burst out of the kitchen with a large salad plate. "What a day. I feel like I've been on the go since the minute I got up." She set the plate down on the counter and turned for the coffee urn, pouring a couple of cups before she plunked down on the stool next to Tricia.

"And have you been on the go since dawn?"

"Yes. The new Chamber secretary started today. I talked it over with her and let her know that she may not be my starting quarterback when we move into the new office space, that I would probably need someone full-time to take that position. Thank goodness she seemed fine with it." Angelica stabbed a piece of lettuce, dipping it into the small container of dressing that sat on the side of her plate.

"Have you had a chance to talk to Chief Baker yet?"

Angelica winced. "No. He never got back to me after I left a message last night, and I'm not going to call him again, either. What's the big deal, anyway? You've already spoken to him."

"I have. But I don't want him to think you've been keeping information from him that could prove vital to his investigation."

"I don't see how he could think that. He didn't return my call and he has the same computer files I've got. It's up to him to ferret out what's important and what isn't."

"Yes, but you have the perspective to judge that. He doesn't."

"I suppose. Look, if you're so interested, why don't you go over all the files with him?"

"I've done my part: I brought it to his attention. But we agreed that as Chamber president the bulk of it should come from you."

"Well, I really don't want to be involved."

"But you already *are*."

Angelica sighed. "You like all this intrigue. I don't. If you want to compare notes with the man, go ahead and do it." Angelica dipped a piece of lettuce into her salad dressing. "While we're on the subject, have you heard anything new on Betsy's murder?"

"Not exactly. Although I wonder if I've been thinking about her death in the wrong way."

"What do you mean?"

"Well, there are all kinds of reasons why people would want her out of the way. But the suspects keep petering out. I really don't think her husband had anything to do with it. Her sister might have been angry that she'd been cut out of Betsy's will, but I can't picture her killing Betsy over it. They didn't seem close and she apparently has no idea of the estate's worth, so why would it come as a shock that she'd been disinherited? And since Betsy wasn't in ill health, there was no reason to suspect she'd die of natural—or unnatural—causes anytime soon."

"That's true," Angelica grudgingly agreed.

"And even if Bob Kelly is a bit of a rat, I can't see him killing her. By the way, I spoke with him this morning."

"Oh?" Angelica asked warily.

"I told him Betsy had been skimming Chamber funds and he seemed genuinely angry. But that's hardly a motive for murder, since he's no longer the Chamber president."

Angelica was quiet for a long moment. "Just where did you find Bob? Not that I have any real interest."

Oh, yeah?

"He was skulking between the Have a Heart bookstore and the Patisserie. He looked half frozen. He was angry to hear that Betsy was skimming funds, but even more angry with you."

"With me?" Angelica repeated, puzzled.

"He says you've ruined his life."

"Well, somebody had to do it," Angelica said in jest, and cut a cherry tomato in half.

"I asked him about the Chamber member list Betsy kept.

He knew about it, but he swears Betsy collected the information and that he told her to delete it."

"Which makes me think it was something Betsy wanted for her own amusement. Granted, she collected a lot of nasty gossip, but I don't remember seeing anything salacious enough to warrant someone paying to have it suppressed."

"You're right," Tricia admitted and poked at her own salad.

"By the way, just what were you doing gallivanting around the village when you should have been minding the business at your store?" Angelica asked.

"I got a call from Billie Burke. She said she couldn't find you."

Angelica looked up sharply. "Why would she need to?"

"Because Dumpster divers, looking for treasure, had descended on the rental house."

"So what? We'd already been through everything. There was nothing left of value."

"*Au contraire.* One of them found a solitaire diamond ring."

"Don't tease me, Trish," Angelica said tartly.

"I'm not. When I found them there, I immediately called Grant, who came right down from the police station and told them they had to leave. I looked in their bags of loot and saw the ring. It's got to be worth at least a grand. Do you think it could have been Betsy's engagement ring?"

"Maybe. She never wore any rings during the time I'd known her. Do you still have it?"

Tricia shook her head. "Antonio showed up with his contractor just then and I gave it to him." She left out the part about Baker's engagement joke. She wasn't in the mood to be teased by Angelica.

"What's got me puzzled is how those guys knew to come to the rental house and sift through the trash. I didn't tell anyone. Antonio swears that he and Ginny didn't talk about it. That only leaves——"

"Me?" Angelica asked, sounding defensive.

"It's well-known you've got the village's biggest gossip in your employ. Did you mention it to Frannie?"

"No," Angelica answered automatically, but then frowned. "At least, not directly. I did speak to Antonio this morning and the subject did come up."

"Were you in the Cookery at the time?"

Angelica nodded grimly. "Oh, dear. I'm sorry, Trish. I should know better than to talk about sensitive subjects when Frannie's around."

"It's over and done with. I'm just worried the word will reach Joelle. Frannie's the one who called her to say Betsy had been killed."

"Really? I had no idea. But Joelle hasn't got a leg to stand on. Antonio has already spoken with a lawyer. The trash in that house belonged to NRA, no ifs, ands, or buts. Antonio is using the cash we found to pay for the repairs to the building. Apparently they haven't figured out what kind of a structure they want to put in place of the house."

"I thought they had it all figured out."

"According to Antonio, they haven't even spoken to their architect. I guess they're not in a terrible hurry to knock it down, which is good for the Chamber—at least in the short run."

"Antonio invited me to hang around while he talked to the contractor. Are you interested in what they decided?"

Angelica's eyes lit up. "Definitely."

Tricia spent the next twenty minutes updating Angelica on plans for the new office space, including upgrades to the electrical and the kitchen. "They found hardwood floors under that dirty rug in the living room. They're going to sand and refinish them."

"What about the timeline?" Angelica asked, getting up and pouring another coffee for both of them.

"As it's winter, Jim Stark isn't exactly rolling in work. They're going to start tomorrow."

"That soon? Oh, good. I'm so eager to get all the Chamber's baggage out of my storeroom. I feel like I should fumigate the place to eliminate the stench of death, too."

"Does it really smell?"

"Only in my mind," Angelica admitted. "I'll be glad to put all of this behind me and get back to work for the Chamber. I have so many wonderful ideas that will take the organization to a whole new level and I feel like I can't get started until we're in the new office."

"It's only a matter of days now," Tricia reminded her.

"I'm going to need some volunteers to champion certain new committees. Can I count on you?"

Tricia shrugged. "I guess so. I've got nothing else to do in the evenings."

"Good. I'll keep you posted."

Tricia looked at her half-eaten lunch and then her watch. "It's time for me to get back to work."

"You mean sleuthing?" Angelica teased.

"Hardly. Then again, with so few customers, there's not much work to be done, either."

"Are you sure you really need two employees—especially during the slowest time of the retail year?"

"Probably not. But I couldn't bear to lose either of them. And as long as I'm in the black, I'm not going to let either of them go."

"Good for you," Angelica said. "It's too bad other businesses don't feel the same. People need jobs. Jobs feed the economy. Everyone benefits."

"Speaking of my employees, I'd better get back to my shop." Tricia got up from her stool and grabbed her coat. "Thanks for lunch. I'll talk to you later."

Pixie and Mr. Everett were standing at the cash desk conversing when Tricia got back to Haven't Got a Clue. "Looks like a welcoming committee," she commented and took off her coat.

"Sort of," Pixie admitted. "Mr. E and I thought we might want to see if we can simplify the inventory system. Since it's been more quiet than the morgue around here, we wondered if it was okay to play with it for the rest of the day. What do you think?"

"Of course. Miss Marple and I can hold down the fort while you work up in the storeroom."

"Great. Come on, Mr. E, we could get a lot done before the end of the day."

"Would you mind hanging up my coat?" Tricia asked.

"Sure thing," Pixie said, taking it from her, and then she and Mr. Everett headed for the back of the store, where Pixie hung up the coat, and then she and Mr. Everett headed up the stairs to the storeroom above.

With nothing better to do, Tricia bent down to retrieve Betsy's heavy Bible from under the cash desk, where she'd stashed it hours before. It made a distinct *thump* as it hit the top of the glass display case. Tricia turned the leather-clad cover so that the title page was visible. It was a King James Version that had seen a lot of hard use over the years. Tricia flipped through the pages to the center of the book. Based on the family tree, it was well over a hundred years old. For its age, it wasn't in such terrible condition, but it wouldn't be worth much. Too bad Betsy's relatives weren't famous—or infamous—which would have considerably increased its value.

Someone dressed in a camouflage jacket passed by the big display window, walking at a fast clip. It could only be Bob. For someone who claimed he didn't want to be caught, what was he doing walking down Stoneham's main drag in broad daylight? Or, after their conversation earlier that day, had he changed his mind and now wanted to be caught?

Tricia looked back down at the Bible. Pack rat that she was, Betsy had stuffed an inordinate amount of papers, news clippings, and recipes into the book. As she flipped more of the pages, Tricia set the loose pieces of paper aside. The Bible did have nice illustrations, but the binding was in poor condition. She could repair it, but it would take quite a bit of effort and she felt no particular urge to do so, especially since Betsy had probably broken quite a few of the commandments listed within it. That, of course, wasn't the Bible's fault.

The camo-clad figure passed by, going in the opposite direction, walking at a fast clip.

Tricia assembled the papers into a neat pile, set them on the top page, and closed the book, putting it out of harm's way on the shelf below the sales counter. She walked over to the door, taking a look outside. Sure enough, Bob walked by once again, and she stuck her head out to stop him. "What do you think you're doing?"

"Are you alone?" he asked, furtively glancing around.

"Yes. You look frozen stiff. For heaven's sake come inside and have a cup of coffee and warm up."

Bob wrapped his arms around himself, rubbing vigorously. "Thanks, Tricia. I was hoping you'd say that."

Tricia ushered Bob in and closed the door behind him. He pulled off his gloves, rubbing his hands together for warmth, and stamped his feet on the bristle welcome mat. Tricia wrinkled her nose as she passed him. How long had it been since he'd had a shower?

By the time she'd poured a cup of coffee, Bob joined her at the beverage station. She set the cup down before him and pushed the tray with creamer and sugar forward. Bob doctored his coffee and Tricia set a plate of cookies in front of him.

"When was the last time you had a decent meal?" she asked.

"About a week ago. Nikki Brimfield tosses out a lot of good stuff every night, but after a while even cookies and cake get boring. I've been dreaming about a burger and fries."

"You can't go on like this, Bob. You need to face up to whatever it is you're running from."

"I will, I will. I've done a lot of thinking since we talked earlier. I just need to figure out what I'm going to say to Chief Baker."

"Come on, Bob, level with me. What did you do in your past life that is so god-awful that you'd risk your health, *and* your business, to hide?"

Bob looked away and took a deep gulp of coffee, as though it might give him the strength to keep talking. "It was a stupid high school prank. When you're a kid, you do stupid things. You don't think about the consequences or realize that one idiotic move could follow you the rest of your life. I didn't have a father figure to warn me about such things. I thought I knew better than anybody else. I thought I knew it all."

It seemed to Tricia that he hadn't changed much in that regard. "If you don't tell me, I'll go to Stella Craft." Stella was one of Stoneham High School's retired English teachers who, until her retirement some ten or twelve years before, at one time or another seemed to have taught just about every student who walked through that school's hallowed doors. "She's got a mind like a steel trap. And if she's reminded of whatever it was you've done—after years of not thinking about it—it's sure to get out."

Bob seemed to squirm. "Okay, but please don't tell anyone else about it. You have to swear."

Tricia sighed, bored. But she dutifully raised her hand and said, "I swear."

Bob seemed to wrestle with his conscience. He looked like he was going to speak, then frowned, fidgeted a bit, then opened his mouth to speak again—and didn't. The man was positively maddening.

"Come on, Bob, I haven't got all day," Tricia chided.

"Oh, all right. I had a nickname back in high school."

"What's so shameful about a nickname?" she asked.

"The shame is how I acquired it. They called me"—his face grew beet red—"the mooner."

Tricia blinked, and tried to stifle a smile. "The mooner?"

"Yeah. I was in my senior year and a bunch of buddies and I would ride around Stoneham and Milford in George Stewart's Chevy Caprice and moon people."

Tricia struggled to keep a straight face. "And I take it you got caught?"

"Yeah, *I* got caught," he emphasized. "We all did it, but I was the only one who was actually apprehended with my pants down around my ankles. I was arrested for lewd behavior. Got hauled up in front of a judge and everything. My mother wanted to disown me. I've never been so ashamed in all my life."

"What was your sentence?"

"A hundred hours of community service."

"And did you complete your punishment?" Tricia asked.

"No. After graduation, I skipped town. I didn't come back for almost twenty years. By then everybody seemed to have forgotten about it. But I knew if I was ever arrested that the truth would come out and I might get tossed in jail—and have my reputation ruined."

"How much of your sentence did you complete?"

"About ten hours. I was supposed to pick up trash, dig holes, and other kinds of manual labor. It was hard work. *Really* hard work."

"That's why they call it punishment," Tricia said, but Bob had no comment. "Where have you been hiding for the past week?"

He shook his head. "Oh, no, I'm not telling you so that you can get me and another person in trouble."

"I've already promised I wouldn't talk about your problem to anyone. I assume you've been hiding at one of your properties."

"Yeah, and after a week my welcome has worn pretty thin."

"Look, Bob, why don't you just turn yourself in? You might have to complete your community service, but I doubt they're going to toss you in jail for this or for vandalizing Stan Berry's house."

"Fat lot you know," he said, sounding forlorn.

"Have you consulted a lawyer?"

He shook his head. "No."

"Then you have no clue what is liable to happen to you."

"With my string of bad luck, they'll likely toss me straight in jail and throw away the key."

"I think you're overreacting. But would doing a few days' jail time be preferable to losing your business? I'll bet your clients are getting pretty annoyed at not being able to reach you. You're playing right into NRA Realty's hands. If you don't show your clients some tender loving care, NRA will swoop down and sign them up."

Bob's entire body seemed to sag. "I guess you're right." He looked up, turning his sad green eyes on her. "Would you broker a deal for me with Chief Baker?"

Tricia always was a sucker for green eyes. "I'd be happy to."

"Thank you. And please don't tell Angelica about this. I've had about all the gloating from her I can stand."

"I promise not to tell Angelica," Tricia said, which was too bad, because about now Angelica would probably *love* to have a good laugh at Bob's expense. "Have you got your cell phone?"

Bob nodded. "Yeah, but I left the charger at home. The battery's dead."

"Then how can I contact you?"

"How about I contact you tomorrow morning? Nine o'clock at the back of your store?"

"What's wrong with me calling the chief right now?"

"I have a couple of things to take care of before I'll be ready to face a jail cell, although I guess I could come back in an hour or so."

"All right. I'll see what I can do," Tricia promised. "Will you be all right out there on the mean streets of Stoneham?" Bob didn't pick up on her sarcasm. Instead he polished off the last of his coffee and stuffed a few of the cookies into his jacket pocket. "I'll be back in an hour. Thanks for the coffee."

"You're welcome."

Bob turned for the exit. "Could you take a look—to make sure there aren't any cops out on the street?"

"Sure," Tricia said and led the way to the door. She stuck her head outside and looked from right to left. Not a soul in sight. "All clear."

Bob pulled his knit cap down low over his brow. "Thanks again," he said and slipped out the door, quickly heading south down the sidewalk. Tricia shut the door and shook her head. She glanced over to the shelf above the register where Miss Marple sat with all four of her legs tucked under her. "What do you make of that?"

Miss Marple gave a bored "*Yow*," and shut her eyes.

"I agree," Tricia said. She moved to stand in front of the sales desk, and picked up the art deco phone, dialing Chief Baker's personal number. It rang twice before he picked up.

"Grant, it's Tricia."

"To what do I owe the pleasure? Have you reconsidered my Friday-night dinner invitation thanks to me chasing away your Dumpster divers?" he asked eagerly.

"Sorry, no. I told you, I already have plans. But I do have something else to offer you."

"And what's that?"

"Bob Kelly."

"Kelly? Have you been harboring him?" Baker asked sternly.

"Of course not. But I have seen him around the village and I did manage to speak with him. He's tired of hiding. He wants to turn himself in. But he's also worried about a transgression from his past."

"I know all about the mooning," Baker said, without humor, "and that he never completed his community service."

"Is he liable to get jail time for a youthful indiscretion?" Tricia asked.

"That'll be up to a judge. Kelly has done a lot for this town over the years. I can't see him going to jail at this point—over that or the new charges that are likely to be filed against him, but he might have his original sentence doubled, tripled, or even quadrupled."

"I think he's already come to that same conclusion," Tricia said.

"When will you talk to him next?"

"He said he'd return to my store in an hour. What's the best way to handle this? Should I call you to pick him up or take him directly to the police station?"

"I'd prefer not to lose him again. I'll set up a stakeout to catch him."

"Do you really need to do that? I mean, the man is already deeply ashamed of what happened in the past. Couldn't you just pick him up here?"

"Well, okay," Baker grudgingly replied. "I'll show up in an hour. And thanks for taking this on."

"I hate to think of Bob standing out in the cold for yet another day, and goodness knows where he's been going at night to stay warm."

"He's been extremely foolish, that's for sure."

There was no arguing that. "Okay. I'll see you soon. And thank you—for Bob . . . and from me."

"Right." The connection was broken and Tricia hung up the receiver. If Bob had been a woman, Tricia would have called him a diva. Why couldn't he have just faced up to his past like a man instead of hiding in the shadows for the past week?

In an hour's time it would no longer be her concern.

One down, one to go.

How much longer would it take to wrap up Betsy Dittmeyer's murder?

TWENTY

Since Haven't Got a Clue hadn't had a customer in hours, Tricia decided to shut down the beverage station for the day. She dumped the dregs, emptied the grounds from the basket, gathered the sugar and nondairy creamers, putting them away before she took out the disinfectant spray and cleaned the counter. With that done, she returned to the cash desk, where Betsy's big Bible still sat.

A figure passed the window and stopped in front of the door. Tricia recognized the woman in the red ski jacket and quickly stuffed the Bible under the display counter once more. The door opened, the bell over it jingled cheerfully, but the look on Joelle Morrison's face was dour. "Where's Angelica?" she demanded.

"Hello, Joelle. What brings you here so late on this chilly afternoon?"

"Where's Angelica?" she asked again, more firmly. This was not the perfectly coiffed, well-dressed wedding planner Tricia had come to know. Instead, Joelle looked a bit crazed, with wind-chapped cheeks that were nearly the same shade as her jacket, and with no hat her hair looked as though it might have gone through a Mixmaster.

"I have no idea. She might be at the Cookery—"

"I've already been there."

"—or at Booked for Lunch."

"I've been there, too."

"I don't know where else she'd be at this time of day. Can I help you with something?" Tricia asked, not sure she really wanted to spend time with Joelle in her present mood.

"I heard the house across the street from the bank has been sold, along with a lot of Betsy's things that were stored there. Betsy's treasures belong to her heirs, *not* Angelica."

"From what I understand, Betsy had plenty of time to clear out her stuff before the house was sold. She signed off on several certified letters that told her to clear out her stuff or lose it. She chose to lose it. Everything was documented, and the house was sold with the contents intact. Whatever was stored in that house legally belongs to Nigela Ricita Associates—not Angelica."

Joelle's eyes blazed. "I heard she'd taken charge of clearing out the house."

"Who told you that?"

"Frannie Armstrong."

Of course.

"Angelica has rented the house for the Chamber of Commerce. She and others"—Tricia had no intention of mentioning her own role in the purge—"worked to clear it. The contents have been removed. The Dumpsters were taken away a couple of hours ago."

"What did Angelica find?" Joelle demanded, a harder edge entering her voice.

"Trash, a lot of newspapers, and a few old books—not vintage, and not worth much of anything."

"Did you find our family Bible?"

"Bible?" Tricia hedged. "What does it look like?"

"It's quite old and large. The cover is brown leather with a big brass hasp. It belonged to my great-great-grandmother."

"Is that what you were looking for at Betsy's house?"

"Yes. It has great sentimental value. It shouldn't be thrown away or sold to the highest bidder. It belongs to *me*!"

"But you said Betsy disinherited you."

Joelle's eyes blazed with fury. "It turns out Betsy never changed her will. She left everything to me. I have the only copy. There were no others."

"Are you sure?"

"Of course I'm sure," Joelle said, but didn't sound at all certain. "If you see Angelica, I'd appreciate you giving me a call—or have her call me." Joelle dug into her purse and came up with a business card for her wedding planning services. "Tell her to call me day or night."

"I'd be glad to," Tricia said and accepted the rather battered card.

Joelle abruptly turned and left Haven't Got a Clue by slamming the door, and without a good-bye or a backward glance. Tricia stepped over to the big display window, craning her neck to follow Joelle's progress as she made her way up Main Street until she turned right, probably to pick up her car at the municipal parking lot.

Once she was certain Joelle wouldn't be making a return visit to her store, Tricia pulled the bulky Bible out from under her cash desk to have another look at it. As Joelle had said, it was big and brown and bulky. Stashed between the pages of the book were more folded sheets of paper, recipes, and a number of death notices cut from newspapers. Tricia extricated all the loose papers before taking time to study them. Some of the recipes were so old that the paper they were printed on disintegrated despite her gentle handling. Next she sorted everything into three piles: useless, unsalvageable, and of possible interest. It was the latter she consulted first. Unfolding one of the pieces of white paper, she found a hand-drawn genealogy chart. Before she could look at it, though, the door opened once again and Bob Kelly darted inside, looking over his shoulder before shutting the door.

"He's not here yet?" he asked.

"You mean Chief Baker?"

Bob nodded.

"No. But he'll be here in a few minutes."

Bob bit his lip, and though he'd just come in from the cold she could see a bead of sweat forming at his left temple.

"Why don't you take your coat off and relax until the chief gets here."

"I'm not sure I can go through with this," Bob said and began to pace in front of the cash desk.

"Listen, Bob, you can't keep this up. Now, you asked me to arrange this meeting—though I'm still not sure why you couldn't have just walked over to the police station and turned yourself in—so you should at least have the gumption to follow through with your plan."

"You don't know what it's like to feel hunted. Right now I haven't got a friend in the world."

"And whose fault is that?" Tricia asked.

Bob looked close to tears. "I've been on the run for so long, I've forgotten how it feels to live like a real human being."

Who did he think he was? Harrison Ford in *The Fugitive*? The charges against him were really quite petty.

"Bob, you're only making things worse for yourself. Now please, sit down and relax."

"I guess you're right," he said and took a seat in the readers' nook.

No sooner had he sat down, when the door opened and Chief Baker entered the shop. "Tricia," he said, tipping his hat, saw Bob sitting in the nook, and headed straight for him. "Mr. Kelly."

Bob stood. "You've got me, Chief. I'll come along quietly," he said, his voice filled with drama, and held out his hands, palms down, ready to be handcuffed.

"I'm not going to cuff you," Baker said. "If you'll come along quietly, I'll take you to the station, fingerprint you, and then release you on your own recognizance."

"You mean, I'm not going to the big house?" Bob almost sounded disappointed.

"I highly doubt it. But you will have to answer to the charges against you. I suggest you consult an attorney."

"I can go home and sleep in my own bed tonight?" Bob asked.

"You don't have to, but you're not staying in my jail overnight."

"Oh." Bob had never looked more downhearted.

"However, I do want to talk to you about Betsy Dittmeyer, but that should only take an extra ten or twenty minutes. With a little luck, you'll be home in time for your dinner."

"Okay," Bob said and shuffled over to the door. "Let's get this over with."

Baker shot Tricia a parting glance. "Thanks for helping out with this."

"Anytime," she said with a grin.

No sooner had the door closed behind them when Tricia heard footfalls on the stairs. At the back of the shop, the door marked PRIVATE opened and Pixie and Mr. Everett stepped into the store. Pixie held a sheaf of papers in her hand.

"Hey, Tricia, you'd better have a look at this updated inventory list." She walked up to the counter and handed the small stack of pages to Tricia, who flipped through the alphabetized list.

"This looks great, but are you sure this is the entire list?" she asked, puzzled.

"Yep. And it includes the two boxes of stock I unpacked earlier this week, too. When was the last time you checked the storeroom for inventory?" Pixie asked.

Tricia heaved a guilty sigh. "Christmas?" she guessed.

"Despite it being so dead around here, we've actually sold a lot of books since then. Did you call that number for the estate liquidator that I gave you earlier?"

"Shoot, with everything that's been going on, I forgot all about it."

"Well, unless you want to start selling coffee instead of books, we're in desperate need of more stock," Pixie said.

"You're right. I'll call the number first thing tomorrow morning."

"Why wait? Do it now," Pixie pushed.

"You're right, of course." Tricia bent down and found the Post-it note, but instead of calling, she turned back to her employees. "You're right about it being dead here today. I think I'm going to close shop early today. You guys may as well head on home."

"That's very generous of you, Ms. Miles," Mr. Everett said.

"Ditto that," Pixie said. She didn't have to be asked twice to leave early. She did an about-face, retrieved both her own and Mr. Everett's coats, and came back to the front of the shop.

"By the way, I finally figured out where I know the dead lady's sister from," Pixie said as she shrugged into the sleeves of her coat.

"Oh?" Tricia asked.

"Yeah. She used to be in the same kickboxing class as me over at the fitness center up on the highway."

"Used to?" Tricia asked, the hairs on the back of her neck bristling.

"I haven't seen her there in a couple of weeks," Pixie said and tucked her hair into her beret.

"Did you ever speak to her during the class?"

Pixie shook her head. "There's like twenty broads there. Who has the time?"

"Do the women at your class go there for self-defense or for exercise?"

"A little of both. When you do it right, you work up a hell of a sweat. It's a great way to keep fit. Burns a lot of calories." She pulled on her gloves.

Tricia felt her mouth go dry. Angelica's door had been kicked in. The door to Betsy's kitchen had been kicked in, too.

"Are you sure we can't do anything else before we leave?" Mr. Everett asked. "Vacuum, perhaps."

"The rug hardly needs it, as it's essentially only been the three of us walking on it," Tricia answered offhandedly.

"That's true. Well, off we go. See you tomorrow, Tricia," Pixie said.

Mr. Everett pulled on his leather gloves. "Good evening, Ms. Miles."

"Good night," Tricia called, and shut the door, locking and bolting it. She turned the OPEN sign to CLOSED and pulled the blinds before she went back to the sales desk, where she lifted the receiver on the old phone and dialed the number Pixie had written down.

She bit her lip with indecision. Had Baker finished dealing with Bob yet? Maybe she'd give him another ten minutes and then call to tell him what Pixie had just shared about Joelle. Was she being paranoid to hope he'd put out an all-points bulletin on the woman?

Yes, in fact, it was just plain silly. Instead, she consulted the note Pixie had taken for checking on the collection of used books, called, and made an appointment to see them the following morning. As she hung up the phone she remembered that she and Angelica had had an appointment to look at some books six days before, but Betsy's murder had taken precedence. Well, nothing like that could possibly happen again.

Now that she knew Joelle wanted to get her hands on Betsy's Bible, Tricia hefted the book back onto the sales counter and opened it to the center, thumbing past the illustrations, which included Moses parting the Red Sea, John the Baptist, and Christ's agony on the cross. Depressing. She flipped a few more pages before coming back to the chart chronicling Betsy and Joelle's forebears. Sure enough, she could count back far enough to their great-great-grandmother, but the chart only had space enough for four generations.

Tricia set the handwritten chart of later generations down beside it and compared the two. Names, birth dates, and death dates didn't tell the story of the people who were now dust. What had they been like? Doing a little math, she found that the women died young, many the same year the last of their children had been born. Had they died in childbirth? How sad.

Tricia turned her attention back to the newer chart. Not only was there a line from John Morrison and Elizabeth Tanner flowing down to Betsy and Joelle, but another line attached John Morrison to Ruth Dittmeyer and to their son . . . who was just a year older than Betsy.

The name?

Gerald.

TWENTY-ONE

An astonished Tricia stared at the names before her. She tried hard to remember Jerry's face, comparing it with her memories of Betsy. Yes, now that she knew the truth, they did share similar features. Worse, they'd had a daughter. A daughter with birth defects that had eventually caused her death. Had they known at the time of their marriage that they were half brother and sister? Betsy's parents must have given her the Bible. Along with all her other interests, could genealogy have been one of her hobbies? Had she made the chart showing her name and that of her ex-husband, or had she paid someone else to fill in the blanks?

It didn't matter. And even if Betsy had made that discovery, was it worth being killed for? That was a mighty big leap of logic. And yet . . . why was Joelle so adamant that she get her hands on the book? She and Betsy hadn't been all that close. What other reason could Joelle have had to account for her obsessive search for the Bible?

Then Tricia remembered what Jerry Dittmeyer had said when she met him just days before: he was engaged and his lady love was expecting a child.

Joelle and Jerry?

No, it just didn't seem possible. But why else would Joelle be so keen to obtain the Bible?

Joelle was eager to plan a wedding for Tricia. Had she been planning to do the same for herself?

Tricia studied every scrap of paper that had fluttered loose from the Bible and found nothing else of significance.

She gathered them all up and set them aside, all but the genealogy chart. What was she supposed to do with it? Why was it so important to Joelle? Did she know the significance of what was listed on it? Betsy didn't talk much about herself to strangers, and since she and Joelle weren't close, would she have shared with her sister what she knew about her father's love child?

If Joelle and Jerry were a couple, and if she was indeed pregnant with his child, was that baby as doomed as its older cousin/sibling? Joelle was in her forties, not an optimum time of life to become pregnant.

Had Betsy discovered that Jerry and Joelle had been doing more than just seeing each other? Did she not only feel a sense of betrayal, but fear for any child they might have? Could that be the reason she'd cut Joelle out of her will? Had Betsy ever told Jerry of their shared parentage? Could she have shared that news with one of them after finding out Joelle was pregnant? It was the perfect excuse for murder,

and explained why Joelle was desperate to hide—or destroy—
the evidence.

Someone knocked on the shop door, but Tricia ignored
it. Couldn't whoever it was read the sign that said the store
was closed?

She stared at the paper before her. Should she call Chief
Baker, telling him what she knew, or sit on it for a day or two
and hope there was another, more viable suspect in Betsy's
death?

The knock came again, harder this time.

"We're closed!" Tricia called.

Miss Marple stood up from her perch behind the register,
looking nervous. Tricia looked over her shoulder. "Don't
worry, Miss Marple, we aren't going to let that person in."

"Open up!" a male voice demanded. Even muffled, Tricia
was pretty sure she recognized it: Jerry Dittmeyer.

Uneasy, Tricia picked up the phone and dialed the Stoneham police station. The knocking grew louder still, and then
Tricia realized Jerry wasn't knocking, he was kicking the
door. Miss Marple jumped down from her perch and ran to
the readers' nook, hiding under one of the chairs.

"Please state the nature of your emergency," came Polly's
dispassionate voice.

"Send someone quick! Somebody's breaking down my
door."

"Remain calm," Polly said, sounding a little bored.
"What's your name and address?"

"You know darn well it's Tricia Miles, 221 Main Street
in Stoneham—" But before she could say anything more, the
door flew open, and Jerry barreled in, with Joelle right behind him.

The wind came roaring in with them, sending all the papers on top of the cash desk flying.

"There it is!" Joelle hollered, advancing on Tricia.

Tricia grabbed the book and shoved it under the cash desk. "I don't know what you're talking about."

"The hell you don't. Give it to me, it's mine," Joelle screamed.

"Give her what she wants," Jerry said, "and there won't be any more trouble."

"You've already kicked my door in. That's trouble enough, and I intend to press charges."

Joelle didn't seem concerned and stamped up to the back of the cash desk, cornering Tricia. For a moment, Tricia thought Joelle was going to hit her, but instead she grabbed the Bible, carelessly holding it over the cash desk, and proceeded to shake it, but no papers fell from its pages. Tricia had already removed them all. For something that was supposedly so precious to her, Joelle treated the old book roughly. She let it drop on the counter with a loud *thump,* and turned crazed eyes on Tricia. "Where is it?"

"Where is what?"

"You know what I'm talking about. Betsy told me her deepest secret was hidden in this Bible. She told me I'd never find it, and she was right. How could I know she stored her crap in that rental house? You must have taken what was inside it. Where is it? Give it to me!"

Tricia knew exactly where the missing genealogy chart was—on the floor right behind Joelle—but she had no intention of telling her.

"What is it you're looking for, Jo?" a nervous Jerry demanded, circling behind Joelle to stand next to the chart.

"I'm not sure. But Betsy threatened to use it against me."

"So what? She's dead. Let's go. I'm already in trouble for kicking in this door. I'm not going to jail for something so petty."

Joelle seemed ready to burst into tears.

It was then Jerry caught sight of the folded paper on the floor. Tricia shoved Joelle aside and made a grab for it, but Jerry intercepted her and sent her flying backward. Before she could right herself, in a flash, Jerry unfolded it, realized its significance, and pulled a lighter from his jacket pocket. He lit it.

"Jerry, no!" Joelle shrieked as Jerry backed up a couple of steps until he was free from the cash desk. He held the paper in the air, his expression triumphant.

"Don't be stupid, Jerry," Tricia cried. "You might burn that piece of paper, but it won't be hard to re-create it. It's based on public records."

"Shut up!"

"Jerry, stop it," Joelle cried. "You're being irrational. Let's get out of here before the cops show up."

"That's right, Jerry. I called them when you started kicking in my door."

So where on earth were they?

Joelle lunged forward, but Jerry backed up several steps. "Give me that paper," she demanded.

"No!" Jerry cried.

Joelle made a grab for it and Jerry fell backward over Sarah Jane's carriage, landing on his rear end. With a harsh *whoosh,* the dried faux leather that covered the old doll carriage burst into flames like a torch. Jerry sat there, stunned, staring at the flames, while Joelle made a mad grab for what was left of the paper—then screamed.

"I'm on fire!" Joelle cried, shaking her arm in the air, which only caused the flames to grow.

Instead of leaping forward to help her, Jerry backed up, looking terrified.

"Jerry—help me. Help me!" Joelle shrieked.

Sarah Jane was engulfed in flames, her head melting before Tricia's eyes. She righted herself and lunged forward, shoving a screaming Joelle onto the carpet. She pushed her, rolling her over and over across the floor for what seemed like endless moments until Joelle crashed into the back of one of the upholstered chairs in the nook. At last, the flames were extinguished.

"Jerry, help me get her out of here," Tricia called, but when she looked up she saw that Jerry had disappeared. The shop door was open, and the cold wind that whistled through it fed the fire. She could feel the blistering heat on her back.

Joelle's coat sleeve was gone, her flesh glistening from the burns. A frantic Tricia grabbed her under her arm, causing her to scream, and hauled her to her feet, dragging her toward the exit. The air was already foul with smoke and Tricia coughed as she pulled Joelle out of the burning store.

Once outside, Tricia saw several people standing on the sidewalk, gawking.

"What happened?" Mary Fairchild, Tricia's next-door neighbor asked, looking terrified.

"Jerry Dittmeyer set my store on fire. Call 911."

"Thank God you're safe," Mary cried as Tricia pushed a reeling Joelle at her.

Tricia gulped fresh air, which seemed to clear her head, and she was seized with a terrible thought. "Miss Marple!" she cried and turned back to the shop door.

"You can't go back in there," cried Michele Fowler, who had suddenly appeared on the scene, with her cell phone in one hand and grabbing Tricia's arm with the other.

"The hell I can't," Tricia said, twisted away, and plunged into the smoke-filled store once again.

If the lights were still on, Tricia couldn't tell; the thick black smoke was a smothering curtain. She dropped to her knees and, coughing all the way, began to crawl to the readers' nook, where she'd last seen her beloved cat. She pawed under each of the chairs, but couldn't find the cat. "Miss Marple, Miss Marple!" she cried, and was seized with a terrible coughing fit. Pulling the neck of her sweater up over her mouth and nose, Tricia began to crawl around the floor. Where could the cat be? Had she run to the washroom? Could she have escaped out the open door to safety?

"Miss Marple, please come out!" Tricia wailed, but she doubted the cat would even be able to hear her over the roar of the fire. There was nothing left of Sarah Jane's carriage, and flames licked the south wall and several shelves of vintage mysteries. Too stunned to even cry, Tricia knew she had to get out of the store before she was overcome by the smoke. But she'd never forgive herself if she saved herself and left Miss Marple to die.

She inched her way across the rug, losing track of where she was in all the smoke, and smashed her forehead into the side of the cash desk. Blood cascaded from the wound and into her eyes, but she had only one thought on her mind—to find her cat.

She crawled behind the cash desk, groping around the floor, and finally touched something fluffy—Miss Marple's tail. The cat didn't move. Was she already dead?

Tricia scooped up her cat and stuffed her limp body inside her sweater and began to crawl, backing out from behind the cash desk. Tears and blood mingled, robbing Tricia of her sight, and she used the wall to guide herself to the open door. She crawled through the aperture and strong arms grabbed her, hauling her across the frozen sidewalk and into the street. She'd lost her shoes.

Sirens wailed, echoing off the buildings, and the Stoneham Fire Department's rescue squad screeched to a halt along the curb. Seconds later, more strong arms hauled Tricia toward the vehicle, and she found herself sitting on its bumper, her feet freezing in the stiff breeze and an oxygen mask pressed against her face.

She coughed and coughed, thought about throwing up, and had to shake her head in order to think clearly. "My cat. My cat!"

"Calm down," the EMT advised. "We'll find your cat."

Tricia pulled the mask away from her face. "You don't understand, I've already got her." She lifted her sweater and pulled out the small limp cat. Another EMT took Miss Marple from Tricia, and jumped inside the ambulance.

"She's dead. I know she's dead," Tricia cried, and started to cough again, but the remaining EMT pressed the mask back to her face and proceeded to work on the cut on her forehead. Across the way, she saw another ambulance and more EMTs working on someone in the street. Was it Joelle?

"Tricia!"

Angelica clawed her way through the crowd of rubberneckers, to reach her sister. "Oh, my God. What happened?" she demanded, throwing her arms around Tricia. She was crying so hard her mascara ran down her cheeks in black rivulets.

"I'm okay," Tricia said, but speaking those words only made her cough harder.

"Keep the mask on your face," the EMT directed, towering over her with a no-nonsense expression.

"Miss Marple is dead," Tricia cried. "I tried to save her but it was too late."

"Please, ma'am, keep the mask on your face," the man said once more.

"You don't understand, my cat is dead!" Tricia cried, and even to herself she sounded like some hysterical harpy.

"No, she's not," said the EMT from inside the rescue vehicle. Tricia half turned and saw the man holding on to Miss Marple in a very undignified manner, but the cat was dazedly looking around, still limp, but definitely alive. He pressed the oxygen mask back on the cat's head and seconds later Miss Marple began to struggle in his embrace.

"It's a miracle!" Angelica cried.

"Let me hold her," Tricia cried and realized she was shivering violently—unsure if it was from the cold or shock.

"Only if you keep that mask on your face," said the man standing in front of Tricia.

The EMT inside the ambulance bent down and handed the cat to Tricia. Afraid Miss Marple might be frightened and try to escape, Tricia lifted her sweater and tucked the cat inside once more. A moment or so later, Miss Marple's head popped out the top of Tricia's sweater, and she took in her surroundings. "*Yow*," she said weakly.

"Don't worry, sweetie. Your aunt Angelica has some shrimp in the freezer. I will serve you one hell of a good kitty dinner tonight."

Chief Baker's cruiser rolled to a halt, with more sirens screaming in the background. Tricia and Miss Marple watched as the big fire engine pulled up in front of Haven't Got a Clue, with firefighters jumping out. Two of them smashed the big display, while another two hooked their hoses to the closest fire hydrant and went to work.

It was then Tricia realized she might lose everything she owned. She rubbed her chin on Miss Marple's head, realizing the most important thing in her life had been saved. Still, as she watched the firefighters work, she knew that life as she'd known it might never be the same.

TWENTY-TWO

Twinkling stars punctuated the dark sky and all was silent in this little section of southern New Hampshire. After all, it was well after midnight and even the Dog-Eared Page had closed down many hours before. Tricia stood on the sidewalk in front of Haven't Got a Clue, taking in the sooty residue that clung to its faux stone façade. The large display window that had shown off some of Tricia's stock was now covered with brand-new pieces of ugly plywood.

Gone. For all intents and purposes, Haven't Got a Clue was history. And though the fire had been contained to just the first floor, chances were most of her other possessions, like clothes, her computer, jewelry, and especially her personal collection of mysteries, were smoke damaged and essentially ruined.

Tricia huddled into Angelica's too-large cloth coat, which reached her knees, along with a pair of her too-big shoes. Joelle had suffered third-degree burns on her right arm and side, but she would survive. She'd been in shock when she'd given a statement to Chief Baker, corroborating Tricia's speculation. It was easy enough to find Jerry Dittmeyer— he'd gone straight home to pack a bag and flee, but in his haste he'd run a red light. He was being ticketed by the Milford police when the APB went out on him.

Tricia wondered at the stupidity of some people. There was still so much she didn't understand about what had happened, but she guessed she would learn in time.

She huddled deeper into the coat and thought back on the rest of the evening.

Angelica was as good as her word and had taken Tricia and Miss Marple in, giving the cat a large selection of goodies to eat, including pâté, shrimp, and small bits of a variety of cheeses. Miss Marple sampled each and looked up at Angelica with what looked like adoring eyes, saying a quiet *"Yow"* in gratitude.

Still, Tricia and Miss Marple needed to find temporary digs, since Sarge seemed to feel he'd morphed into a grey-hound and that Miss Marple resembled a rabbit just perfect for the chase. Both Christopher and Baker had offered their homes to Tricia. She thanked them, but gave each an emphatic no for an answer. Instead, tomorrow she'd call Karen Johnson—and maybe even Bob Kelly—to find an interim place to live. The coming days would be filled with much paperwork and many errands. She'd have to go to Nashua to buy new clothes, too. The entire situation seemed totally overwhelming, and she felt tears fill her eyes once more.

"What are you doing out at this time of night?"

Tricia turned to find Angelica standing right behind her, looking stern. "I needed to see it again, to think about my future."

"You can rebuild."

"I know," Tricia said softly, and sniffed. She really needed a tissue. As though reading her mind, Angelica dug into her jacket and pulled out a pocket pack, peeling out a clean tissue and handing it to Tricia.

"The most important thing is that you're safe, and so is Miss Marple," Angelica said kindly.

"Would you have gone back into a burning building to save Sarge?"

"It would be the stupidest thing in the world to risk life and limb for a dog but, yes, I probably would."

Tears leaked from Tricia's eyes and Angelica threw an arm around her shoulder and pulled her close. "You are made of strong stuff, little sister. You will come out of this a stronger person."

Tricia let out a shuddering breath. "I sure hope so."

"Do you want to know what I found out after they took you to the hospital to get checked out?" Angelica asked.

Tricia nodded.

"You and Chief Baker might not be an item anymore, but he still holds you very highly in his regard."

Tricia sniffed. "Do you think so?"

Angelica nodded. "I know so."

"So what did you learn and why didn't you tell me sooner?"

"There was no hurry, but if you want to hear it now—out here, standing in the cold—I'll tell you."

"Yes, please."

Angelica turned to stare at the sooty building before

them. "Betsy was furious when she'd learned her ex-husband and sister were lovers. Joelle had been thrilled to find out she was pregnant, and the first person she'd shared her news with was her older sister. But instead of joy, Betsy had threatened to cut Joelle out of her will and taunted her with hints of her shameful secret, letting her know that proof of it was hidden in that old family Bible you found.

"Of course, Jerry knew the secret. When their daughter was born with multiple birth defects, the couple had undergone genetic testing. They'd had to face it, and it had nearly destroyed their marriage."

"But why did they stay together?" Tricia asked, sickened by what she was hearing.

Angelic shrugged. "I guess at first they'd stayed together for the sake of their child, and afterward it was just easier to pretend they didn't share a parent."

"How could Jerry do such a despicable thing—knowing what had happened to his own daughter?"

"Denial is a very strong motivator. The guy was no George Clooney. Maybe he wasn't very lucky in love, either, and when Joelle was on the rebound from Stan she might have gone looking for solace in the arms of someone familiar."

Tricia shook her head, wishing the odor of burned wood wasn't so strong.

"Even knowing how his daughter had suffered, that rat Jerry became involved with Joelle and had panicked when she told him she was pregnant. He'd thought she was too old and begged her to get an abortion, but I guess Joelle figured it was probably her only chance to experience motherhood and was determined to go through with her pregnancy."

"Poor Joelle. What a foolish choice she made to get involved with her ex-brother-in-law."

"Grant told me that Jerry confessed he'd intercepted Betsy when she'd gone to empty her wastebasket behind the Cookery. She thought she had the upper hand and let him accompany her to the storeroom, where they'd argued. Incensed, he'd chased her around the storeroom and when he caught her, tried to choke the life out of her. He maintained that Betsy had pulled the bookshelf over on herself, and that she wouldn't have died but for that—something Grant didn't believe for a second."

Angelica shrugged. "It seems Betsy had planned to tell Joelle the whole sordid truth on the day of her death, but Jerry made certain she would never talk to Joelle again."

The stupid, stupid man.

"It all seems so pointless," Tricia said.

Angelica nodded.

Tricia's gaze returned to the ruins of her once-beautiful store and her throat tightened with despair. All her hard work, all her hopes, all her dreams, had literally gone up in smoke. Insurance would take care of the financial loss, but what about the emotional loss?

Tricia couldn't tear her gaze from the building's stone façade that she'd paid so much for and was now a wreck. "I'm so grateful for the invitation, but I can't stay with you, Ange."

"I know, but you know you'd be welcome to camp out at my place for as long as you need to."

"I know."

Angelica patted Tricia's back. "Tomorrow we'll make the rounds. We'll get you some new clothes, new shoes, and see if we can hunt down an apartment or a sublet. And, most important, we'll get you to a bookstore that sells mysteries. If I know you, you won't be happy until you're surrounded by books once again."

"And after that, what? How will I spend my days? What will happen to my employees?"

"Frannie has been itching to take a vacation, so Pixie and Mr. Everett can either come to work for me or work temp for the Chamber for the next couple of months."

"That's very kind of you. But what about *me*? What am I supposed to do?"

"You'll go online, visit thrift shops, and start to rebuild your inventory for the grand reopening of Haven't Got a Clue. And if you're willing to pitch in, there'll be plenty of work at the Chamber to keep you occupied. I've got big plans to expand our reach and it'll take an experienced businesswoman like you to help me set things up. What do you think?"

"It sounds okay," Tricia said, feeling a tiny bit less stressed.

"This time of uncertainty won't last forever," Angelica promised. "Maybe if we sweet-talk Antonio, he'll get us in touch with the people who helped Nigela Ricita Associates cut through the insurance red tape when they bought the site for the Dog-Eared Page. You might even be back in business in time for the first tourist bus that arrives in May."

Angelica was being incredibly optimistic, but her comforting words had given Tricia a much needed shot of hope.

"Come on back to my place. I've got some homemade cookies stashed away for an emergency—and I'd say this counts as one. I'll also make you a cup of my super-duper cocoa that'll have you sleeping like a baby. And when you wake up in the morning things won't look quite so horrible and you'll feel a whole lot better. I promise."

Tricia doubted that but allowed Angelica to guide her back toward the Cookery. Angelica went in first and Tricia paused before entering, turning to take in the apartment atop the Dog-Eared Page. Dressed in only pajama bottoms,

Christopher stood in front of his window. It seemed like every light in his apartment was lit so she could see him in perfect detail. He waved, and then blew her a kiss.

Tricia turned without acknowledging him, and entered the Cookery without a backward glance.

TWENTY-THREE

The Brookview Inn looked as homey and charming as a Thomas Kinkade painting that Valentine's Day evening, with the glow of soft lamplight spilling from the windows overlooking the wide and inviting porch. Tricia and Angelica trundled up the freshly shoveled walk, climbed the stairs to the inviting porch, and entered the welcoming lobby.

Angelica smiled. "This old inn has never looked better, don't you agree?" she asked as she unbuttoned her coat. Tricia couldn't remember a time when Angelica's disposition had been so sunny for so long, and for some reason, her good humor didn't even seem forced.

"Yes," she agreed and meant it.

The sisters surrendered their coats to the cloakroom attendant and headed toward the French doors that opened out of the inn's dining room. As they waited for the hostess, Tricia looked around the crowded room. Every table was occupied and Tricia realized that she recognized quite a few of the dinner patrons, nodding a greeting and receiving smiles, nods, and waves in return.

"Good grief! I just remembered! Weren't you supposed to pick up the cake for tonight?" Angelica asked.

"Don't worry. I did that this afternoon while I was out running errands. Nothing is going to spoil Mr. Everett's happy day. Did I tell you he'd already started helping me with my Internet orders? I might finally make that part of the business actually pay for itself—and it'll be the first part of the business that reopens. I just hope that when the time comes he still remembers how to operate the program."

"I'm sure it'll be just like riding a bike. Oh, look, there's Russ and Nikki," Angelica said and waved. They waved back, smiling.

"I spoke to Russ the other day. He was pretty upset about the baby," Angelica whispered.

"Not anymore," Tricia said.

"What do you mean?"

"I paid Nikki a visit this morning. I told her everything you said about how she could hire a manager and keep the Patisserie going until her little one goes to school, and then she could pick up where she left off. It's a win-win situation; she'll still have an income stream and can take care of her baby."

"She's a pretty smart woman. I wonder why she didn't figure it out for herself?"

" 'Forest for the trees' syndrome?" Tricia suggested. "I'm just glad that when I reopen, I'll still be able to buy thumbprint cookies for my customers—as well as the occasional coconut cupcake for myself."

The hostess soon returned, recognized them, and immediately led them to the best table in the house, where Grace, Mr. Everett, Pixie, Ginny, and Antonio were already seated. A silver ice bucket with a bottle protruding from it sat to one side.

"Hello, all," Angelica called brightly and took the empty seat next to Antonio. Tricia settled in beside Pixie. Everyone was decked out in their best party wear. Pixie had pulled out all the stops and wore a bright pink and black, low-cut silk dress, her hair piled high on her head and dripping with rhinestones. Ginny's little black cocktail dress—which seemed to strain at her belly—seemed positively boring in comparison. Antonio, handsome as ever, wore a tux, outshining the guest of honor's dark blue suit. As always, Grace was the epitome of understated sophistication, from her solitaire diamond stud earrings, to her gray silk, long-sleeved gown. Even Angelica looked extra-smart in a bright pink blouse under a black wool pantsuit, making Tricia feel downright dowdy in a white open-necked blouse and dark slacks, which half an hour earlier had still sported their sales tags.

"Sorry we're late," Tricia said, although they were only tardy by a minute or two.

"We were early," Mr. Everett said with a smile.

"My dear Tricia," Grace began, "we haven't had a chance to speak since—" She stumbled over what else to say, looking embarrassed.

"It's okay to mention the fire. It's a fact."

"How are you holding up?" Grace asked and Tricia could swear there were tears in her friend's eyes.

"Surprisingly well," Angelica answered for her. "Tricia will land on her feet in no time flat."

Angelica had e-mailed their parents to tell them about the fire and their father had immediately called Tricia's cell phone. "Your mother is too upset about almost losing you that she can't come to the phone," he'd lied.

"That's okay, Daddy. I understand," Tricia had said without rancor.

"Do you?" her father had asked. It almost seemed as if he'd known that she, too, was now in on the family secret. But, of course, they didn't speak of it.

"I honestly do," she told him.

Tricia idly wondered if she'd ever speak to her mother again. Since the fire, she wasn't sure if she cared anymore. She certainly wasn't going to lose another minute's sleep worrying about their lack of a loving relationship.

"What have we here?" Angelica said, inspecting the bottle in the ice bucket. Her eyes widened. "Dom Pérignon?"

"A birthday gift to Mr. Everett from my employer," Antonio explained.

"But Nigela Ricita doesn't even know Mr. Everett," Tricia protested. "Does she?"

"I've never made her acquaintance," Mr. Everett agreed.

"I told her I was invited to the celebration and she insisted on sending a bottle to the table," Antonio explained.

"I'm liking this broad more and more all the time," Pixie said, and pushed her glass closer to Antonio.

"Ah, but we are not yet ready to pour," he said smoothly. "There is still so much I do not know about the circumstances of the fire."

Tricia gave Angelica a pained look.

"I think we can discuss it at another time. We don't want to talk about unpleasant subjects on Mr. Everett's birthday and spoil his day," Angelica said.

Antonio looked justly admonished. "I do apologize, Tricia."

"No need," she said, but had been glad of Angelica's intervention. "How do you like working for the Chamber?" she asked Mr. Everett, who'd spent the afternoon at the Cookery, helping the new receptionist get ready for the big move.

"I thoroughly enjoyed it. I've set up next month's breakfast meeting for them here at the inn. I also made an appointment for the auditor to come in and look at the books. It's too bad the Chamber is closed on weekends, but I'm already looking forward to Monday."

"I hope you're not going to abandon me when Haven't Got a Clue reopens," Tricia said.

"Fear not, Ms. Miles, working for you is my first love."

"It is?" Grace asked with raised eyebrows.

"Er, my second love," Mr. Everett corrected, and everyone laughed.

"How did you make out at Booked for Lunch, Pixie?" Tricia asked.

"Piece a cake," she said with a wave of her hand. "It was fun. I've been a waitress on and off most of my adult life. When I wasn't . . . you know, doing other, more physical, work. And Tommy let me have two pieces of cake after my shift waiting on tables was over. I could get used to that."

Everyone at the table fought to stifle a laugh.

"And how about you, Tricia?" Grace asked. "How did you spend your day?"

"Running errands. Thanks to Antonio, tomorrow I move into one of the bungalows out back—at least until I can find a more permanent location. It'll be months before I can move back into my apartment."

"We are very happy to welcome you to our Brookview family for as long as you need us."

"And he gave her a very nice price break," Angelica added with a smile.

"I really appreciate that," Tricia said.

The couple at the next table set their napkins down and rose from their seats. Like vultures ready to pick bones clean, two busboys immediately descended and cleared the table. With blinding speed, a fresh clean tablecloth was in place, with clean water goblets, wineglasses, and sparkling place settings of cutlery.

"This way," said the hostess. Tricia looked up to see Christopher and Chief Baker making their way to the recently vacated table.

"Ah, Tricia. Fancy seeing you here," Christopher said, sounding delighted.

"What on earth are you two doing here?" Tricia demanded, just a tad annoyed.

"Since we couldn't have dinner *with* you, and since we came so close to losing you last night, we decided to call a truce and at least have dinner in the same *place* as you," Christopher said.

Angelica poked a finger against Tricia's ribs. "Isn't that darling?"

"No, it isn't," Pixie answered, giving the men a sour look as they took the recently vacated seats. "Sounds like stalking to me."

"On the contrary," Christopher said, "who wants to be alone on Valentine's Day?"

"Not me," Baker said, "although I have to admit sharing my evening with Christopher isn't my idea of a fun date."

"We decided to unite and are ready to help with anything you need. Moving, errands, cat sitting. You name it, we'll do it," Christopher said with what sounded like pride.

"That's very generous, but no thank you. Would you please excuse us so we can go back to celebrating Mr. Everett's birthday?"

"I had no idea. Happy birthday, Mr. Everett," Christopher said and Baker nodded in agreement. Mr. Everett waved a polite thank-you.

The men took their seats, and almost immediately a waitress showed up to take their drink orders.

Meanwhile the conversation resumed at the party table. "Has anyone heard how Joelle is doing?" Ginny asked, taking a sip from her water goblet.

"According to Frannie, she's in the burn ward at St. Joseph Hospital in Nashua—doing as well as can be expected," Angelica said.

"What about Ms. Dittmeyer's ex-husband?" Mr. Everett asked.

"He's sitting in the Hillsborough County lockup charged with murdering Betsy, and for arson—at least for setting the blaze at Tricia's store," Angelica answered. "But I wouldn't be surprised if he was charged with setting the fire at Betsy's house, too. It'll probably take time for them to tie him to that fire."

"That slimy bastard deserves to rot in jail, what with burning up Sarah Jane and Haven't Got a Clue," Pixie practically spat.

"Did you know the fireman rescued Joelle's family Bible?" Angelica said, and turned to face her sister.

Tricia shook her head. She hadn't been allowed back into the store to see what was salvageable and what needed to go straight into a Dumpster, which was okay as she wasn't quite ready to face that task.

"Chief Baker has it," Angelica continued. "He may or may

not send it to the hospital for her. She may need it to comfort her in the days ahead."

"That's right," Baker put in, and everyone at the table turned to look at him. He ducked his head guiltily, finding his menu of infinite interest.

"As I was about to say," Angelica continued, with a pointed glare leveled at the next table, "apparently, Joelle's going for genetic counseling and will have her baby tested as soon as possible."

"Joelle was pregnant?" Ginny asked, aghast.

Tricia nodded. "It seems to be catching."

"Catching?" Grace asked.

"Yes, Nikki at the Patisserie is also pregnant." Everyone turned to look at Nikki across the dining room. She noticed them and gave a cheerful wave.

"My word, perhaps there's something in the water," Grace suggested.

"I sure hope not," Angelica said.

"Me, either," Pixie agreed.

"And what if the outcome for Joelle's baby isn't good?" Grace asked with trepidation.

Angelica shrugged.

Ginny forced a smile and cleared her throat. "I think you might have something there, Grace, about there being something in the water, because as it turns out . . . Antonio and I are expecting a baby in late August."

"You are!" Grace called out, absolutely delighted, and reached over to touch Ginny's hand. "Oh, I'm so pleased for you both."

"Congratulations!" Pixie squealed.

"I can't wait to throw you a baby shower!" Angelica cried,

got up from her seat, and scampered around the table to give Ginny a hug.

"And what do you think of our news, Tricia?" Antonio asked, unable to keep a smile from his lips.

"I'm ecstatic, but I must confess I already knew."

"So I heard," he said under his breath.

She leaned closer to speak to him. "I hope you're not angry."

"Not at all," he said, keeping his voice low. "For some reason, Ginny was afraid I might make her stop working, or that our employer would replace her. She may do as she wishes. She does not need to be on the premises every day to manage the store, especially if we can find someone like Pixie or Mr. Everett to help out."

"No poaching my employees," Tricia warned him.

"It never crossed my mind," he said with a smile she didn't quite trust.

"Hey, Antonio, is now a good time to pour the wine?" Pixie asked.

"I think so," he admitted, turned for the champagne bucket, and withdrew the bottle. A few moments later, he'd popped the cork and gotten up to fill everyone's glasses.

"I propose a toast," Antonio said, raising his glass. "To Mr. Everett. May this be the best birthday he's ever had."

"Hear! Hear!" they all said, and drank. Ginny, of course, toasted with ice water.

Mr. Everett blushed and took a sip of his champagne.

"I have a special request of you and Grace," Ginny said. "Antonio and I have no relatives in the area. Would you mind terribly being honorary grandparents to our baby?"

Tricia wouldn't have thought it possible, but Mr. Everett blushed an even deeper shade of red. He risked a glance at

Grace, who nodded enthusiastically. "We would be delighted."

Everyone took another sip before Angelica raised her glass. "I propose another toast. To Tricia."

"To me? Whatever for?" Tricia asked.

"To you and Haven't Got a Clue. Without you, Ginny would have never met Antonio. Without you, Mr. Everett and Grace would never have gotten together. Without you—I would have never come to Stoneham along with my own brand of business acumen. It's all because of you that the entire town has blossomed."

"I think that one sip of wine has already gone to your head," Tricia said, but the others would hear nothing of her protests.

"Thank you for being a great boss," Pixie chipped in.

Antonio held up his glass. "May the wait for reopening your store be short, and may you be twice as successful as before."

"Hear! Hear!" everyone said, including Christopher and Chief Baker, who'd again been eavesdropping at the next table.

Tricia felt her cheeks grow hot, but nonetheless smiled. She may have lost just about everything in the fire, but Jerry Dittmeyer couldn't take away one of her most valued treasures, the friendship she shared with everyone at the table. She raised her own glass and drank to the future—whatever it might bring.

ANGELICA'S RECIPES

SPANAKOPITA

½ cup olive oil
2 large onions, chopped
2 (10-ounce) packages frozen chopped spinach,
    thawed, drained, and squeezed dry
2 tablespoons chopped fresh dill (or 2 teaspoons
    dried dill)
2 tablespoons all-purpose flour
2 (4-ounce) packages feta cheese, crumbled
4 eggs, lightly beaten
salt and pepper

1 (24-ounce) package phyllo dough
¾ pound butter, melted

Preheat the oven to 350°F. Heat the olive oil in a large saucepan over medium heat. Slowly cook and stir onions until softened (do not overcook). Mix in the spinach, dill, and flour. Cook for approximately 10 minutes, or until most of the moisture has been absorbed. Remove from the heat and mix in the cheese, eggs, salt, and pepper. Lay the phyllo dough flat and cut into long strips (about 2" wide); brush with the melted butter. Place a small amount of spinach mixture at the bottom of each piece of dough. Fold the phyllo into triangles around the mixture. Place filled phyllo dough triangles on a large baking sheet. Brush with butter. Bake for 45 minutes to 1 hour, or until golden brown.

Yield: Varies

BLUE CHEESE POPOVERS

2 large eggs
1 cup milk
2 tablespoons butter, melted, plus more to grease
     the tins
1 cup all-purpose flour
½ teaspoon sea salt
⅛ teaspoon ground black pepper

1 ¼ ounces blue cheese, crumbled
1 tablespoon fresh thyme, roughly chopped (or 1
    teaspoon dried thyme)

In a large bowl, briskly whisk the eggs, milk, melted butter, flour, salt, and pepper until smooth. Whisk in the cheese and the thyme. Place the batter in an airtight container and chill for 2 hours or overnight.

Preheat the oven to 425°F. Butter the mini muffin tins. Fill each cup to the brim with the chilled batter. Bake the popovers for 15 to 18 minutes until puffed and golden. Repeat until all the batter is used. Serve warm.

Yield: Varies

CREAM OF TOMATO SOUP

3 tablespoons butter
1 medium onion, chopped
2 tablespoons chopped garlic
5 tomatoes, chopped
2 tablespoons pepper
2 cups water
5 tablespoons cream
salt, to taste

Melt the butter in a large fry pan. Add the chopped onion and garlic and sauté until the onions are translucent. Add the chopped tomatoes. Sprinkle with pepper. Add the water and let the mixture boil for 10 minutes. Remove from the heat and blend the mixture in a food processor or blender to a puree. Transfer the puree back to the pan. Whisk in the cream and season with salt to taste. Serve hot.

Yield: 2–3 servings